Praise for CHARLES

NOVELS BY CHARLES MCCARRY

Christopher's Ghosts
Old Boys
Lucky Bastard
Shelley's Heart
Second Sight
The Bride of the Wilderness
The Last Supper
The Better Angels
The Secret Lovers
The Tears of Autumn
The Miernik Dossier

CHARLES MCCARRY

THE MIERNIK DOSSIER

OVERLOOK DUCKWORTH
New York • London

First published in paperback in the United States in 2007
by Overlook Duckworth, Peter Mayer Publishers, Inc.
New York & London

NEW YORK:
The Overlook Press
141 Wooster Street
New York, NY 10012
www.overlookpress
For bulk and special sales, please contact sales@overlookny.com,
or write us at the above address.

LONDON:
Duckworth
30 Calvin Street
London E1 6NW
info@duckworth-publishers.co.uk
www.ducknet.co.uk

Cataloging-in-Publication Data is available from the Library of Congress
A catalogue record for this book is available from the British Library

Book design and type formatting by Bernard Schleifer
Manufactured in the United States of America
ISBN 978-1-58567-942-3 (US)
ISBN 978-0-7156-4736-3 (UK)

3 5 7 9 8 6 4

For Nancy

On pense à moi pour une place, mais par malheur j'y étais propre: il fallait un calculateur, ce fut un danseur qui l'obtint.

—BEAUMARCHAIS *(Le Mariage de Figaro)*

This narrative is set in the middle years of the cold war; the year could be 1959. Travelers familiar with that time, and with the scenes in which the story takes place, will recognize landmarks and atmosphere and attitudes. But they will search in vain for familiar figures. No character is intended to resemble any person who ever lived, and no event is based on fact.

THE
MIERNIK DOSSIER

INTRODUCTORY NOTE

The attached dossier is submitted to the Committee in response to the request by its Chairman for "a complete picture of a typical operation."

The file includes:

a) agents' reports, including those of intelligence services other than our own;

b) written communications exchanged by the principals outside security channels;

c) transcripts of telephone conversations and of other conversations that were recorded by listening devices;

d) certain other documents, e.g., surveillance reports, diary entries, biographical sketches;

e) footnotes supplied by our Headquarters.

Apart from a minimal number of footnotes, which were considered necessary to a full understanding of the material, no comment or interpretation has been provided. It is hoped that the documents will, as it were, "draw their own picture" of this operation.

No changes have been made in any of the documents, except that some have been shortened so as to exclude extraneous material, and each of the principals has been assigned a single fictitious name. In the original documents, they were, of course, identified under a variety of cryptonyms, identification numbers, etc.

For reasons that will be understood by the Committee, the means by which certain of these documents came into our possession are not specified.

The genuinity of all material in this file may be assumed.

1. **INTERNAL COMMUNICATIONS FROM THE FILES OF THE WORLD RESEARCH ORGANIZATION.**

To Mr. Khan

The Polish Ambassador has requested, in a conversation with me today, that we not renew the contract of Mr. Tadeusz Miernik when it expires next month. The Ambassador explained that Mr. Miernik's professional skills are required by the Polish Ministry of Education.

May I have your advice as to whether we may accede to the Ambassador's wish (which has the effect of a formal request from the Polish government) without undue inconvenience to the Organization?

8 May   DIRECTOR GENERAL

To Director General

Mr. Miernik's work can be assigned to another official without undue inconvenience. I venture to add that I should, in the ordinary course of events, have recommended a permanent contract for Mr. Miernik, whose performance over the past two years has

---

*World Research Organization: A specialized agency of the United Nations, in Geneva, Switzerland. It carries out research on social questions (e.g., crime, discrimination, medical care, political organization) and publishes reports that take into careful account the sensitivities of its 101 member nations. WRO has a professional staff of 400, representing 71 nationalities. The Organization has always attracted large numbers of Intelligence operatives from a wide variety of countries. Employment by WRO is regarded as excellent "cover" because it provides diplomatic Immunity and, in the eyes of the host country, professional respectability. WRO is typically the base, rather than the target, of intelligence agents who are unwittingly employed by it.

been of the highest quality.

Mr. Miernik has, moreover, expressed a strong interest in remaining with the Organization. He considers that he has personal as well as professional reasons to remain in Geneva.

If you wish me to do so, I shall be happy to discuss these reasons with you, or to arrange for Mr. Miernik to do so himself.

11 May   H. KHAN
                                          Chief of Political Research

To Mr. Khan

Would it be convenient for Mr. Miernik to state his case to me in writing?

15 May   DIRECTOR GENERAL

To Director General

Mr. Miernik would welcome the opportunity of discussing his case with you. He prefers not to commit his arguments to writing.

15 May   H. KHAN
                                          Chief of Political Research

To Mr. Khan

The Director General would be pleased to see you and Mr. Miernik in his office at three o'clock on Thursday, 18 May.

16 May   N. COLLINS
                                          First Assistant

2. REPORT BY NIGEL COLLINS, FIRST ASSISTANT TO THE DIRECTOR GENERAL (WRO) TO A BRITISH INTELLIGENCE SERVICE.

Tadeusz Miernik and his chief, H. Kahn, today (18th May) made their case to the Director General that Miernik be retained in the Organization under a permanent contract. Khan confined his arguments to an affirmation of the professional competence of Miernik and then asked to be excused from the remainder of the conversation.

2. After Khan's departure, Miernik stated with some emotion that he had reason to believe that his government wished to arrange his return to Poland so that he might be tried on political charges and imprisoned. Miernik denies that he has engaged in any activity that runs counter to Polish national interests. He believes, however, that the security services have looked upon his friendships with foreigners (i.e., Westerners) "with their usual demented suspicion." He fears for the welfare of his sister, a university student in Warsaw who is his only living relative.

3. The Director General made no immediate response to Miernik's plea. He (the D.G.) is annoyed with Khan, whom he regards as an excitable and rather naive man, for having placed him in the uncomfortable position of judging whether the Ambassador of a member state (Poland) has sinister motives towards Miernik.

4. The D.G. asked me, after Miernik had departed, what I thought about the Pole's fears. I replied that I was sure that these were, at least in Miernik's mind, quite genuine. The D.G. replied, after a moment of rather comic thought: "I can hardly ask the Ambassador to guarantee to me that Miernik will not be shot by his secret police!" He delayed a decision on Miernik's contract, which expires on 30th June, until the middle of next month.

5. Is it possible to confirm that Miernik does in fact have a sister in Warsaw University?

2 (A). NOTATION, IN DIFFERENT HANDWRITING, AT THE FOOT OF THE FOREGOING REPORT.

22nd May. Warsaw replies that no female named Miernik appears on the rolls of Warsaw University. Other Polish universities?

28th May. Not on rolls of any other Polish university.

3. BIOGRAPHICAL SKETCH OF TADEUSZ MIERNIK (FROM OUR FILES).

Tadeusz Miernik was born on 11 September 1929 at Krakow. His father, Jerzy, was a university graduate who worked before World War II as a manager of a meat distributing firm. During the war he was connected to the anti-German underground. From 1947 until his death five years later, he was employed in a managerial capacity by a state enterprise. The mother, Maria Prokochni, was killed by a strafing airplane during the Soviet-German battle for Poland in 1941. Her son claims to have witnessed this incident.

Miernik was educated at Warsaw University, which awarded him a doctorate in history. He taught Polish history at Warsaw University for a brief period, until he was awarded a fellowship at a Soviet university. Two years after this fellowship expired, he appeared in Geneva and was granted employment under a temporary contract at the World Research Organization.

Miernik speaks fluent English, Russian, and German, as well as good French. His circle of acquaintances includes many persons of Western nationality. In general, he has avoided political discussion, but he has implied that his strong religious beliefs conflict with Communist teachings. He claims to be a Roman Catholic and regularly attends mass. He has stated that his mother intended him for the priesthood, and that he regrets that political circumstances in Poland prevented his entering on this vocation.

Miernik is a sedentary man whose only exercise is walking. He appears to be of studious habit, and he has told friends that he is writing a social and political history of a tropical country, which he refuses to identify on grounds of scholarly discretion. It is believed that the country in question is either Sudan or Ethiopia. (This judgment is based on an examination of books that he has removed from various libraries.)

Physical description: 5 feet 9 inches, 200 pounds. Black hair, brown eyes. Wears eyeglasses at all times. Three-inch surgical scar on inner right forearm (no explanation). Heavy beard but clean-shaven. Clumps of hair grow from subject's ears. Very strong body odor.

Idiosyncrasies: Fastidious personal habits. Does not smoke. Drinks moderately as a usual thing, but has been known to become drunk. When intoxicated, undergoes personality change, becoming garrulous and physically very active (dances, challenges companions to arm-wrestling contests, etc.). No known sexual abnormalities. No known liaison with any female.

4. **REPORT BY PAUL CHRISTOPHER, AN AMERICAN UNDER DEEP COVER IN GENEVA, TO A U.S. INTELLIGENCE SERVICE.**

Tadeusz Miernik phoned me early this morning (19 May) to ask that I meet him in the Parc Mon Repos at 11:30 A.M. He explained that he wished to talk to me alone before we joined Nigel Collins, Léon Brochard, Kalash el Khatar, and Hassan Khan for our usual Friday lunch. Miernik sounded over the phone even more shaken than he usually does. (I have mentioned in earlier reports that his normal tone of voice is one of acute distress. I continue to wonder if he sounds like that in Polish, as well as in English, French, and German.)

I found Miernik standing by the edge of the lake with the usual bag of stale bread in his hand. He was feeding the swans. All three buttons of his coat were carefully fastened, and he wore the look of a man who is phrasing his last will and testament. Nothing unusual there: he always looks like that.

Miernik has a way of beginning conversations with a non sequitur, if you know what I mean. "Only a month ago," he said, "one of these beautiful swans killed a child with a blow of its beak. You saw the newspapers? The child was feeding it. It fractured the child's skull. Can you tell, by looking at the swans, which is the murderer?" He scattered the last of his crusts on the water and turned his big face to me while he wiped his hands with a handkerchief. "No," I said. "Can you pick out the guilty swan?" Miernik smiled (a movement of the muscles that always suggests the awakening of Boris Karloff in Dr. F.'s laboratory) and said, "Perhaps the swans know, but they will not talk." (I give you this extraneous detail so that you will perhaps appreciate the oracular quality of Miernik's conversation: layers within layers, sorrows within sorrows.)

We walked together along the lakeside. It was a sunny day. The park was full of pretty girls and other people. We could see Mont Blanc and the other high mountains, covered with snow. There were sailboats on the water. Miernik trudged through the crowd with his hands clasped in the small of his back. I have noticed before that scenes of beauty and happiness seem to fill him with melancholy. His eyes moved over the girls, over the children, over the old people. He wore a smile like that of an actor who has renounced the woman he loves because he knows that he is going to die in battle. "All this is not for me!" Miernik seems to sigh. But he adores observing the middle class in its leisure. "These people have the illusion that happiness is a right that cannot be taken away," he said.

All the benches were occupied by noontime sunbathers, so Miernik led me to an empty place on one of the lawns. I leaned against a tree, waiting for him to say whatever it was that he had rehearsed. (I don't mean to be flippant; his English is fluent, but studied.) Miernik turned his back to me and looked at the lake. When, at length, he turned around, he was again wearing his doomed smile. "There is something I do not want to discuss at lunch," he said. I waited. "I wish what I am going to say to remain absolutely between you and me," he said.

"All right."

"My contract at WRO expires at the end of next month."

"I know. You told me."

"I have learned that it may not be renewed."

"Is that important? It's a dull job."

"Important to me. You are an American. Perhaps you won't understand what I am going to tell you.

"I'll do my best."

"It will not be renewed because the ambassador of my country has demanded that it not be renewed."

"Demanded? He can't tell WRO what to do."

"He can tell them that they will lose the goodwill of my country if they do not do as he asks. My well-being is a small thing to WRO. The Organization survives by avoiding trouble. If I am trouble, it will avoid me."

"How do you know what the Polish ambassador has demanded?"

"I know," Miernik said.

"All right. Then why should the ambassador care one way or the other about your contract?"

"He does not. The ambassador is a government servant. Perhaps he guesses the reasons behind his instructions. Unless he is very stupid, he guesses.

"Tell *me* the reason."

"Warsaw, someone in Warsaw, wants their hands upon me. Or perhaps someone farther east wants that."

"Miernik!" I put disbelief in my voice, not to encourage him to tell his story, because he was obviously going to do that anyway. I meant to shake his performance, if that's what it was.

"You scoff," Miernik said. "They wish to arrest me, to question me, to imprison me. Perhaps more than that."

"What on earth for?"

Miernik went on as if I hadn't spoken: he had hit the rhythm of his role. *"Arrest, question, imprison,"* he said. "You cannot possibly hear in those words the . . . *echoes* that a Pole hears."

"Probably not. But why you? Do you live a secret life you haven't told me about?"

Miernik grimaced. "A joke to an American. Something else to a secret policeman. Knowing you is enough to convince them that I work for American intelligence."

(Don't be startled by this remark. He meant to joke. Maybe he does think that I work for you—it's probable, even, that he thinks so. But he wasn't provoking me here. His tone was: *That's how ridiculous they are.* He was keeping up the appearance that he does not suspect me by assigning the suspicion to the Polish secret police, who are known idiots.)

"But if you don't work for the Americans, and I assume you don't, then why are you worried?"

"To them, innocence is an illusion. They don't like my nose. That's enough."

(Miernik has an unlovable nose: meaty, red, with a tendency to run.)

"If all this is true, then you have a problem," I said.

"You don't think that it's true?"

"Why shouldn't I? But is Poland really run by lunatics who'd lock you up for no reason at all?"

"You can't quite conceive of that, can you?"

"I've never been to Poland."

Miernik turned his back again. He blew his nose and cleared his throat into his handkerchief. This is one of his mannerisms when he is under stress.

"My dear friend," he said, "I do not think that I can go back to Poland."

"Then don't go. Ask for asylum here. The Swiss will fix you up. They've done it in more doubtful cases than yours.

"I must go back."

"You just said that you couldn't."

"Poland is my country."

"Which wants to put you in jail for no reason.

"Perhaps not. Once it was suggested to me that I could be use-ful, in a patriotic way. When I was at the university. Perhaps they want to frighten me into something like that."

"You won't know until they try, will you?"

"Perhaps not even after."

"Intrigue, Miernik. Everywhere intrigue."

Miernik paid no attention to this remark. "Most of all," he said, "there is another factor." He fell into a silence.

(I might say at this point, for the benefit of those who sit inside, reading these reports—there *is* someone like that, isn't there?— that there is a certain amount of strain involved in holding con-versations with people like Miernik. Two sets of reactions operate at all times. I pretend to like him, for your purposes. I *do* like him, for reasons that have nothing to do with your requirements. I lie to him, for your reasons. And I lie to him so that he will not sus-pect that I am lying to him. I assume that he feels and does the same. In Miernik's case, all this would be more bearable if he did not take himself so seriously. Of course, I don't know whether he is taking himself seriously, or whether he is just pretending to do so in the name of professionalism. If he is a professional, then this narrative is laughable. If not, it's not.)

"There is my sister," Miernik said.

"What's her name?" I asked this quickly.

Miernik hesitated. You will think that he was selecting a name that he'll be sure to remember the next time I ask. It might have been that, or it might have been his normal citizen-of-a-police-state reaction: a man who asks for information, even innocent information, is to be mistrusted.

"Zofia," he said.

"Where is she?"

"In Warsaw, at the university. She is studying art history."

"She is alone?"

"You know that my parents are dead. She is alone."

"Can't she come out? Pretend to be going on vacation?"

"One passport to a family is the rule. I have ours."

"Would they bother her if you didn't go back?"

"Perhaps not immediately. Eventually, if they want me badly enough. She is my only relative. She is younger. I feel a great deal for her."

"Tadeusz, I don't think we can settle this before lunch. We ought to start walking toward the restaurant."

"It helps to talk about it. You would like Zofia. We don't look alike."

"That's reassuring."

Miernik laughed for the first time. He does not joke about his appearance (his looks distress him, I think), so I assume that his laughter indicated, or was supposed to indicate, affection for his sister.

"She thinks I am too protective. I interviewed her boyfriends when she was sixteen. Before that, in the war, we all tried to make her feel as safe as possible. The winter that the Russians came, the Germans retreated in a hurry. In a snowbank around the corner from our house they left two dead German soldiers. They were just boys. Their faces were frozen—eyes open, mouths open, tongues very swollen. They lay in the snow on our path to school. During the entire winter, I took Zofia by a longer way so she wouldn't see the dead Germans. I would go out every morning to see if they were gone. They were not. The Russians wouldn't bother with them, the Poles would not touch them. They were not hauled away until spring, when they might smell. Zofia was angry with me over all that extra walking. I never told her why we went the long way to school. Why should a little girl know?"

"Have you ever explained?"

"No. I suppose she's forgotten. She was only seven."

We walked through the park again, Miernik with his hands behind him like a monk. I put my hand on his shoulder.

"Do you want to talk about this later?"

"Yes. Your lack of sympathy does me good."

"You can call me."

Miernik said that he would.

You see the alternatives in this situation, I know. But I will list them anyway:

    1)   Miernik's story is true, and he really is deciding whether to go back to Poland and, perhaps, to prison. If he doesn't go back, he'll have to ask for asylum in Switzerland.

    2)   He is in touch with the Poles (or the Soviets), and is under instructions to defect, *and* believes that I can put him in contact with the right Americans.

If (1), it's a sad story. If (2), it's very elaborate, hence very Polish.

Let me know how you want to handle this.

5. **INTERNAL COMMUNICATIONS FROM THE FILES OF WRO.**

Personnel

The Director General wishes to know the date of expiry of the passport of Mr. Tadeusz Miernik.

19 May   N. COLLINS

                                     First Assistant

Mr. Collins

The passport of Mr. T. Miernik, issued by the Polish Consulate in Bern, expires on 2 July. As the passport is not renewable, Mr. Miernik must apply for a new one before the date of expiry.

19 May   T. RASTIGNY

                                      Personnel

6. REPORT BY LÉON BROCHARD, A FRENCH NATIONAL EMPLOYED BY THE WORLD RESEARCH ORGANIZATION, TO A FRENCH INTELLIGENCE SERVICE (TRANSLATION FROM FRENCH).

There was a curious incident today (19 May) at the lunch that has become a weekly habit for Collins, the Englishman; Christopher, the American; Miernik, the Pole; el Khatar, the Sudanese; Khan, the Pakistani; and myself. The central figure in this incident was Miernik, though Khatar, Khan, and Collins were also involved.

Miernik and Christopher arrived together at the restaurant. The rest were already there. The talk was lively as usual. Khatar told an amusing story about Fenwick, the Englishman who is an Assistant Director General of WRO, whom he is trying to induce to call him (Khatar) "Your Royal Highness." Khatar is a prince of a Muslim sect in his country. Khatar's family still keeps slaves, including apparently some intellectuals; he says that Fenwick has the makings of a useful slave. "Fenwick would be quite happy with us as a slave, all our slaves are," said Khatar. "But first he must be trained not to call me 'my dear chap.'"

Miernik seized on this bit of frivolity with great resentment. He read Khatar a lecture on the evils of slavery. "Did you learn nothing at Oxford?" Miernik demanded.

"I learned that it is inconvenient to be without slaves," said Khatar.

Even Khatar, who usually is oblivious to the behavior of others, was taken aback by the ferocity of Miernik's attack. The Pole would not stop talking. It seems that Khatar's father, for political reasons, recently married his son, *in absentia,* to the thirteen-year-old daughter of another black prince. The father sent this new bride by airplane to Geneva. She is now living in Khatar's apartment.

Miernik, going there for dinner last week, was introduced to the girl. Khatar requires her to sit on the floor beside the table, and he tosses her scraps from his plate. Apparently this is the only food she receives. Miernik upbraided him for this behavior.

"Be cheerful, Miernik," said Khatar. "She will go back to Sudan as soon as I can bring myself to consummate the marriage."

Collins said, "Look, Kalash, why don't you send your Swiss girl away for an evening, and do the deed? Then you won't be offending old Miernik when he comes to dinner."

Khatar, who regards himself as quite the most handsome black in the world, laughed. "She is circumcised," he said. "It's a dry experience, my dear Nigel. When I have her, I shall have to be prepared by Nicole. But once she has prepared me, Nicole will not let me go.

At this, Miernik threw down his napkin and left the table. He strode to the door, then came back, red in the face. "Kalash," he cried, "you are a disgusting savage!"

Khatar was quite undisturbed. "It seems that Miernik has no respect for my culture," he said.

"None whatever, if you are its product," said Miernik, and left the restaurant. There were actual tears in his eyes.

Christopher went after him. Everyone except Khatar was enormously embarrassed. Collins, of course, could not let the matter lie.

"Kalash," he said, "you mustn't take old Miernik too seriously."

"I thought that he was quite serious. He was crying."

"It's nothing to do with your sex life, really," said Collins.

"Perhaps he ought to arrange a sex life of his own, then," said Khatar. "They are too moralistic, these Communists."

"Miernik has a good deal to be serious about," said Collins.

"He is very worried," said Khan.

Collins gave Khan a warning look. But the Pakistani went on: "Miernik thinks that he is in danger."

"Really, Hassan!" Collins said.

"You do not believe him?" asked Khan.

"That's neither here nor there. It's an official matter."

"A human matter, I should have said. Is the D.G. going to do anything for him, or not?"

"I really don't know."

"He must do something. It's unthinkable that Miernik should have to go back."

"Back where?" asked Khatar.

"To Poland," said Khan.

"That is where he comes from," said Khatar. "Why shouldn't he go back?"

"Because he is not a royal highness. The Poles are bringing pressure to have him returned. They think that he is a spy, I gather, because of his friendships with us. They wish to put him into prison.

I asked Collins, "Is this true?"

"I have no idea," said Collins.

"That is what Miernik thinks," said Khan. "That is what he told the D.C. in your presence, I believe."

Khan was agitated. Collins paid him no attention.

"If that's so, then Miernik had better sleep with some girls before he goes," said Khatar. "He may not have the chance after he's clapped into the dungeon."

"I assure you," said Khan, "it is not funny."

"No," said Collins, "I suppose it isn't."

I deduced from Collins' reaction to this conversation that what Khan said was substantially true. Collins is expected, as First Assistant to the Director General, to be a tomb of discretion. But there was no mistaking that he was disturbed and embarrassed by Khan's spilling of secrets at the luncheon table.

Neither Miernik nor Christopher returned to the restaurant. Khatar, as usual, had no money. I paid the extra portion of the bill, and a claim for expenses is attached.

7. EXCERPT FROM TRANSCRIPTION OF A CONVERSATION,
   PHOTOGRAPHED BY A MOTION PICTURE CAMERA AND
   DECIPHERED THROUGH LIPREADING, BETWEEN VASILY
   KUTOSOV, AN OFFICIAL OF THE SOVIET EMBASSY IN
   PARIS, AND PIERRE MAILLARD, AN OFFICER OF A FRENCH
   INTELLIGENCE SERVICE. DATE AND PLACE OF CONVERSATION
   (TRANSLATED FROM FRENCH): 21 MAY, PLACE DU
   CARROUSEL, PARIS.

MAILLARD: One more thing, rather unimportant perhaps.

KUTOSOV: Perhaps. Tell me.

MAILLARD: We have a report from a low-grade agent in Geneva concerning a Pole named Miernik.

KUTOSOV: Given name?

MAILLARD: Tadeusz. The report says that the Poles are bringing pressure to have this man returned to Poland. The man says that he fears that he will be imprisoned for espionage.

KUTOSOV: What sort of espionage?

MAILLARD: It is not specified. He has a large circle of foreign contacts.

KUTOSOV: What sort of foreigners?

MAILLARD: I know of an Englishman, a Sudanese, a Pakistani. And, of course, an American.

KUTOSOV: Ask for more information.

MAILLARD: It's difficult. We have no direct interest.

KUTOSOV: Find a way.

8. **REPORT BY A POLISH NATIONAL CONTROLLED BY A WESTERN INTELLIGENCE SERVICE (EXCERPT).**

Other matters discussed by the Deputy Foreign Minister of the USSR in his conversations with the Deputy Foreign Minister of the Polish People's Republic:

. . . The Russian presented an optimistic report of progress made by the Soviet diplomatic arms in Africa. It is the view of the Foreign Ministry of the USSR that the potential exists in many African countries for the replacement of current and future reactionary native governments by more progressive elements. Poland may play an important role in this development.

It is considered that a Polish personality, operating unofficially, might find it possible to give assistance and advice to progressive elements in African countries who, for reasons of discretion, cannot deal openly and directly with the diplomatic missions of the USSR and other Socialist states. A Pole who has a reputation as an anti-Communist and a history of conflict with the Polish government would be ideal for this role. It is considered essential that such a person should possess Western citizenship, or at least a bona fide travel document issued by a Western state.

Countries of prime interest are Kenya, Tanganyika, Somaliland, Ethiopia, Sudan.

It was agreed that this project should be discussed by responsible officials in the two ministries, with the participation of the ministries of state security of the two countries.

23 May

9. CABLE RECEIVED BY THE U.S. CHIEF OF STATION, GENEVA,
   FROM HIS HEADQUARTERS.

1. CHRISTOPHER SHOULD PURSUE MIERNIK MATTER TO DETERMINE HIS
   INTENTIONS. POSSIBILITY MIERNIK MAY BE ATTEMPTING TO PROVOKE
   CHRISTOPHER INTO REVEALING SELF. INSTRUCT CHRISTOPHER TO
   MAKE NO REPEAT NO SUGGESTION HE CAN FACILITATE DEFECTION
   THROUGH CONTACTS WITH US GOVERNMENT. CORRECT POSTURE
   FOR CHRISTOPHER IS THAT OF CONCERNED FRIEND POWERLESS TO
   ASSIST.

2. HEADQUARTERS DISINCLINED ENCOURAGE DEFECTION UNLESS CAN
   ESTABLISH MIERNIK IS OPPOSITION AGENT WITH SPECIFIC MISSION. IN
   THIS CASE COULD JUSTIFY FACILITATING HIS MISSION AS MEANS NEU-
   TRALIZING MIERNIK THROUGH SURVEILLANCE AND MANIPULATION
   HIS SOURCES.

3. NO INTEREST IF MIERNIK DILEMMA GENUINE.

10. EXCERPT FROM THE DIARY OF MIERNIK (TRANSLATION FROM
    POLISH).

19 May. In the park today I spoke to P. [Christopher] about my
situation. He offered no assistance. I think that his sympathy is
aroused, however. His American manners make him seem more
open than anyone plausibly can be. At lunch I made a scene with
K. [Khatar] over some joking remark he made concerning slavery.
My emotions are raw, and I overdid it. Must write to apologize.
Now, of all times, he (and all the others) are important to me.

11. LETTER FROM MIERNIK TO KALASH EL KHATAR.

19 May

My dear Kalash,

I wish to apologize for my unforgivable behaviour at lunch today. In justification I can only say that I was much disturbed by a personal matter, and I am afraid that I permitted this to colour my reaction to your joking remarks.

As you know, I have the greatest respect for.the culture of your people. Also, I have very great affection for you in spite of the fact that you are a member of the ruling class!

I hope very sincerely that you will consider that I never said to you the things that I said.

Several of our friends will be coming to my flat on Sunday night at eight o'clock for the small party I mentioned to you last week. I very much hope that you will reaffirm our friendship by coming along to the party, bringing with you whomever you wish to bring.

Your affectionate and very contrite friend,
[signed] T. Miernik

12. REPORT BY CHRISTOPHER.

The disintegration of Tadeusz Miernik went public Sunday night at a party in his apartment. Miernik invited a small group of people up for drinks. Usually these affairs of Miernik's are anything but wild; the party on Sunday was an exception. Miernik himself made it so.

I arrived a little late and found Collins, Brochard, Khan, and three girls already on hand. Of the females, the most noteworthy was Ilona Bentley, Collins' companion. She is half English, half Hungarian. She has black hair to her shoulder blades and a face that will be ruined before she is thirty. It is not yet ruined. A light burns under her skirt.

It was apparent early in the evening that Miernik had noticed all this. Ilona sat on the floor at Collins' feet. Miernik sat opposite, saying nothing, his eyes fixed on the girl. He wore a suit, a vest, a tie, polished shoes. Everyone else, just back from the mountains on a Sunday evening, wore sweaters and corduroys.

For his guests Miernik had provided Polish vodka, and nothing else. The vodka, several bottles of it, was chilled in ice buckets. Miernik kept one bucket beside his chair, and he filled the glasses out of the dripping bottle as soon as they were emptied. He insisted that the stuff be drunk Slav style: no sipping, right down the hatch with a cry of good luck.

This sort of drinking did not bring good cheer to our company. Among them, in addition to the melancholy Miernik, we had a concentration camp survivor (Ilona); a man who saw his three young brothers murdered by a Hindu who decapitated the little corpses and hung the heads around his neck on a string (Khan); a victim of mass rape by Russian troops (Brochard's girl, an Austrian named Inge); and a veteran of the Maquis (Brochard).

Brochard was attempting to lighten the mood by singing bawdy songs. This failed because no one else knew all the French words, and because Collins wanted to hear about Brochard's experiences as a boy guerrilla.

Brochard's Maquis group operated, during the war, in the country around Geneva. He comes from a small town in the Jura. He joined the Maquis as a runner when he was only twelve. Apparently the Resistance felt that the Germans were not intelligent enough to suspect children. Brochard found out different when he was thirteen. He was arrested by a German patrol, which seized him as he bicycled from one village to another at two o'clock in the morning. The Germans took him to their headquarters, where he was questioned by a Wehrmacht officer. Brochard managed to get rid of a kitchen knife that he was carrying (against orders) in the waistband of his trousers. He pushed the knife downwards and shook it out the leg of his pants. He cut himself on the thigh in the process.

The German officer stood him in front of his desk and questioned him in a harsh voice. "I think that he must have been a schoolmaster in civilian life," Brochard said, "because he had the technique perfect. I, of course, was filled with heroism: the Boche would not get any secrets out of me. The only secret I knew, really, was the one I was carrying in my mind. I had been told to tell a certain man in Gex that Marcel wished to sell his cows. The Resistance used these ridiculous formulas for their messages. They were always sending news about cows to people who had no conceivable interest in cows. The Germans could not guess the meaning of the code phrase, of course. But they could shoot anyone who spoke such phrases. The messenger was dead, but the secret was safe. The joke was, the message usually meant no more to the recipient than to the Germans. Our clever agents were always forgetting the code, so they would have to call up the sender on the telephone and ask what he meant by 'Marcel wants to sell his cows.' At thirteen, I hadn't figured this out.

"The German officer wanted an explanation of my riding around on a bicycle at two o'clock in the morning. I knew that I must tell him something. I searched for a cover story. I couldn't think of anything. My leg was bleeding, I could feel the blood filling my shoe. I thought I might faint. I stood there daydreaming about a daring rescue: I pictured my gallant comrades of the Maquis bursting through the windows with machine pistols blazing. I saw myself picking up the weapon of a fallen rescuer and riddling the German.

"The German said, 'I am going to call your parents in here to find out why they permit a child to roam about on a bicycle in the middle of the night.' He was outraged that I wasn't asleep as I should be. He thought I was a bad boy. It was humiliating that he should think only that, when I was a hero of the Resistance. I thought of a story that I believed would keep my parents out of it.

"'Herr Hauptmann,' I said, 'I'll tell you what I was doing if you agree not to tell my mother and father. I was making love to a girl in the woods.'

"'Making love to a girl!' bellowed the German, and stood up so suddenly that his chair went squealing over the floor. He was outraged. He strode around the desk. I think that he was going to strike me. Then he saw, on the floor at my feet, a puddle of blood from the cut that the knife had made.

"'What the hell is *that?*' he cried. 'Take off your pants.'

"I tried to avoid this. I refused. He sent for two soldiers. They leaned their rifles against the wall and pulled off my trousers.

"It was a very German scene: *'Take off that boy's trousers!'*— *'Jawohl!'* No questions, no hesitation, no smiles, a serious order to be obeyed.

"Blood was running down my leg. The soldiers were careful not to get it on their uniforms. The officer brought the lamp from his desk and tipped it so that the light fell on my wound. It was a small cut. 'How did you come by that?' he demanded. He shone the light on my genitals. 'You have no hair!' he cried. He grinned in triumph; I was outwitted. Obviously hairless boys cannot make love in the woods. Then he stopped and stared at my hairless parts again. His expression became grim. He told the soldiers to go out of the room.

"'Léon,' he said. 'You are clipped.'

"He had seen that I was circumcised. Everything was pushed out of my mind by a sudden shame. I knew that I could not be a hero in the German's eyes now. He knew I was a Jew. He knew that my parents were Jews. I might say that he knew more than the French people in our village knew, because my father had stopped mentioning his religion years before. France is not a Jew-loving country.

"I knew we were all as good as dead. We'd be on the next train for Auschwitz. The German poured some alcohol on his handkerchief and gave it to me. 'Wash that cut,' he said. I did so. He left me standing in front of his desk for several minutes. I remained as I was, naked from the waist downwards. He stared at his hands.

"Finally the German looked at me. 'Put on your pants, he said. He wrote me out a pass. 'I advise you,' the German said, 'to keep your pants on in the presence of the German Army. Get out of here.'"

Inge, the Austrian girl, lifted misty eyes to Brochard. "Not all Germans were beasts," she said.

Miernik gave a great snort, like a horse smelling a corpse. "That is a lot of shit," he said in German. "Ilona, isn't that a lot of shit?"

I had never heard Miernik use such a word, I would have been less surprised if he had pulled a gun.

"Which?" asked Ilona. "Léon's story or Inge's proposition?"

"Inge's shit about the Germans."

"I don't know."

"You've had no chance to observe the Germans?"

"I don't suppose that I met the flower of Germany at Belsen."

Ilona, herself a flower at Collins' feet with her white skirt spread around her, reached over and touched Miernik's heavy leg. He was quivering. The black cloth of his suit trembled.

"I've practically forgotten the camp; I was very young, Ilona said. It was hard to think that Ilona—she could hardly have been less beautiful, less fragile at the age of eight—had stood behind the wire in a sack dress, her hair shaved off, guard dogs sniffing her sour prisoner's odor. She smiled apologetically, as if she really regretted that she could tell no horror stories.

Inge stared at Miernik, her face ready to break like a child's. "I remind you that I am Austrian," she said.

"I remind you, my dear Inge, that Austria was part of the German Reich when your lover was having his pants pulled off by German soldiers, while Ilona was in a concentration camp, while my country was being raped by the SS."

"Really, Tad," Brochard said. "Inge was hardly born when all that was going on."

"I was thirteen when the war ended," Inge said.

"Old enough," Miernik cried. He pulled another bottle of vodka from the rattling ice and began filling glasses. Water poured off the end of the bottle, wetting everyone's clothes. Inge pulled her glass aside, and the vodka splashed on the floor beside her.

"I was old enough to be thrown on the ground and raped by a company of Russian soldiers," she said. "They are heroes, I suppose. Was Ilona raped by a German soldier? Did the Germans rape your mother, your sisters?"

"The Germans raped no one. That is an act of life."

"Try it at thirteen," Inge said. "Your act of life! I say shit right back at you."

"Yes, an act of life. An act of spontaneous human beings. Brutal, yes. But *human,* Inge."

"Wild beasts," Inge said. There was no danger of her crying now. She was a victim, too.

"Better a beast than a machine," Miernik said. "I will tell you the difference between the Russian Army and the German Army, since you are too young to remember."

"Inge seems to remember, all right," Ilona said. "Tad, we're all a little drunk."

Miernik remained standing, the bottle in one hand, the vodka glass in the other. He poured himself three quick drinks, throwing his head back to swallow. His hair fell over his forehead.

"The German Army was a machine," he said. "A machine, Inge, a gray machine clanking through mankind. It smelled of steel and petrol. The Germans sat on the machines, like machines themselves. Gray, smelling of the machine shop."

"I know what the Russians smelled like," Inge said.

Miernik, holding Inge's eyes, went around again with his bottle. He poured the vodka into glasses that were already full; it slopped over. He drank out of the bottle.

"The Russian Army," he said. He fell into his chair with his legs spread and closed his eyes. "The Russian Army was like the earth. To see it coming was like seeing the earth move, a great mob of men in brown. It was an avalanche. It buried your Germans. The German Army, to me, is the burnt trucks and tanks in the Polish countryside."

"Tell me how beautifully the Russians sang," Inge said. "You people always tell that."

"The fighting went right by our house," Miernik said. "I went out when it was over, I wanted to give the Russians something. It was snowing. I found a Russian soldier sitting on a pile of rubble. He was eating bread. He had only this piece of bread. He saw me, a boy, and he gave me half the bread. We didn't say a word, we sat there chewing the bread. Black Russian bread. He kept smiling at me. Finally he said, 'I must go. Comrade Stalin has asked us to keep right on to Berlin.' And he picked up his rifle and went."

"And the commissars and the secret police came after him," Inge said. "They haven't picked up their rifles and gone away, have they?"

Miernik opened his eyes. "No," he said. "Those people are still there."

"I should think that you'd want to be with them, those wonderful human beings," Inge said. "You could be a part of the earth, too."

Miernik stared at her. There was no expression in his face at all. He took off his glasses and threw them against the wall. The lenses broke.

"I am going to dance," Miernik said.

He staggered over to the phonograph and started it. Still wearing his coat and vest, dark stains of vodka on his buttoned chest, he began to dance. The room shook, he laughed. He pulled Ilona off the floor. Her black hair swung like a curtain. He placed her on his shoulder and began to spin. She straightened her legs and shrieked like a child on a carnival ride; she put her cheek on top of his head and her hair tangled around both their faces. Miernik was shouting in Polish, his voice loud at first, then blown out by laughter and loss of breath. He fell with Ilona on top of him. She lay there for a moment, then kissed him on the forehead and got up. She stood over him with her legs apart, smiling down on him.

Miernik lay on the floor. He still had no breath. In a moment he gathered enough to shout, *Ilona Ivanovna, I forgive you!*

He sucked in more breath and cried, pointing his finger at each of us in turn, *"Léon Léonovich, I forgive you! Hassan Hassanevich, I forgive you! Paul Alexandrevich, I forgive you! Nigel Andreevich, I forgive you!"*

Miernik staggered to his feet and lifted Inge off the sofa. She tried to pull away. He lifted her by the waist so that her face was in front of his own. "Even you, Inge—what was your father's name?"

"Peter."

"Inge Pyotrovna, I forgive you!"

The doorbell rang. "That must be Kalash," Miernik said. "I will go and forgive him."

He opened the door to a Swiss policeman. "We have a complaint," the policeman said. "There is too much noise."

Miernik would have embraced the policeman, but Brochard stepped between them. "The noise will stop at once," Brochard said.

"Papers," the policeman said.

Brochard reached for his pocket. "Not yours. His," the policeman said.

"This gentleman is a functionary of WRO," Brochard said. "He has a diplomatic identity card."

Miernik reached over Brochard's shoulder and gave the card to the policeman. The policeman wrote in his book and gave it back.

"There will be a formal complaint unless the noise stops," he said. "I advise you to put this man to bed."

"Je vous pardonne," Miernik said.

Brochard went into the hall with the policeman and shut the door. Miernik sat down on the floor. His head sagged. He leaped to his feet and flung open the door. Brochard and the policeman were walking up and down the hallway, deep in conversation. The smile on the policeman's face went out at the sight of Miernik.

"Do you speak German?" Miernik said to the policeman. The cop stared at him. Brochard let go of the policeman's elbow and threw up his hands.

"Of course you do," Miernik said, in German. "You smell like a German. Like gasoline. Gasoline burns. Remember that, you damned machine."

"You will come with me," said the policeman.

"I have diplomatic immunity," Miernik said.

"You cannot insult the Swiss police."

"I have just done so. I don't like the color of your uniform."

Collins and I pulled him back into the room. He struggled with us. Ilona put her palm on his cheek. "Tad," she said, "come and sit with me." He followed her to the sofa.

Inge was putting on her coat. "He's cracked my ribs," she said. "He's a bloody Mongolian."

We went into the hall to talk to the policeman. He asked for all our papers and wrote our names in his book. "You are witnesses," he said. "I have no more to say at this time." He went down the stairs.

Collins watched him go. "I don't think that the copper is going to forgive Tadeusz Jerzyvich," he said.

Inge came out the door. She gave Brochard a look, and he followed her out. "There's nothing to do," he said.

"Mongolian," Inge said.

Inside, Miernik lay on the sofa with his head in Ilona's lap. "He's asleep," she said.

"Fifteen minutes too late," Collins said. He beckoned Ilona away from the sofa. She smoothed back Miernik's hair and stood up.

They all left. I took off Miernik's shoes and tried to loosen his tie. He opened his eyes.

"Would you agree that I've been a fool?" he said. "You were carried away by vodka. We all forgive you. (This business of "I forgive you" is an in-joke at the expense of the Russians. Miernik imitates them: "I had to shoot your mother, Ivan!" "I forgive you, Igor!")

"That policeman will make a report to the WRO. No contract after that."

"Yes. And he may file charges, diplomatic immunity or no diplomatic immunity. There's a law against insulting the police in this country."

"In all countries."

"Almost all. It's a sad world."

"What about America? What is the law there?"

"You can say what you want to the cops. If they don't like it, they break your skull."

Miernik turned over and put his face in the cushions of the sofa. "Tonight I lost everything," he said. "My contract, my Swiss asylum."

"We're both losing sleep," I said.

"I must become an American. That is the solution."

"I don't think you can. You're a Commie rat."

"I am a Christian and a lover of truth."

Miernik sat up. His hair fell into his face. His suit, in spite of everything, was still neatly buttoned. He looked odd without his glasses.

"Paul," he said, "I am lost. I have insulted the Swiss police. You should have stopped me.

"You were too quick for me. Léon and Nigel both tried to stop you.

"No Swiss asylum now. I am in their files as a troublemaker. The Polish wheel turns against the Swiss wheel, and Miernik is in between."

"You'd better go to bed."

"I'd rather go to America.

"With your background, you'll have to go by Russian submarine."

"I die. You joke. That's the American answer to the Polish question."

"You won't die, Miernik."

"You don't think so?"

"I think you've had a lot to drink."

"I will die, my friend. You will live. Do you know why? Your passport is green, mine is brown."

"Go to bed."

Miernik got up and searched for his glasses. He examined the broken lenses and put the frames in his breast pocket. He began to laugh.

"I am now seeing the humor in this situation," he said. "You are *bored*. Victims bore you. Would you save me if I were less of a bore?"

I didn't answer. Miernik smelled his own armpit. "I've always thought that I smell like a corpse," he said. "It's a Central European malady."

I said good night. In the street, I looked up at his window. He was moving around inside, clearing up the mess of the party. When he opened the sash to let in the air, I saw that he was wearing glasses again—an extra pair, no doubt.

13. REPORT BY AN AMERICAN SURVEILLANCE TEAM IN GENEVA.

Kirnov* emerged from Hotel du Rhône at 0312 hours on 22 May. He proceeded on foot to the corner of Boulevard Georges Favon and Rue du Stand, where he unlocked a gray Simca Aronde with registration number BE 80987 and drove away.

Chase vehicle kept subject in sight northbound across Pont de la Coulouvrenière, then eastbound on Rue de Lausanne, south on Avenue de France and the quais to the Pont du Mont Blanc. Subject then proceeded to the left bank and through a number of small streets in the vicinity of the Parc de la Grange. This was interpreted as a maneuver to spot our surveillance, and we accordingly ceased following so as to avoid detection.

We made new contact four minutes after breaking it, in Place

---

* A Brazilian national of Polish-Russian birth who is believed to have contacts with Soviet intelligence. He travels frequently in Eastern Europe with the ostensible purpose of negotiating contracts for the purchase of goods manufactured in Western countries.

Neuve. Kirnov parked and locked car and proceeded on foot to 21-bis, Rue Saint-Leger.

He buzzed an apartment inside this building from the entryway and was admitted. After his buzz, a light appeared in a third-story window, fourth from west end of building. Subject entered the building at 0331 hours.

At 0334 hours, Bamstein entered the building with a passkey and proceeded to the third floor by way of the fire stairs. Bamstein attached a contact microphone to the door of Apartment 23, which had been identified as the apartment with the lighted window.

Apartment 23 is occupied by Tadeusz Miernik, a Polish national employed by the World Research Organization.

The microphone, which was left in place until 0348 hours, picked up nothing but the sound of typing. Microphone was removed when a voice, identified as Kirnov's, said "Good night" in Russian. This was the only spoken word overheard by Bamstein.

Kirnov and a second white male assumed to be Miernik walked together to the elevator shaft. Bamstein, concealed in the stairway, overheard indistinct conversation in Russian. Bamstein was able to identify the name "Zofia" spoken several times by Miernik. Also the phrase "Don't worry, I will see to her," spoken by Kirnov.

Subject left building at 0351 and returned to his own residence by a circuitous route.

14. TELEPHONE CONVERSATION BETWEEN MIERNIK AND A FEMALE CALLED "ZOFIA" (GENEVA PTT—CORNAVIN BRANCH TO WARSAW 18754) (RECORDED 22 MAY AT 0635 HOURS; TRANSLATION FROM POLISH).

MIERNIK: Hello, Zofia? Zofia?

"ZOFIA":   Tadeusz? Why are you calling?

MIERNIK: Must I have a reason to call my sister? I am lonely for you.

"ZOFIA": And I for you, Tadeusz. How is Geneva?

MIERNIK: Beautiful. Beautiful. Spring is here.

"ZOFIA": Warsaw is beautiful, too. Perhaps you cannot remember.

MIERNIK: I remember every day. Zofia, I would like a little holiday.

"ZOFIA": So would I. It must be the weather.

MIERNIK: With you, I mean. Can you come to me here?

"ZOFIA": How? I have my studies.

MIERNIK: Have you a passport?

"ZOFIA": No, I have no passport.

MIERNIK: I should love it if you could get one and come to me for a few days. We will go walking in the Jura.

"ZOFIA": Why not the Alps? *(Laughter)*

MIERNIK: There is snow in the Alps.

"ZOFIA": The Jura, then. I wish that I could, Tadeusz.

MIERNIK: Perhaps you can. Apply for a passport. I long to see you. Write to me when you are coming.

"ZOFIA": I will try, if I can arrange my studies and a passport.

MIERNIK: I will wait for your letter. Good-bye.

"ZOFIA": Good-bye, Tadeusz.

15. **LETTER FROM ILONA BENTLEY, ADDRESSED TO AN ACCOMMODATION ADDRESS IN BERLIN USED BY A SOVIET INTELLIGENCE SERVICE (TRANSLATION FROM RUSSIAN).**

Darling Heinz,

Spring has come to Geneva, and I am foolishly happy about it. The city's face has changed in a week from that of an old man to that of a young girl with flowers in her hair. Blossoms everywhere, smiles everywhere. It hardly seems possible that a month ago the wind they call the *Bise* was blowing down the lake, that the bridge railings were curtained with ice, that people were so distressed that one read almost every day of another suicide. (The Swiss are bizarre suicides, they always find some way to do it that not even a Hungarian would have imagined: one man suffocated himself in January by placing a transparent plastic bag over his head, sealing it around his throat with a large rubber band. "He drowned in his own breath!" said *La Suisse.*)

My little love affair continues. I see him every day. He says nothing of his work. I accuse him of being interested only in an affair of bodies. He laughs. He is not always a gay lover, he has black moods when he will not speak. The state of the world troubles him; he believes that civilization is going into a long night, that the bomb will be dropped, that history is one long prank designed to be played on our generation. On this subject he will not laugh. I never see him on Saturdays. He gets into his car and goes to the Alps. He wears climbing clothes, but perhaps this is a disguise. I accuse him of meeting some wild girl on a mountainside. I have threatened to follow him to see if this is true. I can see that the threat disturbs him. Do you think that I should do this? I should not confront the other girl, if there is one. I should hide behind a tree and watch, perhaps take pictures. Tell me, dear Heinz, if this is what a jealous woman should do?

My lover and I went to an extraordinary party on Sunday night. Our host was M. (You remember that you thought you knew this man.) He became very drunk and did a wild dance, spinning like a trained bear with me in his arms. It was quite exhilarating, in a way. However, M. has the most extraordinary body odor I have ever smelled. It rose from him in waves. The stink *pulsed;* it was almost visible. The police came and our host insulted them. I am afraid that there will be repercussions. It was silly, because the policeman meant to do nothing except warn about the noise. Yet M. made a terrible fuss. It was ugly, self-destructive. I thought that he must have *wanted* trouble. Perhaps that is too fanciful—I am studying abnormal psychology at the moment.

I made the mistake of being sympathetic to M. I even kissed

him, in a sisterly way, as he lay panting on the floor after our dance. Now, to my astonishment, he has phoned to ask if I will dine with him. He is a friend of my little friend's. Men are such traitors! His company is very dull. Nevertheless, I said that I would go out to a restaurant with him. It may be interesting. I wonder what the effect would be if I told my lover of this engagement. Of course I shall not tell him. Let him be spared the suspicion he has caused me. It will be amusing to deceive him a little with a man who smells like a corpse. If anything truly amusing happens, I shall write to tell you all about it.

Always your affectionate friend,
[signed]   Annelise

16. REPORT TO WASHINGTON BY THE AMERICAN CHIEF OF STATION IN GENEVA (22 MAY).

1. It is our preliminary judgment, based on Christopher's reporting and certain other information, that Tadeusz Miernik is attempting to defect to a Western country for operational reasons dictated by the Polish intelligence service. The possibility that the Soviets may be involved in this operation cannot be ignored.

2. Miernik is conducting a stagy show of despair for the benefit of Christopher and other Westerners (e.g., Nigel Collins and Léon Brochard, both of whom are assumed to be agents of their respective national intelligence services). Miernik's intention seems to be to arouse the sympathy of his friends on a personal level, and the interest of their intelligence services on an official level. The technique has been used before by the Poles. The elaborate nature of the "trimmings" (representations to the WRO by the Polish ambassador, the convenient expiration date of Miernik's passport, the alleged existence of a hostage sister in Poland) is characteristic of Polish operations.

3. Outside of his personal contacts with Christopher and his

other friends, Miernik has behaved in a most rational manner. He has continued to function in his job. He has arranged an assignation with Collins' mistress (though the reason behind this may be operational, it's possible that the girl is his cutout). Except for the breakdowns in personal discipline that Christopher has conveniently witnessed and reported, Miernik has maintained his normal schedule and his usual behavior, with two significant exceptions.

4. These two exceptions are his clandestine meeting with Kirnov in the early hours of the morning and his telephone call to Warsaw a little later the same morning. Many of the phrases in this conversation, ostensibly with his sister, could be construed to be a code for telephone use ("There is snow in the Alps," etc.). If our assumption is correct that Kirnov is a Soviet agent, then there is only one logical explanation for his meeting with Miernik. If Kirnov is clean, then there really is no explanation why he should call on Miernik between three and four o'clock in the morning and spend the entire visit pounding on a typewriter.

5. It can be assumed that Miernik has some immediate operational assignment that depends on a successful defection. If his defection were authentic, or if he were being defected as a long-term asset to the Poles, he would presumably just walk into an embassy and ask for asylum.

6. Please advise whether we should attempt to determine Miernik's possible assignment through closer surveillance, including audio surveillance of his apartment and telephone.

17. TRANSCRIPTION OF A CONVERSATION BETWEEN MIERNIK AND ILONA BENTLEY (LISTENING DEVICE LOG; 26 MAY).

(Door opens and closes. Indistinct voices of two subjects. Sound of ice tray being emptied. etc.)

MIERNIK: I behaved very badly to Inge. I'm sure Léon is angry.

BENTLEY:	Why should he be? Everyone has strong feelings. Léon understands that, if anyone does.
MIERNIK:	But the French are so preoccupied with themselves.
BENTLEY:	I suppose that the Poles are not. Or the English, or the Eskimos. You shouldn't whip yourself, Tadeusz.
MIERNIK:	Humanity should make a treaty with itself never to talk about the Germans.
BENTLEY:	I'll sign it.
MIERNIK:	You must have more feeling about them than you let on. I can't believe . . .
BENTLEY:	As I said, I was young.
MIERNIK:	But old enough to remember.
BENTLEY:	When I am reminded, yes.
MIERNIK:	I'm sorry. We'll talk about other things. The Polish Question.
BENTLEY:	That hasn't been answered?
MIERNIK:	Not for the Poles. You know the story about the Frenchman, the Englishman, the American, and the Pole who were asked to write about elephants? The Frenchman wrote about the sexual life of the elephant, the Englishman about the way the elephant treated small dogs, the American about the mass production of elephants. The Pole wrote a twenty-thousand-word monograph entitled "The Elephant and the Polish Question."
BENTLEY:	*(Laughs.)*
MIERNIK:	You are extremely beautiful.
BENTLEY:	When I laugh?
MIERNIK:	At all times. Was your mother dark like you?
BENTLEY:	Yes. My father was fair, like Nigel. English fairness.
MIERNIK:	As soon as I say you are beautiful, you mention Nigel.

BENTLEY: That is the Hungarian part of me. Subtle.

MIERNIK: I like Nigel very much. I wonder if you do not find him frivolous.

BENTLEY: Why should I? He's sort of solemn.

MIERNIK: That side of him I have never seen, except when he is doing his job. Then he has the Foreign Office manner. He glows with secrets, there is a dynamo of class privilege smoking under his good manners. But at all other times he does nothing but joke.

BENTLEY: They learn all that at school in England. It means nothing.

MIERNIK: You find it attractive?

BENTLEY: I find it irrelevant.

MIERNIK: In Nigel's case only, or in the English as a whole?

BENTLEY: I'm English.

MIERNIK: Half.

BENTLEY: Half, then. But I don't notice English manners particularly. I notice yours.

MIERNIK: Mine? Why?

BENTLEY: Because they are different from my own.

MIERNIK: And from Nigel's?

BENTLEY: Yes. He would never mention any unhappiness he may have had. You mention little else. It's a difference in cultures more than personality.

MIERNIK: Perhaps he has never been unhappy in the way that I have been unhappy.

BENTLEY: Nonsense. Everyone is unhappy.

MIERNIK: Even you?

BENTLEY: Even I.

MIERNIK: Even the beautiful are unhappy. That is very disillusioning.

BENTLEY: You're an idiot.

MIERNIK: No, it's important that the ugly, the miserable believe
             that the beautiful are serene.

BENTLEY: What an idea. The Edwardians thought that nothing
             gave the poor greater pleasure than the sight of a rich
             man. That's an odd viewpoint for a modern
             Communist.

MIERNIK: You think I'm a Communist?

BENTLEY: Well, aren't you?

MIERNIK: No.

BENTLEY: Why on earth not?

MIERNIK: Why on earth should I be?

BENTLEY: The Polish Question. Surely that's a Communist
             question from now on?

MIERNIK: No.

BENTLEY: But they control your country. They will go on con-
             trolling it for the rest of your life, unless Nigel is right
             and the bombs go off.

MIERNIK: The bombs?

BENTLEY: The H-bomb. The Americans will fry us all.

MIERNIK: Nigel thinks that?

BENTLEY: Don't you?

MIERNIK: No. The Americans do not make horror.

BENTLEY: Ha! Ask the Japanese.

MIERNIK: The Americans were out of character when they did
             that. They say it saved lives because they didn't have to
             invade. Perhaps they're right.

BENTLEY: They were simply trying to keep the Russians out of
             Japan. Pure capitalist thinking. They wanted a client
             state in Asia. Markets.

MIERNIK: Ilona, I think you are a Communist!

BENTLEY: Would that be so terrible, if I were?

MIERNIK: Ugly. It would be ugly. Tell me that you aren't.

BENTLEY: All right. I'm not. Am I less ugly now?

MIERNIK: Infinitely.

BENTLEY: You interest me. Your emotions are so generalized. The Polish Question, the Germans, the Communists. What do you feel as an individual towards other individuals?

MIERNIK: Everything. Despite my nose.

BENTLEY: Your nose? What's wrong with your nose?

MIERNIK: *Cyrano, c'est moi.*

BENTLEY: Nonsense. It doesn't matter in a man. Even Cyrano found that out. He got Roxane in the end, didn't he?

MIERNIK: Truth in life and truth in art are not the same.

BENTLEY: You think women don't like you?

MIERNIK: I think that it's safer to assume that they don't.

BENTLEY: What nonsense.

MIERNIK: A matter of experience. I should be terrified to kiss you.

BENTLEY: My God.

MIERNIK: It's true. Your beauty frightens me.

BENTLEY: Frightens you? Really frightens you?

MIERNIK: Yes.

BENTLEY: Come here.

MIERNIK: I think not, Ilona.

BENTLEY: Come here.

MIERNIK: The beauty and the beast. I'll get you another drink.

BENTLEY: Come here.

(A pause in the tape. Male voice groans.)

BENTLEY: Did that terrify you?

MIERNIK: A little.

BENTLEY: You're going to sit down again? You're going to stop?

MIERNIK: What else should I do?

BENTLEY: You really are afraid. You're really afraid.

MIERNIK: I told you I was.

BENTLEY: That's very exciting. Is your heart beating very fast? Let me feel. No, under the shirt. Yes, feel that. It's leaping in its cage, poor heart.

MIERNIK: Ilona, you're cruel.

BENTLEY: Tell me that later. Here, put your hand there. On my skin. My heart isn't at all like yours, is it? Do you feel anything?

MIERNIK: It's a very calm heart.

BENTLEY: There, now feel it. There is no cloth in the way now. Move your hand. You've touched breasts before. Haven't you?

MIERNIK: Yes.

BENTLEY: Wait. Now you can touch everything. Get up. Take off your clothes. Take them off. Quickly. You're covered with hair. That's very exciting. You *are* a beast. No, stay standing. I'll take off your shoes. You're very big, bigger than Nigel. He has no hair, just a little there and around there. He has no skin at the end. The end of yours is moist. It smells like the forest, like ferns in the forest.

MIERNIK: Ilona, my God.

BENTLEY: Come down on the floor. Take off your glasses. Put your face there. Kiss. How do I smell? Do you like that smell? Is it a forest smell? Is it a sweet taste? Not inside so much. Find the place. Find the place. There. Sweetly, do it sweetly. Now kiss my mouth. Yes. Taste yourself, taste myself. Turn over. Let me see it. It's beating too, like your heart. Feel the wet, feel the warm. You're beating inside me like a heart. Now you're happy. Now you're beautiful.

(Long pause in tape.)

BENTLEY: You make love with your eyes closed.

MIERNIK: I do?

BENTLEY: You do. Why do you close your eyes?

MIERNIK: I don't know. Don't you?

BENTLEY: Never. I watch faces.

MIERNIK: What do you see?

BENTLEY: I don't know. Pain.

MIERNIK: You saw pain in me?

BENTLEY: I think so.

MIERNIK: It was not pain, Ilona.

BENTLEY: Did all this surprise you?

MIERNIK: It positively astonished me.

BENTLEY: You didn't say so.

MIERNIK: There's a time for keeping quiet.

BENTLEY: Did my talking disturb you?

MIERNIK: I never heard anyone talk like that.

BENTLEY: Sometimes I say worse things.

MIERNIK: Like what?

BENTLEY: You'll hear in a minute.

MIERNIK: Say only beautiful things. You are too beautiful.

BENTLEY: Would you say I'm good at it?

MIERNIK: Yes.

BENTLEY: So are you, my lad. It's all that hair, and the smell of you.

MIERNIK: Thanks.

BENTLEY: I'm trying to make you laugh. One should laugh after sex. Between sex.

MIERNIK: Laugh?

BENTLEY: Out of the joy of it. It's all we have, Tadeusz. Bits of flesh that fit together.

MIERNIK: We have more than that.

BENTLEY: You think so?

MIERNIK: Why did you do this, Ilona?

BENTLEY: Because I wanted to. I wanted to see your face.

MIERNIK: Nothing more than that?

BENTLEY: I've told you. That's enough. In fact, that's everything.

MIERNIK: I don't think so.

BENTLEY: You thought so five minutes ago, didn't you?

MIERNIK: That was five minutes ago.

BENTLEY: Yes. I'll make you think so again in a minute. Keep your eyes open this time.

18. INTELLIGENCE REPORT FROM THE AMERICAN STATION IN KHARTOUM.

1. The revolutionary-terrorist organization calling itself the Anointed Liberation Front (ALF) plans to move during June and July from its training ground in the Darfur highlands in western Sudan to a variety of large villages and small cities. Teams of trained men, usually numbering from three to seven, will carry out the assassination of important public figures, disruption of communications, small-scale attacks against police outposts, and exemplary punishment (i.e., torture and assassination) of those who refuse to cooperate with the ALF.

2. The leadership of the ALF consists of two Sudanese of unusually good educational and social background. Both were trained in the USSR in ideology, organization techniques, weapons, demolition, and communications. Of these two, one whom we have code-named *Firecracker* was recruited by us before his departure to the Soviet Union. He has remained our prime source of information about the ALF, although we have penetrated the organization with several other agents of lower rank.

3. Firecracker states that the ALF is well equipped with subma-

chine guns, grenades, explosives, and other small weapons. All weapons are of American or Belgian manufacture. The weapons, together with medical supplies and other materiel, were dropped by parachute into the Darfur region from unmarked DC-3's painted gray. Six Land Rovers, with false Sudanese registration, were driven across the border from Egypt and through the desert. A number of camels were purchased with funds provided before Firecracker and his companion left Moscow. Total funds currently available to the ALF are estimated by Firecracker at £5,000 (US $14,000).

4. In the six months since the return of the two Sudanese agents from the USSR, approximately one hundred men have been recruited and trained as three-, five-, and seven-man teams. Strict compartmentation of teams has been observed, so that the members of one team do not know the names or faces of those in any other team. The teams follow the Soviet practice of using code names even within the teams or cells, so that members know each other only under *noms de guerre*. Firecracker has been able to furnish us with true names for 61 of those involved.

5. The objective of ALF is to arouse an Arab resistance to the central government. After the terrorist stage, it is expected that this Arab organization will merge with the non-Arab resistance that has been attempting to operate in the South. The ALF theater of operations will be confined to an area north of a line running from El Fasher in the West to Om Ager on the Ethiopian border. This area includes about half the territory of Sudan, and most of the major population centers.

6. ALF, as its name suggests, hopes to pass itself off as a revolutionary religious movement in the Mahdist tradition. At the moment it has attracted no figure of sufficient stature from the Islamic community to serve as its leader. Firecracker reports that the ALF is under heavy pressure from Moscow to recruit such a figure.

7. The information in para. 6 is confirmed by radio messages from Soviet control in Dar es Salaam to ALF. We continue to

intercept and decode this radio traffic with the aid of transmission schedules and a code key supplied by Firecracker.

8. We believe that this operation has reached a stage where a decision must be made by Headquarters as to whether we should continue this project strictly as an information-gathering activity, or whether action should be taken to gain control over the ALF with a view to neutralizing it.

19. REPORT BY COLLINS TO A BRITISH INTELLIGENCE SERVICE.

Prince Kalash el Khatar stopped by my flat on the evening of 23rd May in order to borrow a sharp knife. (Because of his position in the religious nobility, he is much in demand among Muslims to preside over the ritual slaughter of the goats and sheep that are eaten by Mohammedans at this time. Apparently Ramadan, the annual Muslim fast, has either just ended or is about to commence.)

2. Khatar invited me to accompany him on a trip to his home in the Sudan. His father has bought an air-conditioned Cadillac and has instructed Khatar to see that the car is delivered to him at his palace in western Sudan. This involves driving it from Geneva to Naples, accompanying it aboard ship to Alexandria, and then driving it down the Nile and across the desert to the house of el Khatar. The whole trip would take about a month. Khatar anticipates that we might meet some bandits along the way, and he asked whether I might be able to get my hands on a couple of Sten guns. "We shall only need them in Egypt, where the population is not Arab," said Khatar. "Once we are across the frontier, you will be quite safe so long as you are with me." Khatar assures me that he has been schooled since earliest boyhood in desert navigation, so there is little chance that we shall become lost in the trackless waste that lies between Khartoum and his home. "If you become lost in the desert," he says, "you just go back to where you started

and begin the whole trip again. It is quite simple. I will teach you to read the stars, in case we become separated."

3. Khatar intends to invite Paul Christopher, the American, to accompany him. He believes that Christopher will be able to make repairs on the Cadillac if anything goes wrong with it. Further, he thinks that Christopher must be a good shot and an expert out-doorsman. "Americans are very good with motors and firearms," Khatar says. (The belief that Christopher is any sort of mechanic is, I think, an illusion. But he may be able to shoot a submachine gun well enough, since he was a parachutist in the American Army.) I have no doubt that Christopher will go along on this journey if it materializes.

4. One other companion is being considered by Khatar. This is Tadeusz Miernik, the Pole. Miernik, as I have reported, is about to lose his passport and perhaps his position at WRO. I mentioned these difficulties to Khatar. He waved them away. "I will tell our Ambassador here to give Miernik a Sudanese passport," he said. Khatar wishes to take Miernik along because the latter, it appears, has a scholarly interest in Sudanese history and culture. Khatar alleges that Miernik has for some time been writing a book on this subject. "He distracts me with his questions about the look of the country, and what he calls social dynamics," Khatar said. "I hope to shut him up by letting him see it all with his own eyes.

5. I asked Khatar when he intended to begin the journey. "The car will be ready in June," he replied. "We can leave as soon after that as we wish. As soon as we have the Sten guns." Procuring these weapons apparently is going to be my responsi-bility. I explained that automatic weapons are not easy to come by. "Oh, it's not so difficult. Half the zealots in Sudan have them," Khatar replied. I asked why he was so determined to have machine guns. "It is better to have them just now," he said. "There are madmen in Sudan. Everyone knows that." I pressed him for further details. "One of the forms of social dynamism in the desert," said Khatar, "is banditry. Part of the local colour, always has been. And just now there are a lot of silly bastards

who think that they're revolutionaries. The Russians gave them guns and bombs and told them to go and kill people. Naturally, people in Cadillacs are very desirable targets. I rather like the picture of old Miernik hosing down a bunch of black Communists with a Sten gun out of the window of an American limousine. If we turn up the radio and the air conditioner, it will be quite like the telly, won't it?"

6. Subject to your approval, I agreed to go along on this trip. I should be glad of any assistance you may be able to give in obtaining three or four Sten guns, with ammunition.

20. **REPORT BY THE AMERICAN CHIEF OF STATION IN GENEVA (26 MAY).**

1. Search of the apartment of Tadeusz Miernik has discovered an extensive file of information on Sudan. A card file with more than 700 entries lists important personalities in that country, together with detailed information on tribal matters, transportation system, principal public buildings, power stations, etc.

2. A large number of books in Arabic were found. It is speculated that Miernik reads and/or speaks Arabic, a fact that he has not disclosed to Christopher or, as far as we can determine, to any of his other friends.

21. **DISPATCH FROM WASHINGTON TO THE AMERICAN STATIONS IN GENEVA AND KHARTOUM.**

1. Information from a highly sensitive source in Warsaw indicates that a Polish national will be put into Sudan under joint Polish-Soviet control as principal agent advising an indigenous Communist movement.

2. Headquarters believes that the movement in question is the Anointed Liberation Front.

3. Headquarters believes, further, that the Polish national in question may be Tadeusz Miernik. (See Geneva's reporting, this subject.)

4. We have arranged for the delivery of an automobile in Geneva as a gift to the Amir of Khatar, head of the Bakhent Muslim sect. The Amir has instructed his son, Prince Kalash el Khatar, who resides in Geneva, to accompany the car to Sudan.

5. A trained U.S. agent (Christopher), controlled by Geneva, will accompany Khatar and the automobile.

6. Through the intervention of Christopher, Miernik will be invited to join Prince Kalash on this journey. This arrangement will provide for close surveillance of Miernik by Christopher.

7. After Miernik's arrival in Sudan, Khartoum should facilitate his contact with the ALF and keep watch on Miernik's activities through existing assets within this organization.

8. No operation against the ALF will be considered until Miernik is in place and until documentary evidence has been developed by Khartoum that he, as a foreign Communist agent, is controlling the activities of the ALF.

9. When the conditions of para. 8 have been fulfilled, Headquarters will issue further instructions.

22. FROM THE FILES OF WRO.

To Mr. Miernik

The Director General has decided not to renew your temporary contract when it expires on 30 June.

The Director General has asked me to express his gratitude for the excellent work you have done during the term of your temporary contract, together with his best wishes for the future.

2 June   N. COLLINS
                                     First Assistant

Note for the file

The Director General, on 2 June, informed the Polish Ambassador of his decision to let the temporary contract of T. Miernik lapse. The Director General asked for assurances that the Polish consulate will, if so requested, renew the passport of Mr. Miernik. The Polish Ambassador replied that this was "a routine matter" in which he could not intervene. He added that Mr. Miernik would undoubtedly wish to return to Poland, where employment awaited him, and would therefore have no immediate use for a valid passport. If in future Mr. Miernik wished to travel again, his application for a passport would be treated like that of any other Polish citizen.

2 June   N. COLLINS
                                           First Assistant

23. REPORT BY CHRISTOPHER.

Miernik's distress is complete. His contract with WRO will not be renewed and the Poles will not reissue his passport. He came to my apartment just before midnight yesterday (2 June). I was in bed, reading, when the doorbell rang; it kept ringing until I opened the door. I was not surprised to find Miernik with his finger on the bell. Collins had told me earlier in the day what had happened to him, so I expected that he would turn up to discuss his problem.

Although his clothes are faultless—suit pressed and brushed, shirt clean, vest and coat buttoned, shoes shined—Miernik always manages to look disheveled. His thick body, the huge head set crooked on the shoulders, the big sad face with its strange nose and great hairy ears give him the look of an animal dressed up for a child's tea party. He was sweating a lot and his breathing was audible, as if he had walked very fast up the fire stairs.

Miernik began talking as soon as I opened the door. "I suppose you know the news," he said. "Nigel informed me this afternoon. He called me into his office and shuffled his papers, which had my fate written across them. 'My dear Miernik,' he said, 'I'm afraid it's Poland for you. Really, I had to laugh—he seems to think my anxiety is a joke. Your friend Collins has another side you've never seen. When he is on duty he is as cold as a fascist. He treated me as a British district officer would treat a native. I asked him—very quietly, very calmly, Paul—if he had any idea what this meant to me. He raised his eyes to the ceiling. 'Really, Miernik,' he said, 'you must try not to be so theatrical. The worst that can happen is that you'll spend a short time in custody, and then you'll be let out. Things will be back to normal for you in no time at all.' A short time in custody! Things will be back to normal! His idea of hell is his public school."

"Did he really call you 'my dear Miernik'?"

"Of course he did. What else would he call me? When I lost my papers, and therefore my identity as a functionary of WRO, I crossed over into another existence. Nigel's friend Tadeusz vanishes. Miernik the statistic takes his place. Before my very eyes I became a dossier. I no longer have blood. I become a paper man. I am what Nigel Collins and the other bureaucrats write on my new paper skin: *Take away his passport. Put him in jail. Kill him.*"

Miernik said all these things before he had advanced far enough into the room to reach a chair. I put a drink into his hand and sat down. There was no point in saying anything to him. He emptied his glass, which contained about four ounces of neat whiskey, in a single gulp—and let a tremendous fart.

His face reddened and he clubbed himself on the forehead with his fist. "Aaaah!" he cried, throwing his glass against the wall. "Even before a firing squad I would be a joke."

Miernik opened a window and began fanning the air with a magazine to drive the smell he had made out of the room. I gave him another drink. "That's not necessary," I said. He went on fanning.

"I shouldn't have got you up for this," he said. "I'll go away in a minute."

"Stay as long as you like."

His mouth opened in a grin, showing stainless steel teeth at the back of his jaw. "Are you offering to hide me in your attic like a Jew?"

I laughed. "If necessary."

Miernik, still standing with his arms hanging loose, gave me a solemn look; his jokes never last very long. "You really would do that, wouldn't you?" he said.

"I don't think it's come to that yet, has it?"

"No. I am not in Poland yet."

"Maybe you never will be."

"My dear Paul, what do you imagine I am going to do—ascend to heaven on a sunbeam?"

"There are more than a hundred countries in the world. Surely one of them will have you."

"The U.S.A., for instance?"

"Anything is possible. Walk into the embassy and ask for asylum."

"Wonderful. I will find some Nigel with an American accent who will make two telephone calls and advise me to go back to Poland, where, after a short delay of perhaps twenty years, I can once again lead a normal life."

"I think you're being a little hard on Nigel. It wasn't easy for him to tell you what he had to tell you. Maybe he was just embarrassed."

Miernik, scowling, shook his head. Even at the hour of his doom, his compulsive neatness took hold of him. He got down on all fours and began picking up the fragments of the glass he had thrown against the wall. He disappeared into the kitchen and I heard the glass fall into the wastebasket. When he returned he had regained his composure, though he was still breathing audibly, drawing his breath in through his nose. Even more than usual, he had the air of a man who is recovering from a mortal insult.

"My friend Paul," he said, "I want to discuss this situation seriously. What am I to do?"

"Doing the obvious really is as impossible as you say it is?"

"The obvious? Returning to Poland?"

"Yes. Are you sure it would be so terrible if you did go back?"

"You sound like Nigel."

"I suppose so. It's hard to accept that they really want to destroy a man like you.

"A joke of a man? Believe me, they have no sense of humor."

"They must know something about you that I don't know."

"They know things about me even *I* don't know. They are artists, these secret police. They make a file. Into it they put their suspicions. To justify one suspicion they must find another, and another. The file gets fat. A thousand lies equal one great truth, just like a novel. When the dossier is fat enough, they send the man to the butcher."

"How can you know that?"

"It's natural for me to know it. I grew up in a society you cannot comprehend because it hasn't happened to you Americans and English yet. You haven't lived in the future as we Poles have done. From childhood, out there in the future, you learn two languages—one is heard with the ear, the other with the back of the neck. They are after me all right. I hear it here." He touched the nape of his neck.

"You want me to help you."

"How can you help me? You say yourself the Americans don't want me."

"I think there are easier countries for the citizen of a Communist country to get into right now, yes. I don't think you'd have a chance with the people in the American embassy."

"Then what can you do for me? Put a bed in your attic?"

"How would you like to go to Africa in an air-conditioned Cadillac?"

This was the first mention of the trip to Sudan I had made to Miernik. He treated it as a bad joke, and I was not surprised that he did so. It must have sounded like more American frivolity. He began to talk in a loud voice, going back to his own subject, refusing to hear me. Finally I managed to interrupt him.

"That was a serious suggestion," I said. "Khatar's father has bought a new Cadillac, and Kalash is going to drive it down to Sudan."

"*Drive* it to Sudan?"

"Drive it to Naples, take ship to Alexandria, drive it down the Nile and across the desert. It will take about three weeks. Do you want to go?"

"On what date?"

"In about two weeks' time, Kalash says. But you know Kalash."

"I would have to go before my passport expires. That is July 2."

"That means your passport will expire while you're in Sudan. Do you want to be stateless in Khartoum?"

"Kalash could fix something," he said. "Down there he is a royal highness."

"Maybe you could be a slave. You'd come in handy if the old prince wanted to have a little talk with a Polish tourist."

Miernik laughed. "Some Polish tourists would be very interesting to a man who keeps a harem. Maybe this is not such a bad idea."

He cheered up very quickly, a little too quickly perhaps for a man who is going to find himself in the middle of the desert without a passport. He began to rub his hands together, always in Miernik a sign of joy.

"I have always wanted to see Sudan," he said. "It is an extremely interesting place, you know. The populations, the religion, this ancient society cut off from water, living where no men should be able to live. Not only have they lived, they have been conquerors, even. Fascinating."

"You seem to know a lot about it."

"I have studied it for years. One of my secrets, Paul. I want to write a book about it. I even studied Arabic at one time, a little."

"You speak it?"

"Read it a little. I suppose I would speak it with a Polish accent."

"That should give Kalash something to laugh about."

"Kalash. He is no longer very friendly to me."

Miernik was plunged again into gloom. He reminded me of his outburst in the restaurant a couple of weeks before. "I insulted him. Royalty does not like that."

"Kalash probably didn't even notice. He'll take you along if you want to go. He'll even get you Somali girls—that's what he's promised Nigel and me."

"Nigel is going?"

"Of course. He wouldn't miss a trip like that."

"Then the trip is out for me."

"Because Nigel annoyed you today? Don't be an ass."

Miernik closed his eyes. "It has nothing to do with that. But I could not spend three weeks in a Cadillac with Nigel."

"Why not? He's the best man in the world on a trip."

"It's something I am not free to discuss. It would be painful for me. I cannot go."

He got to his feet. His glass had left a ring of moisture on the coffee table. He took out his handkerchief and wiped the table and the bottom of the glass. He staggered halfway across the room before catching his balance with a frown.

"Paul, I say good night."

I did not quite know how to handle this. According to your calculations, Miernik should have leaped at the chance to go to Sudan. At first, he had done so. Now, for no reason he cared to explain, he had decided that he would not go.

I thought I knew the reason. "What have you done," I said, "fucked Ilona?"

(Be calm! There is no way Miernik can possibly know that I heard the tapes you have of the great love scene. My tone was joking.)

The effect of my remark was about what I would have expected if I had driven a spear into Miernik's spine. His whole body jerked, his face flushed. I think sometimes that he *is* a tortured Catholic; I don't know what else could produce such a paroxysm of guilt. Miernik sat down again.

"Nigel knows this?" he asked. "Ilona has told him?"

"You mean you *have* slept with Ilona?"

Miernik began to grin. For an instant he looked positively jaunty. "You will not believe this, Paul, but *she* asked *me*. An extraordinary girl."

"How was she?"

"Very generous, very—inventive."

"I congratulate you."

Miernik's grin got broader. He was more than a little drunk. "Thank you, but I did nothing except surrender. I think she wanted me to die happy." He rose and began to pace. "The question is, why did she tell Nigel?"

"You don't know that she did. Why should she?"

"Oh, I know. Why else would he have treated me so badly today? He was joyful about everything that happened to me. At the time I wondered if he knew, but I tried to believe he did not. Guilt—I felt *guilt*. Standing in front of Nigel's desk I felt that my fate had been given to me by God for having betrayed a friend. Very odd, the human conscience."

"Dieu te pardonnera, c'est son métier," I said. "A minute ago you looked pretty pleased with yourself, old man."

Miernik shrugged and spread his hands. "She is *something*, Paul. Now I really will say good night."

"You'd better think about the trip with Kalash. I think it's your best chance as things stand now."

"I don't think so," Miernik said. He was smiling again. "Nigel has started to smoke a pipe. How can I lock myself up in a car all the way to Khartoum with someone who blows smoke up my nose?"

He shook my hand and left.

COMMENT: In the above conversation, Miernik showed flashes of humor for the first time since I've known him. Maybe this is the comedy of desperation, and then again it's possible he knows something I do not about his situation. If he is serious about avoiding the trip to Sudan, I see no point in going myself. Do you want me to try to change his mind (a move he would be waiting for if your suppositions about him are correct), or have you some alternate temptation you'd like to try on him?

Please advise.

24. TELEPHONE CONVERSATION BETWEEN TADEUSZ MIERNIK AND ILONA BENTLEY (RECORDED 3 JUNE-AT 1955 HOURS).

MIERNIK: Ilona? Here is the hairy beast.

BENTLEY: Miernik? *Quelle jolie surprise.*

MIERNIK: I waited a week to phone you. I thought you'd admire my self-control.

BENTLEY: I thought you were making a very slow recovery.

MIERNIK: Maybe I will never recover.

BENTLEY: You sound very sick and sorrowful.

MIERNIK : Yes, I suppose I do.

BENTLEY: That's very flattering. Good-bye.

(Connection broken here. Miernik dials again; Bentley answers on tenth ring.)

MIERNIK: Ilona, I want to talk to you. Don't ring off.

BENTLEY: Why not? I don't seem to make you very happy.

MIERNIK: Is making me happy so important to you?

BENTLEY: Making people unhappy is not what I like.

MIERNIK: It's not you. Hasn't he told you what's happened?

BENTLEY: He? Who?

MIERNIK: Your Englishman.

BENTLEY: Nigel? What's happened with you and Nigel?

MIERNIK: He gave me the sack. My government is taking away my passport.

BENTLEY: *(Laughs).* Oh, that. I thought it might be something else.

MIERNIK: You say "Oh, that?" This is not merely "Oh, that," Ilona. If I go back to Poland, I go to prison. If I remain here or anywhere without papers I cease to exist. A man without a passport simply vanishes from life. He is a fugitive from everyone.

BENTLEY: I know. It's terrible. I'm very sorry, Tadeusz, truly I am.

MIERNIK: What did you think I was talking about? There could be something worse?

BENTLEY: Not worse, more embarrassing. I thought perhaps you and Nigel had been comparing notes.

MIERNIK: Ilona!

BENTLEY: Men are men. I know how you can be.

MIERNIK: I cannot be like that. But I think your Englishman suspects something. He is very, very cold to me.

BENTLEY: Suspects something? How can he suspect anything unless one of us gives him reason?

MIERNIK: Have you given him reason?

BENTLEY: I haven't seen him.

MIERNIK: Are you sure?

BENTLEY: What the hell is this, a police interrogation? What I do is my affair—not Nigel's, and not yours either, my friend.

MIERNIK: I apologize. I didn't mean . . .

BENTLEY: All right. I am not a piece of property.

MIERNIK: I have been wondering.

BENTLEY: Wondering what?

MIERNIK: If you would like to have dinner again. Tonight.

BENTLEY: I've eaten.

MIERNIK: Now you are angry.

BENTLEY: No, just not hungry.

MIERNIK: Tomorrow, then.

BENTLEY: I won't be hungry tomorrow either, I'm afraid.

MIERNIK: I see. Once was enough.

BENTLEY: There is something I call Ilona's Law. "Enjoy the experience but watch out for the aftermath." I see it proved every day.

MIERNIK: Not with everyone with whom you have an experience, I expect.

BENTLEY: The vast majority.

MIERNIK: It's a new experience for me to be in a majority of any kind. I don't like it as much as I always thought I would.

BENTLEY: Miernik, you must stop feeling sorry for yourself all the time. With you, if it isn't politics it's sex. Why don't you just live and make the best of things like everyone else?

MIERNIK: A good question. I think I won't see you again. I thank you for everything.

BENTLEY: Look, Miernik, if you want to . . .

MIERNIK: Now it is I who say good-bye.

(Conversation terminates at 2006 hours.)

25. FROM MIERNIK'S DIARY.

5 June. Ilona phoned me at the office this morning and invited me to lunch. She drove me at an incredible speed out to Genthod to a restaurant beside the lake. We ate *filets de perche* and drank a great deal of Mont-sur-Rolle, sitting under the plane trees. Ilona ate her fish with her fingers, very rapidly. A ring of grease around her mouth from the fish. Why are the beautiful never disgusting?

The more bestial they are and the more cruel, the better we love them. Ilona was—not contrite, but sorry she had been unkind when I phoned her Saturday night. She said I caught her at a bad time. She said she is like Nigel, all joy one moment and all black despair the next. When their moods coincide all is well. They must be marvelous lovers, or so I kept thinking as she chattered. We sat side by side on a bench. Watching her eat, I became sexually aroused. I hadn't the courage to tell her this: she would have regarded it as a delightful new perversion.

Ilona wishes to be my friend. She says that friendship is the most extreme emotion of which she is capable. She calls her affair with Collins a sexual friendship. Ours, I think, is not to be that any longer. I am in difficulty and everyone must rally around, she told me. What could she do for me? She does not imagine that she can destroy me. She is the only beautiful girl I have ever had; I do not suppose that I will ever have another.

There is no longer any reason not to trust people. This flashed through my mind as Ilona and I talked. For years I have been deprived of half the power of the speech: fear has done this to me, and training and necessity. I have never had the experience of confiding in another human being. Mother died before I had any secrets, Father did not invite confidences, Zofia had to be protected from every kind of truth. But now my stars have freed me. I am between an old world and a new one. I am in a free fall between lives. Until my passport expires and I enter my new orbit, I can say whatever I like to anyone. For three entire weeks I cannot harm myself by being trustful.

Therefore I told Ilona about Christopher's idea of going to Sudan. She was most interested. *(Why is she so inquisitive?* asked the old Miernik. *Quiet! She is only being kind,* replied the new Miernik.) "This is marvelous," Ilona said, "you will go away, no one can touch you in Kalash's desert—you must go, Tadeusz." I said, joking, "Why don't you come too?" Her face changed into that expression, merry and secretive, that women have after making love. "That *would* be interesting," she said, "to spend three weeks under the stars with you and Nigel—and Kalash." (Him, too? I cannot doubt it.)

She plied me with questions about the arrangements, the route, the dates. I know almost nothing about it; I may even have left Christopher with the impression that I am not going. Ilona is right—I *must* go. Duty is duty, and the bridge between the old world and the new. For Ilona it is an adventure—down the Nile, through the desert. Bandits, perhaps. She had a thousand questions; I answered them all. Her hand on my thigh as we talked.

Now, two hours later, the habit of a lifetime comes back to warn me that I should have told her nothing. Suspicion is a disease: guilt's little sister. I cannot be cured of it even by this girl whom I now love. (I realize that I was tempted to refuse Christopher, and therefore refuse my escape and my duty to go to Sudan, because I wanted to stay near Ilona—at least in the same city, if not in the same bed.) I should have told her nothing.

She shook my hand when she let me out of the car. Her skin is always warm and perfectly dry. Her hair was windblown, her lips a little swollen, I suppose from the excitement of fast driving in an open car; she pulls up her skirt like a child when she drives. I don't know whom she will sleep with tonight. Nor, my dear Tadeusz, does she.

> *Entbehren sollet du, sollet entbehren! Das ist der ewige Gesang.* *

26. REPORT BY BROCHARD (EXCERPT).

Finally, for its value as entertainment, I include the following note on a conversation between Nigel Collins and Ilona Bentley that I overheard on the evening of 6 June in the Restaurant Plat d'Argent. It contains some useful information about the Pole, Tadeusz Miernik, and other personalities in whom you have expressed an interest.

---

*"You shall abstain, shall abstain! /That is the eternal song." (A quotation from Goethe's *Faust*.)

In the Plat d'Argent are a number of booths with very high backs. I was seated in one of these with a young woman at about 8:30 when I heard, issuing from the adjoining booth, the unmistakable voice of Collins. He was speaking in what he imagined to be an undertone to a female who I at once realized must be Bentley. These two make no secret of the fact that they are lovers.

"Of course you can't come along," Collins was saying. "How could you think we'd take you? There'll be no room in the car if both Christopher and Miernik come. Besides, you'd likely end up in a harem."

Bentley giggled. "I think I'd rather like that," she said.

"Yes, I suppose you would. Being had by some diseased old Arab who pumps himself full of aphrodisiacs sounds like one of your sexual fantasies. You can do it without my cooperation."

"I haven't noticed that you've been so awfully cooperative lately, dear Nigel."

"Perhaps I need an aphrodisiac."

"I know someone who doesn't."

"Really? How pleasant for you."

"You don't want to know who?"

"Really, Ilona, you don't expect me to rise to that old bait again? You can do as you like."

"All right, we won't discuss the shambles of my love life. Normal people, my dear Nigel, often sleep with the opposite sex at least once a week. Sometimes more often. Does that astonish you?"

"It astonishes me that you should want to go to the Sudan with me if I leave you so frustrated," Collins said.

"We will not be alone. I can creep from tent to tent under the desert stars until my horrible appetites are satisfied."

"Yes, you could do that, couldn't you?"

"Nigel, I don't want to do that—really I don't. I thought it would be rather nice to be with you, away from Geneva, for a time. I've always wanted to see the Nile and the desert. Why can't I come?"

"Because Kalash hasn't asked you to come—and won't."

"Of course he will, if you tell him you want me. After all, Kalash is my friend too."

"Kalash? Your friend? My dear, the thought that a woman might be a friend is impossible to Kalash. He regards you as conveniences. He's an Arab and a prince besides. All you or any female can be to him is a warm place into which he can have a discharge."

"How poetic you make it sound. He *is* awfully good-looking, you know."

"Yes, and Kalash knows it too. He won't have you in his Cadillac. He doesn't need you down there—half the girls of Central Africa are available to him. He has only to pick them off a baobab tree."

This sort of squabbling, a good deal better-natured than it seems when written down, went on for some time. It would appear that Collins, Prince Kalash el Khatar, Paul Christopher, and Miernik are planning a trip by automobile to the Sudan. The ostensible purpose is to deliver a Cadillac to Khatar's father.

However, it appears to me that another purpose is to remove Miernik from Switzerland while his Polish passport is still in force. Collins suggests that Khatar will be able to obtain a Sudanese travel document for Miernik once he is in that country, where the Khatar family has great influence. The date of departure, according to what Collins told Bentley, will be approximately 15 June, but perhaps sooner.

Bentley continued to press Collins to arrange for her to come along. "If you ask Kalash, he will say yes.

"I'm not going to ask him."

"Then maybe I'll find a way to ask him. Would you prefer that?"

Collins by this time was wholly exasperated. "What are you going to do, Ilona, when your bottom wears out? How will you live?"

Then Bentley said something so extraordinary to Collins that I can only believe it was part of the wounding game they seem to enjoy playing with one another. She told him, in her clear voice, that she had been sleeping with Miernik. She described Miernik's body, covered with hair and giving off a strong odor, and in the most minute detail listed the sexual uses to which she had put it.

Collins rose from the table, threw down some money, and left the restaurant. After he had gone, Bentley had a ladylike chat with the waiter. She explained that her friend had suddenly become ill. Sympathy from the waiter.

"Have you any wild strawberries?" Bentley asked. She ate a large portion, with whipped cream, and drank a cup of coffee. Then she paid with Collins' money and walked to the door. She turned and lifted her hand to me. *"Bon soir, Léon!"* she cried, with a reckless smile. She must have known I had heard everything. She really is extraordinarily beautiful.

27. REPORT BY A CLERK OF THE SUDANESE CONSULATE AT GENEVA TO THE ANOINTED LIBERATION FRONT (TRANSLATION FROM ARABIC).

H.R.H. Kalash el Khatar has demanded that visas for entry into Sudan be issued forthwith to the following persons: Collins, Nigel Alexander Spencer (British subject); Christopher, Paul Samuel (U.S. citizen); Miernik, Tadeusz (Polish citizen).

In an interview with the consul, Prince Kalash demanded also that this Miernik be issued with a valid Sudanese passport. The prince furnished photographs of Miernik. The consul explained that Sudanese passports can be issued only to Sudanese nationals, but Prince Kalash was insistent that an exception be made.

The consul, aware of the influence of the prince's family, has instructed me to issue in Miernik's name not a passport but a laisser-passer. The consulate possesses no such document. Indeed, I have never heard of such a document.

On instructions by the consul, issued after I vainly protested this improper giving of documents to a non-Sudanese, I am arranging to have a laisser-passer printed by a local printer.

Because only one such document is being printed, the cost is enormous, and there is no authorization in the consulate's budget for such an expense. The consul, when informed of this fact, chose to ignore it. He told me to "find a means to pay this trifling sum." My own pocket is the only means.

The consul is hardly less arrogant with me than is the prince with the consul. Khatar regards the Sudanese government as a mere convenience to gratify his every whim. He never takes into account the difficulties he creates for us with his behavior. I have written of the insult he gave to the Ambassador of Egypt at an official function last week, when he remarked that the appellation "United Arab Republic" was a "joke." In the prince's view, as he expressed it with the utmost contempt to the Ambassador of Egypt, "Egyptians are not Arabs, they are the descendants of loose females like Cleopatra who offered themselves to a thousand conquerors.

So long as my country continues to give respect and homage to such relics of the exploiting class it will not be free! Meanwhile, in anger, I must issue these visas, falsify this laisser-passer. Such deeds do not humble me, they feed my hatred, increase my thirst for retribution.

(The consul would not tell me why these visas, etc., are wanted by Prince Kalash. Probably he does not know himself, though of course he makes a show of being in the confidence of the great Highness.)

28. CABLE TO WASHINGTON FROM THE AMERICAN CHIEF
   OF STATION IN KHARTOUM.

1. WE NOTE WITH INTEREST HEADQUARTERS DISPATCH CONCERNING IMMINENT ARRIVAL HERE MIERNIK, KHATAR, CHRISTOPHER, ET AL.

2. REFERRING TO OUR OWN DISPATCH CONCERNING ANOINTED LIBERATION FRONT'S SEARCH FOR SUITABLE FIGUREHEAD WE ADVANCE FOR

HEADQUARTERS DISCUSSION AND ADVICE IDEA THAT PRINCE KALASH EL KHATAR MIGHT WELL FILL THE BILL.

3. KHARTOUM REALIZES YOUNG KHATAR HAS NO GREAT REPUTATION FOR ENERGY AND STABILITY BUT THIS SHOULD MATTER LITTLE TO ALF'S SOVIET MASTERS AS HE HAS GREATEST NAME IN SUDAN.

4. FROM OUR VIEWPOINT INSERTION OF KHATAR AS TITULAR HEAD ALF MAKES GREAT OPERATIONAL SENSE: WE KNOW KHATAR DOES NOT SYMPATHIZE WITH ALF OR ANY REBEL GROUP AND WE HAVE EXCELLENT ACCESS TO HIM THROUGH HIS FATHER AND THROUGH CHRISTOPHER.

5. KHATARS FATHER WOULD PROBABLY AGREE SO LONG AS HIS SON'S SAFETY COULD BE GUARANTEED. WE ARE IN POSITION TO MAKE THIS GUARANTEE BECAUSE OF OUR CONTROL OF FIRECRACKER WHO INCREAS-INGLY EMERGES AS STRONGEST FIGURE IN ALF LEADERSHIP AND COULD THEREFORE EFFECTIVELY PROTECT YOUNG KHATAR FROM BODILY HARM.

6. SUDANESE SECURITY SERVICE WOULD HAVE TO BE INFORMED IN ADVANCE OF KHATARS ROLE AS AGENT PROVOCATEUR TO PROTECT HIM FROM SUSPICIONS AND REPRISALS FROM HIS FAMILY'S ENEMIES IN SUDANESE ESTABLISHMENT. AFTER DESTRUCTION OF ALF YOUNG KHATAR COULD BE REVEALED IN PRESS AS HERO SHARING CREDIT WITH SUDANESE POLICE. THIS FORMULA SHOULD RECOMMEND ITSELF EQUALLY TO KHATAR FAMILY WHICH NEEDS CREDIT WITH GOVERNMENT AND TO GOV-ERNMENT WHICH NEEDS CREDIT WITH NUMEROUS AND INFLUENTIAL BAKHENT SECT.

7. ALF ALREADY AWARE IMPENDING VISIT YOUNG KHATAR THROUGH REPORTING OF ALF FOLLOWER IN GENEVA CONSULATE. FIRECRACKER STATES HIS COLLEAGUES REGARD YOUNG KHATAR AS LIKELY FIGUREHEAD AS THEY BELIEVE HE HAS QUARRELED WITH HIS FATHER AND NEEDS MONEY.

8. SCENARIO WE ENVISAGE WOULD INVOLVE RECRUITMENT OF KHATAR AS ALF FIGUREHEAD BY FIRECRACKER. NEITHER OF COURSE WOULD BE MADE AWARE OF THE OTHER'S CONNECTION TO US. IF GENE-VA AGREES WE WOULD USE CHRISTOPHER WHO HAS ESTABLISHED RELA-

TIONSHIP WITH YOUNG KHATAR AS CUTOUT BETWEEN LATTER AND THIS
STATION FOR DURATION OF OPERATION.

9. WE FEEL SOME URGENCY ON BASIS FIRECRACKER'S REPORT THAT ALF
IS UNDER INSTRUCTIONS TO INSTALL FIGUREHEAD LEADER BY MID-JULY.
TERROR CAMPAIGN WOULD BEGIN IMMEDIATELY THEREAFTER. STEPS TO
PREVENT THIS CAMPAIGN MUST BE TAKEN SOONEST IF THEY ARE TO BE
TAKEN AT ALL.

10. WE ATTACH IMPORTANCE TO INSTALLATION OF FIGUREHEAD
WE CAN CONTROL. VALUE OF SUCH INSURANCE SHOULD FIRE-
CRACKER BECOME NONOPERATIONAL THROUGH ACCIDENT OR EXPO-
SURE IS OBVIOUS.

29. REPORT BY CHRISTOPHER'S CASE OFFICER IN GENEVA.

1. Christopher, in a verbal report delivered to the undersigned on
9 June, states that Miernik has abandoned his pretense of reluctance
with respect to the trip to Khartoum. He is now ready to accompany Khatar and Christopher. The date of departure is 12 June.

2. Per instructions, I sounded Christopher out on possibility of
recruiting Khatar as short-term asset for a specific operation. No
details of this operation were communicated to Christopher.
Christopher says as follows: "You are out of your minds." He does
not believe that Khatar would place himself in the position of
working under the discipline of a foreign intelligence service. He
does not believe that Khatar has any political motivation whatso-
ever, apart from a desire to maintain the position of his family in
Sudan. Money would be no temptation to Khatar, who has an
apparently inexhaustible supply of cash from the Bakhent faith-
ful wherever he goes. (Christopher has heard him call up a follower, demand five thousand Swiss francs, and have the money
delivered in an hour's time.) Christopher objects, finally, to
revealing himself as a U.S. agent to Khatar. If instructed to do so,

he would naturally comply, but with serious misgivings.

3. Based on Christopher's reaction, though not on any articulated suspicion, I assume he realizes that our interest in Khatar is connected to the Miernik operation. He has not been told full details of our suspicions vis-à-vis Miernik, nor has he been fully briefed concerning the Anointed Liberation Front. If the operation proceeds as Khartoum envisages, Christopher should be put into the picture to the extent Khartoum deems necessary after his arrival in Sudan.

COMMENT: This officer agrees with Christopher's reservations concerning the recruitment of Khatar by the method proposed by Khartoum. All our knowledge of Khatar confirms Christopher's judgment of him. Absent imperative operational considerations, this officer sees no net gain in causing Christopher to reveal himself to Khatar as this would certainly diminish his value to the Geneva station as a long-term and extremely effective asset.

30. NOTE FOR THE FIELD ON PRINCE KALASH'S CADILLAC.

In addition to standard equipment, the Cadillac automobile delivered on 10 June to Prince Kalash el Khatar for subsequent delivery to his father has the following devices:

1. Two voice-activated microphones, placed 3 inches on either side of dome light beneath ceiling fabric. Microphones feed into two minimum-speed tape recorders concealed beneath the floor of the trunk. Each recorder is capable of storing 70 hours of conversation, and they operate in sequence, i.e., one recorder activates as soon as the other has expended all its tape. Microphones can be activated and deactivated by electronic signaling device so that only vital portions of conversation can be recorded when an agent using this device is present. This device is disguised as a Zippo cigarette lighter.

2. A concealed compartment between the rear seat and the trunk. This compartment was provided at the prince s request. It

is of sufficient size to accommodate an adult of normal size. Access is through the passenger compartment, with back of rear seat removed. This portion of seat will unlatch when electric window cranks on right rear and left front windows are held firmly in "closed" position with ignition *off*. It re-latches when same window cranks are held in "open" position with ignition *off*.

3. Water tanks with a total capacity of 75 gallons have been built into the trunk and engine compartment. A false tank, with visible spout and cap, has been installed in the rear wall of the concealed compartment described in (2) above. This was done to provide an explanation for the obvious false wall of the trunk.

31. LETTER FROM KIRNOV TO MIERNIK (TRANSLATION FROM POLISH).

Vienna, 10 June

My dear Tadeusz,

I can now tell you that the reunion we planned will take place on the sixteenth. As you know, I had doubts that my business would go quickly enough for me to keep to the schedule we discussed, but I now believe that the timing will be convenient.

There was some difficulty in locating the young lady we spoke about, but once I got hold of her she was delighted at the prospect of a holiday. She is well, and she reminds me greatly of her dear mother. She sends you her affection.

We will not meet again before our reunion. I will be traveling a great deal between now and then, so a letter will not find me. If for some reason you cannot keep our appointment, you can reach me by telephone here at 2315 hours on any day through 13 June.

I look forward to this meeting, for reasons you know so very well.

Ever your affectionate friend,
Sasha.

32. REPORT BY COLLINS.

On the eve of departure for the Sudan, Prince Kalash el Khatar continues to press me on the matter of the Sten guns. I think I have persuaded him that it would not be a good idea to transport such weapons across European frontiers where his royal birth is unlikely to influence customs inspectors. He is more or less reconciled to doing without machine guns until we reach Cairo. May I once again emphasize the importance of your making the necessary arrangements for delivery of the weapons in Egypt. Prince Kalash will no doubt wish to accompany me on the purchasing mission in order to inspect the guns, so it will be necessary to arrange what will appear to him as a bona fide purchase, preferably from a non-European. (Prince Kalash wishes to have also 100 rounds of 9 mm. ammunition for his automatic pistol; he proposes to carry this pistol with him from the start of the journey.)

2. The itinerary has been changed somewhat at Miernik's request. Miernik is insistent that we travel to Naples, where we take ship on 23rd June, by way of Vienna. He explains that he has never seen this city and wishes to do so before he leaves Europe. Since Prince Kalash has arranged for Miernik to be given some sort of Sudanese travel document, Miernik has taken to making heavy jokes about his future as a slave in the Khatar household. The fact that a side trip to Vienna is several hundred kilometres out of the way troubles neither Prince Kalash nor Miernik. I shall make telephone contact with our Vienna representative on arrival in that city, probably on 14th June.

3. It is my belief, in which Christopher seems to share, that Miernik has some reason other than tourism for the detour. I shall try to discover what this may be, though of course constant surveillance of Miernik by myself once we are in Vienna is impractical.

33. REPORT BY CHRISTOPHER.

12 June. Until exactly 11:32 this evening, this wasn't a bad trip. The Cadillac is comfortable. We rolled across Switzerland with the radio playing Mozart, attracting looks of desperate hope from girls on bikes (and glowers from their peasant lovers). In order to make time—Miernik seems to be in a hurry to get to Vienna—we ate sandwiches in the car, and kept on until we crossed the Austrian frontier. Collins knew a hotel in St. Anton in the Arlberg, and we arrived at about five in the afternoon. We made remarkable time—Kalash at the wheel all the way, his hand on the horn, slowing down to eighty miles per hour when threading his way among oxcarts on village streets but otherwise keeping to a steady 100 mph. "Tomorrow you drive," Kalash said to me as we pulled into the hotel, "this car is a bit sluggish going up the mountainsides."

We washed, had a beer on the terrace overlooking the Tirol, and ate an enormous meal. Kalash, who changed from European clothes to his splendid robes for dinner, stood the waiters and the other guests on their ears; he is, as you know, six feet eight inches tall and he has the head and the manner of an emperor. The headwaiter, who is old enough to have voted enthusiastically for the Anschluss, had never dreamed that there could be a black who would treat him as Kalash did: "There must be no pig fat and no alcohol in anything I eat unless you want your dishes on the floor." To H.R.H., a lackey is a lackey.

After dinner, Kalash evicted an elderly Austrian from the best chair in the lobby by a simple device. He stood three feet away, absolutely erect in his desert clothes and his turban, and fixed the man, who was bald and rather fat, with a steady stare. Kalash possesses what I think could be called obsidian eyes—almost black and as opaque as volcanic stone. When his victim scurried away, the prince sat down and went immediately to sleep.

Collins went upstairs (I suppose to write his report; I am writing this at two in the morning while my roommate Kalash slumbers on, his thin legs protruding over the end of the bed). Miernik and I played a game of chess. Normally he beats me with little trouble. I defeated him in three straight games, and when I had taken his queen for the fourth time, I suggested that we call it a night. Miernik nodded and crossed the room to the sleeping Kalash. He spoke his name, and Kalash opened his eyes, crossing over from deep sleep to complete wakefulness in the space of a second. "Why don't you go to bed, Kalash?" Miernik asked. Kalash nodded and went upstairs.

Miernik looked around the room carefully. We were alone except for the hotel clerk, who was typing behind his counter at the other end of the lobby, and a couple of old women playing cards in a distant corner. Miernik sat down again and in his methodical way began to put the chess pieces back into their box. Then he folded his hands on the table between us and gazed at me in a way I have come to realize means nothing but trouble. The Black Forest clock over the reception desk had just cuckooed 11:30. Miernik cleared his throat. He blew his nose and wiped his eyes.

"There is something I want to discuss with you, Paul."

11:31. "As you know," he said, "I have a sister still in Poland. She is a student of art history, not a very profitable subject in a people's democracy where everyone's taste conforms to Comrade Khrushchev's, but that is what she is studying. She's six years younger than I am, so she is now twenty-three. I'll show you her picture."

He took a photograph from his wallet. It showed an astonishingly pretty blond girl, smiling into the lens with perfect white teeth. He grinned at my reaction. "That is Zofia Miernik," he said. "She looks like our mother. I favor our father, which shows that God is merciful."

"She certainly is very good-looking."

"Yes. And very sweet and kind. I want you to prepare yourself, Paul, to grant me a great favor. I want you to help Zofia as you have helped me."

11:32. I stared at him and he continued to give me his grimace of friendship, which manages to combine a tremulous fear of rejection with an almost canine look of trust.

"I have made certain arrangements. When we get to Vienna, I want you to continue onward by train or bus for a few miles to the east—across the Czech frontier, in fact."

"Across the Czech frontier," I said in a flat tone of voice. "I see."

"You *will* see, Paul. Hear me out. In Bratislava, only a few minutes inside the border, you will find Zofia having a cup of tea at a certain coffeehouse. You will sit down where she can see you and order a beer, speaking German. The Czechs have the best beer in the world. On the table you will place a copy of this book."

From the pocket of his jacket he produced a paperback copy of Schiller's poetry. "If all is well, Zofia will take a book out of her purse and begin to read it. If *you* believe that all is well, that you have not been followed, you will read *your* book. When you have finished your beer, leave the coffeehouse, turn right, and walk to the fourth corner. Turn left into a small street—I'll give you the name—and there you will see a man in a black Citroën. Get in and show him this book of Schiller. He will drive for a few minutes, and then Zofia will join you."

I was overcome by a desire to laugh, and also by irritation. "Everything is eminently clear so far, Tadeusz," I said. "What do I do after we're all together in the black Citroën?"

"The man will drive you into the country. He knows a place where it is relatively easy to cross the frontier. Of course you will have to wait for dark, and exercise some care. But I am assured you can just walk across through a woods. On the other side, back in Austria, you will find me waiting. We will rejoin Nigel and Kalash at the hotel, have our celebration, and in the morning continue on our way." Miernik leaned back in his chair and gave me a look of anticipation.

"I'm interested in one of the things you've said," I told him. "What sort of a celebration do you plan, exactly?"

"Something splendid, I think. Dinner, champagne."

"And a bottle of mineral water for Kalash?"

Miernik got out his handkerchief again. I watched him go though his wiping ceremony, and when he had his glasses back on his nose I said, "Good night." He gripped my forearm.

"You don't want to do this," he said. It was not a question.

"Miernik, you're crazy. You want me to cross the frontier without a visa on an American passport into the most efficient police state in Central Europe. Then you want me to stroll into a coffeehouse where every waiter is no doubt in the pay of the secret police, flash a book of German poetry at a girl I've never seen in my life, and then escort her across a frontier that's patrolled by soldiers and dogs, strung with trip wires, seeded with mines, and guarded by watchtowers that have searchlights and machine guns on them— all for a glass of champagne and a wiener schnitzel? I think you're trying to get me locked up in a Czech jail for the rest of my life. I give you the short answer to your small request for assistance. No."

"No—listen," Miernik said. "If I thought for one moment that there was any real danger I would never ask you. But I have made arrangements. First, you will have a visa. That has been arranged. Second, no one in the coffeehouse is going to suspect a thing. You look like a German or an Austrian, which means you look like a Czech. You wear European clothes. You speak German with absolutely no accent; in five minutes of listening you will have the accent of the place perfectly."

"The *German* accent of the place? There are no fucking Germans in Czechoslovakia—the regime threw them all out after the war."

"Many people there still speak German. Anyway, you're not supposed to be a Czech. Everyone will think you're an Austrian or a German, a tourist or a businessman."

"For Christ's sake, Miernik. There are no tourists or businessmen in Bratislava. Czechoslovakia is Khrushchev's country estate."

"No, it will be all right. You will only be in public for an hour, at the very most."

"I agree with that. I'm not likely to be in public again for the rest of my life."

"Believe me, Paul, that will not happen. You will not have any trouble. Not with the visa, not with the coffeehouse, not with the frontier. The soldiers will not bother you, they will not turn on their searchlights, there are no mines the way you are going. I tell you arrangements have been made. What I am asking for, really, is an act of friendship that will take no more than a few hours."

"I say it again. No."

Miernik, in the course of this conversation, underwent a change. He stopped cringing. Now he looked at me with a perfectly steady gaze. "If I could do it myself, I would do it," he said. "But I *would* spend the rest of my life in prison, and so would Zofia. I ask you because there is no one else I can ask. I trust you, my friend. You must trust me.

He handed me the book of Schiller. When I refused to take it he closed his hand over mine on the table and gave me a confident smile. "I warn you," he said, "I will not give up. Tomorrow we'll talk again. I know you will do this thing in the end. And we both know why."

Miernik opened the book to a page with the corner turned down and put his finger on a line underscored in green ink. *"Alle Menschen werden Brüder,"** it read. He patted my arm, cleared his throat as if to say something more, but decided not to speak. With one final squeeze of my biceps, he went upstairs. I heard him pause on the second landing to blow his nose.

13 June. Rosy-fingered dawn had hardly tapped on my window this morning when Kalash awakened me. He was dressed in walking shorts and a heavy ski sweater. When you travel it's important to go to bed early," Kalash said. "Otherwise you are tired in the morning and your reflexes are sluggish. I am trying to get some breakfast but I can't get that cretin downstairs to understand me. You must come down and speak German to him."

"What time is it?"

---

*"All men become brothers." (From Schiller's "An die Freude.")

"Five-thirty."

"You won't get anything to eat at five-thirty. The dining room opens at half-past seven. Go for a walk, why don't you?"

"We're going skiing as soon as we have some hot chocolate."

I then remembered that we had agreed, near the end of a second carafe of strong Anstrian wine the night before, that we would do some dawn skiing. There is still snow on the Valluga, the high mountain behind our hotel, and it's possible to have a run down from the cable car station before the sun is too high.

By the time we got downstairs, Collins had organized everything. A table in the lobby was laid with hot chocolate and biscuits, and four pairs of hotel skis leaned against the wall. We found boots that more or less fitted, and went to the cable car station. We rode up with the cooks and waitresses of the mountaintop café. The valley was still in shadow, but as we rose in the cable car so did the sun; the first pink light touched the snowfields and the meadows and the windows of the musical comedy houses with their flower boxes. Miernik put an arm across my shoulders. "It makes one quite sentimental," he said. "How could such a landscape produce Adolf Hitler?" He spoke in German so that our fellow passengers would be certain to understand. They turned their fascinated gaze from Kalash, who had drawn up one bare black leg and dozed off standing on the other leg like a stork, and stared in unison at Miernik.

At the top we inquired about the ski paths and chose the longest; there are no tows at that height, so it's necessary to walk the rest of the way down the mountain when you come to the end of the snow. I paired off with Kalash; he is a fine skier, and I did not want to spoil the experience by having to help Miernik down the path-or to listen to him quite so early in the day. Collins, divining my purpose, kicked his feet into his bindings and pushed off first down the long straight run. Miernik followed him, arms flailing, thick body tipping from side to side as he tried to keep his speed down. I waited for five minutes, hoping that would be time enough for him to get far ahead of me, and started down.

The path turns gently on the breast of the mountain, so that it covers a couple of kilometers. It's a lovely run, with other snowy peaks all around backlit by the sun; the snow was crisp, although there were patches of ice in the shadows of several big rocks. About halfway down I came upon Miernik; he seemed to be all right, leaning on his poles by the side of the path, so I went right by him. Far below I saw Collins dropping down the mountain and a moment later heard Kalash shout something to Miernik. The snow ran out abruptly, but you could see perfectly, so there was plenty of time to stop. Collins was waiting for me with his skis already off when I got to the end. Kalash pulled in a moment after I did. No sign of Miernik. Minutes went by. "Let's not wait.for the silly bastard," Collins said, "he's probably decided to walk down the steep part."

Collins has not been in one of his better moods since the beginning of the trip. He is pleasant enough to Kalash and me, but he barely speaks to Miernik. I have an idea that this has something to do with Ilona Bentley. In the car yesterday, Miernik asked some innocent question about her and Collins flicked him with a look of contempt and ostentatiously changed the subject. Now, with his skis on his shoulder, he began to walk down the dirt path that leads to the bottom of the mountain.

At this moment, Miernik came into sight above us. His poles were tucked under his arm and he was moving very fast. I swore and Kalash watched impassively as Miernik tried to snowplow, lost control of his skis, dropped one of his poles, and went by us right off the edge of the snow. He flew over a patch of jagged gravel and landed on his shoulders at fifty miles per hour on a small meadow of alpine grass. He lay quite still about a hundred feet below us. "It looks as if he's broken his bloody neck, doesn't it?" Kalash said calmly.

By the time we reached him he was up on all fours, feeling in the grass for his glasses. Without the spectacles his face had a naked look. Blood oozed from a scrape on his cheek, and a dribble of pink saliva ran from the corner of his mouth. He was breathing hard. "No matter," he said, "I have another pair of glasses in my bag." Collins reached the scene at this moment, out of breath from his scramble up the steep path. "Miernik, you clumsy ass," he cried, "what do you think you're doing?"

Miernik, still down on his hands and knees, shook his head from side to side, looking more than ever like a wounded animal. It was almost impossible to feel sympathy for him. If ever a man was born to be injured it is Miernik; it occurred to me that this unconscious masochism is his essential quality. It makes it impossible to like him-or to abandon him. Even when he is all buttoned up in one of his black suits, walking through a quiet park surrounded by harmless children and little dogs on leashes, you have the feeling that something terrible is going to happen to him. When it happens, you find yourself nodding your head—you knew it all along. "You'd better feel his bones," Kalash said. "He may have broken something."

Miernik turned his face toward Collins; we hadn't been able to find his glasses, and no doubt he saw nothing but a blur dressed in a red sweater. It is just as well that he could not see the expressions on any of our faces. Collins's was a mask of disgust. "I'm sorry to say that I have not killed myself, Nigel," he said. "Yes, I suppose you are, Collins said. "I'll get some snow for your face; you've got dirt in those cuts."

Miernik was able to walk. He stumbled down the mountain path between Collins and me, leaning heavily on our arms. He was sweating heavily and trembling. Collins held him upright in cold silence, and when we got to the village, he turned away and started back to the hotel. Miernik got little more sympathy from the local doctor, who seems to have been driven into a state of perpetual annoyance by the stupid accidents of skiers. "If you cannot deal with the mountain, you should not be on the mountain," he said, poking fingers into Miernik's stomach and manipulating his limbs. The doctor was still in pajamas. He found a dislocated shoulder and some cracked ribs and bandaged them. "Also," the doctor said, as he pocketed his fee, "you should not have walked in those ski boots. It ruins them."

At the hotel we found Nigel and Kalash sitting in the sun on the terrace with the remains of their breakfast in front of them. Miernik sat down heavily, his arm in a sling and the left side of his face painted bright red with Merthiolate. He groaned. "I'm not going to be very comfortable in the car," he said, "but that can't be helped." Kalash asked about Miernik's injuries; Collins picked up a newspaper and began to read it. Miernik, refusing to eat, stumbled away. When he was out of earshot, Collins put down his paper. "Really, Paul," he said. "How on earth could he do such a thing?"

I shrugged. "We all know he can't ski," I said. "Why did we let him try it?"

"You realize the whole trip is going to be one thing like this after another, don't you?" Collins said. "We'll spend all our time helping him across the street and bandaging his wounds."

Miernik returned, wearing his spare glasses. He had managed somehow to get into a shirt and tie, and he wore a pressed suit coat, the empty sleeve draped over his bad shoulder. Collins said, "I'll pack for you, Miernik, and have your bags brought down. We ought to leave in half an hour."

Miernik nodded. I ordered some tea for him and he began to drink it clumsily, sitting far back from the table because of his sling. When we were alone he glanced around him, squealing the legs of his chair on the floor as he turned stiffly to look behind him, and began to talk.

"Did you think any further about our conversation of last night?" he asked. "I had difficulty sleeping. I dreamt of Zofia, waiting in the coffeehouse all alone. No one came for her. Finally a secret policeman came and began to read a book. She went with him. I saw her go with him. A very bad dream."

"There's something I'd like to ask you," I said. "Did you fall off your skis with the idea that I'd be more tenderhearted if you had your arm in a sling?"

Miernik gave me a shocked look. "Of course not," he said. "I might have killed myself at that speed."

This is true enough. Maybe he didn't know what he was doing on the conscious level, but he makes me wonder. There was such perfection in his victimhood that I began to take bets with myself that some part of his punished brain told him to have the accident. I have played the role of sympathizer for so long that it's beginning to have some reality for me. Watching him struggle with his teacup, observing the flashes of pain playing across his injured face, I began for the first time to think seriously about rescuing Zofia for him.

It might be worth the risk just to see what scene Miernik will play next. That, at least, was the thought I had with the part of me that is a professional agent. The situation is very interesting from that point of view: he has left just enough unsaid to intrigue me. (How did Zofia get from Warsaw to Bratislava? How did Miernik, who professes to have no friend in the world, make all those "arrangements" for visas and a quiet stroll across a fortified frontier?) Of course he must know this, and be counting on it. His attempts to outwit me are annoying as hell. I tell myself that I can walk in and out of Czechoslovakia and confound the son of a bitch by doing so. One American is worth any five Communists.

At the same time I have to keep in mind the possibility that he may be exactly what he says he is. This becomes a smaller possibility every day, but it is still there. Going into Czechoslovakia may be the way to find out. The plot is interesting. There is an artistry to what we are doing: spies are like novelists—except that spies use living people and real places to make their works of art. More and more I want to see what I can do with these characters I've been given.

34. REPORT BY CHRISTOPHER'S CASE OFFICER (FROM VIENNA).

1. Christopher made telephone contact at 2345 hours 14 June and reported to my hotel room at 0245 hours 15 June for an operational meeting. He submitted a written report (attached), which despite its poor organization and extraneous matter provides interesting new light on Miernik.

2. Christopher regards Miernik's request that he cross into Czechoslovakia to "rescue" Miernik's "sister" as operational opportunity. He estimates that Miernik has set up this venture as a means of testing Christopher's willingness to (a) trust Miernik and (b) be manipulated by Miernik. In Christopher's reasoning, a successful "rescue" of the "sister" would increase chances that Miernik will make an overt attempt to recruit Christopher as an asset for the operation Miernik plans in Sudan. Such a move on Miernik's part would certainly be consistent with the clumsy tactics he has used so far with Christopher.

3. To minimize risk, Christopher proposes changes in the scenario Miernik has laid on for the "rescue." Instead of following Miernik's plan, Christopher would enter Czechoslovakia in the secret compartment of Khatar's Cadillac. (He believes that Prince Kalash, who has a diplomatic passport and would presumably have no difficulty in getting a genuine twenty-four-hour Czech tourist visa, could be persuaded to drive the car.) Christopher proposes to bring the girl out overtly, using public transportation. He will require two Swiss passports with Czech visas and entry stamps, made out as if to a married couple, to be used by the girl and himself on exit from Czechoslovakia. He requires also supportive documentation (i.e., driver's licenses, Swiss identity cards, membership cards, and Czech currency). No photograph of Zofia Miernik is available, but Christopher has seen a picture of her and states that she is a common physical type; a believable likeness can be found in the files and used for the passport.

4. Christopher would bypass altogether Miernik's proposed meeting with "the man in the black Citroën." He rightly regards this element in Miernik's plan as a possible attempt at entrapment. On my own discretion I told Christopher of Miernik's contacts with Kirnov, including Kirnov's recent letter to Miernik. It seems possible, in light of Christopher's new information, that this letter was a signal that the "rescue" operation had been arranged. It is not probable that the cutout in the Citroën will be Kirnov himself, but this remains a possibility.

5. Miernik states to Christopher that the "rescue" attempt must be made at 1540 hours 16 June. The time and date cannot be altered. A river steamer departs Bratislava, westbound on the Donau-Danube for Vienna, at 1710 hours. Christopher proposes to exit Czechoslovakia on this boat.

COMMENT: The operation by Christopher does not, in my opinion, present an unacceptable risk. What is lacking is a contingency plan to exit Czechoslovakia alone if his attempt to contact Zofia Miernik fails, or if he decides that he is in danger of arrest. As we have no assets of any kind in the Bratislava area, he would be on his own in any emergency. The only border he can cross is the Austrian. The Vienna station has a standing arrangement with an officer of the Czech border guards at a point 12 kilometers east of Drasenhofen. A night crossing can be arranged at that point on short notice. I propose that a time be set for a clandestine crossing by Christopher on a contingency basis, and that he be provided with the information necessary to find the crossing point before he enters Czechoslovakia. Transport in the form of a motorcycle can be provided for him in a predetermined location in Bratislava.

Because of the short time element, Headquarters is requested to grant its immediate approval for the operation outlined above, bearing in mind not only the risk to Christopher but also the possible dividends of success—i.e., a closer relationship to Miernik with the possibility that he will be encouraged to invite Christopher's participation in his activities in Sudan.

35. CABLE FROM WASHINGTON TO THE ABOVE OFFICER.

1. CHRISTOPHER'S ENTRY INTO CZECHOSLOVAKIA FOR ONE DAY ONLY 16 JUNE APPROVED IN ACCORDANCE YOUR PLAN ON CONDITION ALTERNATE ESCAPE ROUTE IS FEASIBLE AND ARRANGED IN ADVANCE. . . .

36. REPORT BY COLLINS.

Christopher and Khatar went out foraging for girls last evening (14th June), leaving me to entertain Miernik, who is in considerable pain from his injuries but as chatty as ever. Nothing new developed from an interminable conversation. He dwelt on the problem of his sister who is marooned behind the Iron Curtain. Her fate is much on his mind. Bearing in mind our information that no such university student as Zofia Miernik exists in Poland, I asked him a number of questions about her studies. He spun a very circumstantial story about her activities as a student of art history at Warsaw University; she is a painter of some talent; she is beautiful (hard to believe of Miernik's sister, but he has a photograph of a pretty blonde he says is Zofia); his fondest wish is to have her join him wherever destiny may take him. Etc.

2. After breakfast this morning I joined Christopher for a walk around the *Inner Stadt*. Miernik has been talking to him too about his sister. I told Christopher that I regarded Miernik as a mythomaniac, that I did not believe in the existence of the sister. Christopher is unbelievably discreet for an American; he almost never asks a direct question about anything. But my statement startled him, and he put me through a sharp interrogation. I told him only that my doubts were instinctive, not being based on any real information. I don't know whether he accepted this explanation.

3. A bit later in the day I learned from Prince Kalash that there may be a reason for Christopher's anxiety. The prince mentioned casually, in the midst of a description of the Viennese whore he had had the night before, that he is going to drive Christopher over the Czech border tomorrow (16th June)—*and leave him there.* Christopher has told him that he wants to see a Communist country and will return to Vienna by his own means. Kalash does not accept this explanation, but he is quite willing to do as Christopher has asked. "He is probably on some spy mission," Kalash says. I declined an invitation to go along, even with a diplomatic passport.

4. I confronted Christopher with Kalash's information. I must say he is very professional. He must have been devastated by this leak (although I suppose he expected something like it to happen in dealing with Prince Kalash, who is not only an amateur but incapable of keeping a confidence of any kind). But he showed no discomfort whatever. "It's just a one-day tour behind the Curtain," he said. "You can come along if you like. I thought someone should stay with Miernik to keep him from falling out the hotel window." Not surprisingly, no amount of prodding could induce him to tell me more.

5. *Speculation:* Christopher's excursion must be illegal (no American is given a Czech tourist visa) and it must therefore have an operational purpose. I assume that he and I are along on this journey for similar reasons. Therefore what he is doing must have something to do with Miernik. He cannot be taking this extraordinary risk merely to gain information. What would the Czechs, even some Czech controlled by the Americans, know about Miernik that would be sufficiently important and urgent that it could not be communicated in a normal way? It is my belief (again instinctive) that Christopher is going in with the idea of bringing somebody out. Putting together his reaction to my doubts about the existence of Zofia Miernik with Miernik's preoccupation with his sister, I think it is possible that the Americans have laid on a rescue attempt involving Zofia. The purpose obviously would be to cement Christopher's relationship with Miernik.

6. *Recommendation.* That we stand aside entirely from this situation. If Christopher is arrested, as seems likely, I will still be in place. If he does turn up with Zofia Miernik in tow, we will have even stronger reason to believe that Christopher is, as we have always assumed, an American agent, and that his current assignment points to the conclusion that Miernik is up to something sufficiently important to justify Christopher's masters exposing him to very high risks.

37. DISPATCH FROM THE AMERICAN STATION IN VIENNA.

1. In accordance with your instructions, we placed S. Kirnov under twenty-four-hour surveillance during his presence in Vienna 9–13 June.

2. Kirnov registered at the Hotel Ambassador in Kaertner Strasse, Room 816. At 2100 hours on 9 June a transmitter was planted in this room, and audio surveillance of the room telephone was maintained throughout Kirnov's stay at the hotel. Results were negative. Kirnov, as might be expected, used his telephone only for normal calls to room service, valet, et cetera. He entertained no visitors in his room and therefore conducted no conversations. (When alone Kirnov has a habit of singing; the songs are generally in Polish.)

3. At 1320 hours on 10 June Kirnov made a brief call from a public coin telephone in the Café Sacher, Philharmoniker Strasse. Surveillance was unable to overhear the substance of the conversation.

4. At 0127 hours on 11 June Kirnov met Heinz Tanner, a known agent of the Soviet intelligence service, on the Reichsbrucke bridge. Surveillance was unable to approach close enough to overhear the conversation between Kirnov and Tanner, although photographs taken with a telephoto lens and extra-fast film provided positive identification. Kirnov handed an envelope to Tanner at the conclusion of the conversation.

5. At 1750 hours on 13 June Kirnov departed Vienna for Prague aboard Austrian Airlines flight 312. Surveillance was broken off at Vienna airport after the departure of this flight.

COMMENT: Kirnov's behavior throughout the surveillance was consistent with the supposition that he is a trained agent. The choice of meeting time with Tanner (0127 hours) is consistent with the Soviet practice of meeting not on the hour, half hour, or quarter hour, but at an odd-numbered time. The site of the meeting with Tanner, in the middle of the largest bridge in Vienna at a time when pedestrian traffic is minimal, demonstrates good professional judgment. Kirnov used public transportation exclusively while in Vienna; he made no effort to shake surveillance until the night of his meeting with Tanner, when he changed buses, trains, and taxis several times in following an indirect route to his destination. We have no reason to believe that Kirnov was aware of our surveillance. His eluding tactic is interpreted as a routine precaution on his part.

38. REPORT BY CHRISTOPHER.

I have already given the essentials of the Zofia Miernik operation in my verbal report. In the following narrative I'll begin at the beginning and end at the end in the hope of filling in details that may be useful in case anyone else ever wants to do the one-day tour of Bratislava.

Kalash had no difficulty getting a Czech visa. One of his uncles is ambassador to Austria. "My Uncle Embarak sent some little chap hopping over to see the Czechs with my passport, Kalash explained. "Everything is laid on at the frontier. While you crouch in the secret compartment, your air supply slowly running out, wishing desperately for a lavatory, I shall be sweeping through the customs, decadent jazz playing on my radio. Uncle has given me some pennants for the front wings of the car. All will be well."

When on the morning of the sixteenth we went downstairs, the Cadillac was waiting, washed and shined by the servants at Kalash's embassy. Two pennants were attached to the fenders—the flag of Sudan and another one I didn't recognize. "That is a small replica of the battle flag of the Mahdi," Kalash explained. "My great-grandfather, as I may have mentioned to you, led the charge of savages who wiped out Hicks Pasha at Kashgil in 1883. I believe he castrated the senior Englishman with his own sword, which was by that time very dull after hacking at the whites and their tame Egyptians all day. Uncle Embarak has explained the significance of the pennant to the Czechs, so I expect to be cheered at the frontier as the descendant of a very effective anti-imperialist."

Upstairs, there had been an emotional scene as we prepared to leave. Miernik came into our room while we dressed and sat on an unmade bed, watching in silence. As we started to leave, he shook hands with Kalash, who then went downstairs to supervise the loading of a picnic hamper he had ordered from the hotel kitchen. As the door closed behind Kalash, Miernik rose and flung himself across the room at me. With his good arm he embraced me, and he planted a kiss on my cheek. Then he stood back, with his hand on my shoulder, and looked into my face. Behind his glasses his eyes were filled with tears. "My friend," he said huskily, "I await your return." He walked briskly out of the room, like a man hurrying off a train platform after saying good-bye to a brother he knows he will never see again.

Kalash and I started off in the Cadillac at about nine o'clock. By ten we were on the outskirts of the city and well on the way to the border. As soon as we were on the right highway, I turned over the wheel to Kalash, who doesn't like to drive in cities. We rolled over the country along the Donau, making better time than I expected. I didn't want to approach the frontier much before two o'clock, since my appointment with Zofia was at 3:40 and I did not want to spend several hours wandering around Bratislava. We found a side road and followed it, looking for a place to stop and waste some time. Kalash did not take very kindly to the delay. He wanted to see Czechoslovakia, turn around, and get back to Vienna in time to catch the early evening shift of prostitutes. "After six o'clock they are no longer fresh," Kalash said. "You must catch them early or they are covered with footprints." He calculated that he would have to recross the border no later than four o'clock in order to be in the Mozartplatz, where he had arranged to meet a girl he specially liked, by six.

It is impossible in this countryside to get out of sight of a house. This was no small problem, because I wanted to climb into the secret compartment as secretly as possible. Kalash finally just gave up and pulled the Cadillac off the road between two villas about fifty yards apart near the river. He got the hamper out of the trunk and, sniffing suspiciously at the chicken sandwiches for signs of lard, began to eat. I had a couple of sandwiches, but avoided the large bottle of beer Kalash had provided for me: there would be no way to get rid of it in the secret compartment.

As the clock advanced I found it difficult to breathe normally even with the windows rolled down, and I wished that I had taken the tranquilizers you offered me when the passports and money were delivered. The training we are given, and the experience that follows it, are not good preparation for a jaunt behind the Iron Curtain. It is one thing to sit in an apartment in Geneva and calmly discuss the secret police and their prisons with Miernik. It is another thing to put oneself under the jurisdiction of the secret police even for one day. More clearly than you can imagine, I understood why a Miernik would develop nervous habits; even assuming he is play-acting, his performance is based on the reality of truncheons, water torture, testicle crushers. I thought a great deal about János Kádár, sent back to Hungary as a steer eager to please his veterinarian. Kalash did not find me a very responsive companion.

At one o'clock, after making as certain as we could that there were no faces pressed to the windows of the houses on either side of the car, we opened the secret compartment. I manipulated the rear window switch while Kalash worked the one in front. The space behind the rear seat opened like a charm. I had not seen the compartment before I climbed into it. Kalash, catching his first glimpse of the inside, burst into laughter. "We'll have to cut off your legs to get you in," he said, and leaned against the side of the car, overcome with the comedy of this image. I got myself inside by curling up in the fetal position with my hands between my knees and my head on my coat. The fake passports in the inside pocket of the coat dug into my face.

When Kalash closed the trap, the back of the seat slammed into my buttocks; I was frozen into position, unable to move any part of my body except my fingers and my neck. It was pitch black and absolutely silent. The walls are lined with thick felt—soundproofing, I suppose. It's very effective: I did not even hear the motor start. The false water tank extends over the top of the compartment and down the wall facing the trunk. The tank was sweating, so the felt was soaked. In moments the knees of my trousers were wet though, and each time the car hit a bump large drops of water were shaken off the roof, splashing along the whole length of my body.

There was, as Kalash had predicted, very little air. I imagined at first that I smelled exhaust fumes, but I think this was nerves. I went to sleep almost immediately. As I drifted off, my mind told me that I was probably being overcome by carbon monoxide; it told me also that there was nothing I could do about it. Kalash would certainly not hear any noise I made, and there was no way to open the compartment from the inside. (A serious omission in the design, I realized too late.)

I was awakened by a thumping sound on the rear wall of the compartment. The car was stopped. I assumed the border police were pounding on the side of the false water tank. The cap of the tank was removed and a long stick inserted and wiggled around: I heard the water sloshing. It was amazing how keen my sense of hearing became as I lay curled up in the dark, blind and frantic to urinate. I hoped that if they discovered that the tank was false, Kalash would have sense enough to tell them how to get me out. I had no confidence at all that he would do so, and I began to imagine the years ahead in which a Czech commissar rode around the country in this confiscated Cadillac, unaware that the mummy of an American spy was pressed against the small of his back.

The car began to move once more. It stopped again after half an hour (I could read the luminous dial of my watch with one eye: it was 2:35). Nothing happened. Fifteen minutes went by. At one point I heard the cap of the tank being screwed off again. A strange noise, like the faraway lowing of cattle, filtered through the wall of the compartment. I put my mind to the problem of identifying this sound. It was impossible. I was convinced we had been caught.

A long time later, the back seat popped open and a gust of fresh air flooded in. I lay facing the back wall, so I had to come out of the compartment blind. I did not know who had opened the trap; I certainly did not expect it was Kalash. My dominant feeling was not fear but a mixture of guilt and embarrassment. This was one hell of a way to be captured: it was like being found in uniform under a bed by enemy soldiers.

I rolled over and saw Kalash sprawled on his stomach across the back of the front seat. We were in a woods, in a narrow track with trees pressed against the windows on both sides of the car, which was filled with lovely green shade. Kalash held one of his enormous shoes in his right hand. The index finger of his left hand was pressed to the switch on the right rear window. The large toe of his bare right foot was on the switch of the left front window. He is six feet eight inches tall. Had he been half an inch shorter, he would not have been able to reach both switches. He wore a look of intense surprise that he had been able to manage the job at all. I plunged out of the car and emptied my bladder. While piss ran into the dust I wondered idly why our peerless technicians had placed the switches for my mummy-case so far apart.

Had they tiptoed into Kalash's sleeping room and measured him from big toe to forefinger and then designed the car around his dimensions? It's an absolutely foolproof system as long as you have Kalash or Wilt Chamberlain in the car.

Kalash unfolded himself and joined me on the roadside. It was cool under the trees but my clothes were pasted to my sweating body. "You smell rather like Miernik," Kalash said. "I thought I might have to leave you inside. Did you hear me hallooing down the water pipe? I wanted to tell you you were trapped, and so you would have been if I hadn't thought of tripping the front switch with my toe. It required several minutes of squirming to achieve just the right position. The whole experience was most discomforting. Those chaps at the frontier, all wearing funny hats, were suspicious of the water tank. Their officer drew some of it out with a rubber tube and tasted it. They were disappointed that it contained nothing sinister."

We were parked off the Trnava road, ten kilometers from Bratislava. Kalash had kept an eye on the mileage indicator as I had asked him to do, and he had found the track into the woods exactly where I told him it would be. After he left, with the rear seat back in place, I went to the edge of the road and stepped off the 150 paces specified in my instructions. The motorcycle was just where it should have been, fifteen additional paces off the left side of the road under a pile of brush. I screwed in the spark plug, stowed the wrench, and started the machine.

The knees of my trousers were black with water from the walls of the secret compartment, but the wind dried them by the time I reached Bratislava. I attracted little notice, though the road is a fairly busy one—mostly pedestrians and people on bicycles.

Zofia was on time and in place, seated alone in the Olympia Coffeehouse in Kollárovo Námestie. She wore a plain dress buttoned to the throat and her hair was pulled back into a bun. She had done as much as a girl with her looks can do to be inconspicuous. I sat down and ordered a beer; the waiter did not blink an eye when I spoke to him in German. I had parked the motorcycle several blocks away and come on foot. There was no sight of surveillance, but this is hardly necessary in a city where armed police stand on every corner, glowering at all who pass. Through the glass front of the coffeehouse I saw a pair of police with rifles slung over their shoulders. They seemed to be paying no particular attention to me or to the coffeehouse. At four o'clock they were relieved by another team.

I got out my copy of Schiller and read for a few minutes. When I looked up, Zofia was reading her book. I paid and left. The police across the street gave me a routine glance. I walked along the route Miernik had laid out in his instructions, but stopped a block short of Drevena Námestie, the street in which the black Citroën was supposedly waiting. There were no police in sight and almost no one else, except for an occasional housewife going in or out of a bakery on the corner. In moments, Zofia came along, followed by a man in workman's clothes who had his eyes fixed on her buttocks. She has a brisk way of walking with her heels clicking on the pavement and her head held high; I wondered if she had ever been to drama school—it is the walk of an actress. When she saw me she did not hesitate, but strode right up to me with her hand held out. She has her brother's handshake—up, down, moist palm. The workman, with a look of regret, continued on his way.

"This is the wrong place," Zofia said. "We must go on to the next street to find Sasha."

Zofia was in command of the situation, smiling and calm. We might have been childhood friends who met on this corner every day. When I took her arm and began to walk in the wrong direction, her muscles grew tense, but she followed along.

"There has been a small change in plans," I said. "Let's walk for a moment."

We were speaking German. Zofia's voice is low, but it carries very well. "I am not free to accept changes in the plan," she said, smiling into my face. A woman in a kerchief, passing by with a string bag full of bread, looked at us in a startled way and scurried on. At the other end of the street a pair of policemen appeared, and the woman headed straight for them. She seemed to be walking faster than before, and I expected that she would report that a pair of strangers were lurking behind her, talking in a foreign language.

"Those policemen may be here in a minute," I said. "You are a Swiss tourist named use Oprecht. I am your husband, Johann. We live in Zurich, and we entered Czechoslovakia on June 12 at Cheb, coming from Germany." I gave her the wedding ring and, after a moment's hesitation, she slipped it on her finger. When I asked if she was carrying any papers that conflicted with the ones I had for her, she shook her head.

"Sasha took everything," she said.

I told her I had her passport and a wallet full of other papers. "You can tell the police I always carry all the papers because I'm a domestic tyrant," I said.

"Here they come," Zofia said. My back was to the police. "The woman crossed the street without talking to them, but they are coming anyway. They are walking slowly."

We went into the bakery. The girl behind the counter did not understand German. Zofia, smiling, struck up a conversation in pantomime. She and the clerk giggled back and forth over a tray of pastries. Zofia took one, bit into it, made a delighted face, and offered it to me. I took a mouthful and tried to duplicate Zofia's look of pleasure. The police stopped outside the shop and stood side by side, staring though the display window. We went on buying pastries. The girl put the half-dozen we selected into a screw of paper and helped us count out the necessary coins. She showed us to the door and opened it for us. Its little bell tinkled.

The police were still on the sidewalk. Under their caps and crossbelts they were young boys. Zofia, her whole body signaling gaiety and holiday sexuality, gave them a bright smile and took my arm. They let us walk by. Zofia looked up at me, laughed, and put her head on my shoulder. I kissed her on the forehead. One of the young policemen said something in a low voice. The other laughed. They turned around and went back to their post at the other end of the street.

Once around the corner, Zofia slowed our pace. "We must go to Sasha at once," she said. "I don't know what all this business about Swiss passports is supposed to mean, but I know nothing about it. What did my brother tell you to say to me?"

I had forgotten to give her the identifying phrase supplied by Miernik. There had hardly been time to do so, and I began to wonder if there ever would be. Two new pairs of policemen were now in sight at either end of the narrow street in which we were walking.

"Your brother told me to say that Sasha likes to eat his turnips by an open window," I said.

She looked relieved and responded, *"Les couleurs de Princeton sont orange et noir."*

"Well, I guess you are you and I am I," I said.

She giggled. "No one but Tadeusz could have invented *that* greeting."

Zofia's lack of nervousness was having an effect on me. She seemed to feel no fright at all, and that was a good deal more than I could say. Those constant glimpses of police, and the ostentatious curiosity they showed in us, did not make for a relaxed atmosphere.

"We can't stand on corners talking," Zofia said. "We're already five minutes late, and Sasha will have moved the car. It's a long walk to the new meeting place and we have only fourteen minutes. Come."

She set off briskly. I had a choice of following or getting into an arm-pulling match. I followed.

As we walked I told her of the new plan. She set her lips and shook her head, and I could see a resemblance to Miernik. That is one of his gestures. She has others—brothers and sisters sometimes may not look much alike, but they keep the facial expressions and the movements of the body they acquired in childhood.

"What you have in mind will never work. Nobody can cross the frontier on a riverboat," Zofia said.

"People do it every day."

"Not people with false passports. They will *know* who came across at Cheb on June 12. Herr und Frau Oprecht will not be on the list. You can't fool them. They have had too much practice."

It was obvious that I was never going to get her on a river steamer. The psychology of this kind of work is very odd. My first worry was not that the plan had failed, but that she was now in a position to blow my cover to Miernik by telling him that I'd turned up with a pocketful of perfect forgeries. Would this proof of my sponsorship (who but an intelligence agency could produce false passports on such short notice?) ruin the purpose for which we'd taken the risk of going in after Zofia? Obviously Miernik would only bring me into whatever he was doing in Sudan if he could keep up the pretense that I am a good-hearted, slow-witted American. I wondered why we didn't think of this.

Zofia led me through the back streets of Bratislava as if she had lived there all her life. She crossed intersections, cut through parks, turned into alleys with no more hesitation than I would have shown in Boston. We must have encountered twenty teams of policemen; they passed Zofia from one guard post to another in a linked series of hungry stares. At length we turned a corner and there, parked in the shade of a flowering tree that hung over the wall of a little graveyard, was the black Citroën. A small bald man sat in the front seat with his hands on the wheel. There were no police in sight. "You in the front," Zofia said briskly, as she tucked her legs into the back seat and closed the door behind her.

The bald man held out his hand to me. "Sasha Kirnov," he said. "It's very kind of you to go to all this trouble."

Kirnov put the car in gear and moved off through the empty streets. "These Communist towns," he said matter-of-factly, "have the advantage of being very quiet—nothing like the traffic you have in the West. And some of them, particularly here in Czechoslovakia, are quite beautiful. It's a pity you haven't more time. Not many Americans see this part of the world." He turned his head and smiled; he might have been a host, collecting a week-end visitor at the station.

"Zofia and I did a little sightseeing on the way to meet you," I said. "Very interesting rifles on almost every street corner."

"Tadeusz said you spoke excellent German. It's quite perfect—better, alas, than mine. I have to change gears from Yiddish all the time. Did you study in Germany?"

"Yes."

"Remarkable for an American, if you'll forgive such a remark. You people don't have a reputation as linguists."

"No."

"Strong peoples never do. They make others speak their language. How many Romans spoke Helvetian or ancient British? Or Russians any of the languages they now move among? It's natural for the weak to have quick ears."

We were by this time at the outskirts of the city, moving along an empty road. As we rolled to the top of a hill I saw the countryside stretching before us—little copses dotting the fields, horses and oxen working, the distant outline of the Little Carpathians. And, a mile or so off to the left, a high wooden watchtower on the frontier with the sun flashing on the lens of a searchlight.

Zofia touched my shoulder and said, "Excuse us a moment."

There followed an exchange of Polish between her and Kirnov. Kirnov gripped my knee and grinned. "My dear boy," he said, "Zofia was telling me of your plan to take the riverboat. Very enterprising, but it would have been quite fatal. I see your reasoning, of course. It was obvious, to take the boat—so obvious that you thought it would attract no notice. Let me tell you, the Czech police do not think in that way. They always look first of all for the obvious. So you would have been caught in no time. No, no, no. It would never have done. But I congratulate you for being suspicious of us. It shows you are intelligent. One should trust nobody. Because you were suspicious of us, I may say I trust *you* a little more. So it's a gain for all of us, this plan of yours, even though we cannot use it." He looked in the mirror at Zofia. "You will have good company in our young Paul," he said.

Zofia squeezed my shoulder. "I think you're right, Sasha. Getting Swiss passports was very clever, Paul. We do appreciate all your trouble. But Sasha's way is better. You'll see."

All this patting on the head was annoying. "Maybe you'll let me judge that for myself," I said. "I'd like to know right now where we are headed and what Sasha's plan is, exactly."

"Of course you do. What could be more natural?" Kirnov said. "Soon we'll be at a place where we can talk comfortably. We have a little while to wait. Zofia will make us some tea, we will have something to eat, and we will go over the whole thing together. You will know everything."

Kirnov turned the car into a dirt track leading away from the frontier. He drove fast, raising a cloud of dust. The old Citroën snaked over the rough ground, its unlatched hood flapping, its muffler rattling. Kirnov is not much larger than a half-grown child. He sat on a cushion, peering through the spokes of the steering wheel and working the pedals with the tips of his toes. He steered into a woods and followed what seemed to be a cow path at undiminished speed, running over rocks and crossing a good-sized stream, throwing up sheets of water that sprayed through the open windows. He laughed delightedly. At the end of the path we found a small house in a clearing. There were geese in the yard and a goat tied to the fence; the geese set up a racket when the Citroën emerged from the woods. Kirnov turned off the engine.

"The owners are away for the day," he said, "but we can make ourselves at home. Zofia, the tea!" Kirnov helped Zofia out of the car and the two of them strode across the yard, scattering geese before them, and went into the cottage. It was obvious that they were on familiar ground. Still the keen observer, I noticed a lot of tire tracks in the dust near the Citroën and concluded that they had been staying here for some time. I watched the odometer and the landmarks, so I could doubtless locate the cottage on a relief map of the area. These admirable skills did not seem to mean much as I reflected on my situation. Our plan was out the window. I was thirty kilometers from my motorcycle, the riverboat had departed, and I was in the middle of a woods, unarmed, outside a strange house that might very well contain a detachment of security police.

Kirnov came to the door with a bottle in his hand. He smiled cheerfully and clinked the bottle against a glass. "The sun is over the yardarm," he called in English. Kirnov has a jocose quality; you expect him to start tumbling or juggling at any moment. It was impossible to be afraid of such a tiny man. I started toward the house. "Pay attention to the big goose," Kirnov said. "She bites."

Inside, Zofia was pushing twigs into the stove. She laid the table and sliced bread and cheese and a large salami. Her skirt swung with each strong cut of the knife. "Simple food gives the greatest happiness," Kirnov said. He poured vodka for all of us. "To the happy future of this beautiful girl!" Kirnov and I drank. He filled our glasses again. "To our brave American!" This time Zofia drank. So did I.

Kirnov sat down on a kitchen chair and drew his short legs under him. He looked more than ever like a bald child. (He is not a dwarf, though he cannot be much over five feet tall; he is just a very small man.)

"Now you wish to know everything," he said. "Very well. We will stay here until after dark. It is quite safe, everything has been arranged. At ten o'clock we will leave, once again in the car. Very innocent—a little drive along the road to a certain point. There we leave the car. We go through a woods to another point. There we will find a signal if all is well—a beer bottle on a stump. We will be very near the frontier. I will accompany you to the edge of the forbidden zone. A strip of land along the border has been plowed and harrowed, to show footprints. You will have a rake. As you go over the plowed strip, you will rake out your footprints. It will take you four minutes, perhaps five. Then you must cross a small meadow. At the edge of the meadow is a woods. You will be in Austria. Nothing will go wrong. It's a simple plan."

Kirnov put a piece of cheese into his mouth and gave me a merry look of conspiracy. My stomach churned with anger, and I waited for it to subside. It did not subside. I had come here with the idea of running an operation and I found myself being taken for granted by this Polish midget.

"At last I understand," I said. "I am here because you needed someone to rake away Zofia's footprints."

Kirnov stopped chewing. "You are annoyed," he said.

"No. I am astonished that you think I'll accept to go along on this holiday you've planned, knowing no more than you've just told me.

Kirnov stood up. "But surely Tadeusz told you what was involved? You knew before you came that you'd be making a night crossing with Zofia."

"I knew very little else. I still don't. Some things you have left out, Sasha. For example, how close is the nearest guard tower? Are there any mines? Are there any trip wires? What is the schedule of the searchlight sweeps? Are there any patrols? How do we maintain direction going across? What are the frontier guards going to be doing while we stroll by under their noses, gardening as we go? What is your alternative plan if we are discovered? Little things like that."

Kirnov held up his hand. "All those questions I can answer, gladly. In a word, you have nothing to worry about. We have a secret weapon."

"I see. And what might that be?"

"The oldest of all secret weapons. Human nature. In this case, greed. There is a certain officer of the frontier forces who likes money. He has been paid. The exact sum is five thousand U.S. dollars. Pretty good for five minutes work. He is an honest workman. Don't worry. You will not be discovered."

"I'm sorry. That's not good enough, Kirnov. I want facts, not reassurances."

"Naturally," Kirnov said. He hitched his chair closer and beckoned Zofia to sit down with us. "First, to all your questions—there are no trip wires where you will be walking, no patrols, no searchlights. The nearest watch-tower is fifty meters from your starting point. That sounds risky, but it is the essential safety factor. Our man will pay a call to this watchtower at exactly 11:10. He will find something wrong with the way the tower is being manned. He is an officer, he does not have to be logical. He will bring the entire crew to attention and berate them for five full minutes—inspect their rifles, criticize the timing of the searchlight, accuse them of every kind of negligence. At this time, the patrol will be on the other side of the watchtower. They will not see you or hear you. There is no moon tonight. On the Austrian side of the border, on a hilltop beyond the woods, there is a house. There will be a light in the window. You walk straight toward the light. This is important, because you are right—there are mines everywhere except where you will walk. As long as you walk with your eyes on the light, never deviating, you will be all right."

"If I am raking, I'll be walking backwards."

"Yes, but Zofia will be walking normally. She will be your guide. Of course you're right about the raking—we have to hide the footprints so that it will not be known that anyone went across. That's why it takes two persons, one to guide and one to rake. Otherwise, our rich officer would not have the opportunity of spending his dollars."

Zofia smiled proudly at Kirnov. "Satisfied?" she asked me. "With Sasha's good intentions, yes. Do you mind if I ask how well you know this officer you've paid?"

"Very well," Kirnov said. "Oh, very well."

"You've dealt with him before?"

Kirnov turned solemn. "I do not use a girl like Zofia, who is like my own child, as a guinea pig. If I had the slightest doubt that things will go exactly as I have told you, I would not let her leave this cottage. You can believe me when I tell you that."

Zofia rose and put her arms around the little man. "Yes," she said, "you can believe that. Now, Sasha, your tea."

We ate our cold meal in silence by the light of an oil lamp. Zofia kept stealing glances at me. I rewarded her with no smiles, and gradually her air of happiness dissipated. Kirnov produced two large Havana cigars and offered me one. I refused—the idea of smoking a cigar before going over the top was the final touch of incongruity. Kirnov cut his Havana carefully and lit it with a splinter of its wooden wrapping. As he smoked I noticed that he wore a ruby ring on the index finger of his right hand. I realized that his dandyism—the double-breasted blazer, the suede shoes, the precise speech, and now the ring and the Havana—had annoyed me from the start. If headquarters is right in their suppositions about him, he belongs to another era of Russian secret agents. Kirnov belongs in E. Phillips Oppenheim, not in the KGB.

Zofia cleared the plates, giving Kirnov an adoring look as she did so. A guitar hung on the wall, and she took it down and struck the strings. "Sasha taught me to play when I was a little girl," she said. Smiling at Kirnov, she played a tune I did not recognize. He closed his eyes in pleasure. When she finished, he said, "I always see your mother when I hear that song. A woman of gold."

"Have you always known each other?" I asked politely. There seemed no point in adding to the bad atmosphere. I was committed to them for the rest of the evening.

"Always," Kirnov said.

Zofia, with the guitar in her lap, said something in Polish. Kirnov shrugged.

"Sasha was always a friend of my parents," Zofia said. "He is my godfather and Tadeusz's too, which is a little strange because he is of course a Jew. My father and mother did not mention this to the priest when we were baptized, and Sasha had no hesitation in promising to raise us as believers in Christ because he saw nothing wrong in revering a fellow Jew."

"Zofia, no blasphemy. I take my duty seriously. If all those millions of Christians believe Jesus to be God, he is God. All it requires to make a god is belief. Q.E.D."

"So all through our childhood," Zofia said, "there was Sasha, with candy and books and stories of his journeys. He always traveled. A long time would go by sometimes. Where is Sasha? We'd look out the window for him. Then, one day, up the walk would come Sasha, buried under a mountain of dolls for me and soldiers for Tadeusz."

"Books for Tadeusz," Kirnov said. "For Tadeusz, always books."

"Then one day when I was very small, Sasha came to live with us. We woke up one morning, and Mother took us into the sitting room to tell us that Sasha was in the house. But we must never tell that he was there. We knew the Germans were in Warsaw. They wanted to kill Sasha because he was a Jew. So Sasha was going to live in our attic and we would keep him alive. From now on, we could never take any children upstairs. There were many rules, all to keep Sasha from being killed. He remained in the attic for four years, and that's when he taught me to play the guitar."

"I'll tell you an amusing story about that," Kirnov said. "One day in 1943, when I had already been upstairs for more than two years, I was giving Zofia a guitar lesson. It was early evening, just getting dark. You could always tell in those days when it was dusk, even if you had no windows in your room—and of course I had no windows. At dusk the air was filled with the smell of turnips cooking. In a thousand houses, turnips were in the pot—that was all anyone in Poland had to eat. So I smelled the turnips while Zofia tried to learn to play the guitar. I owed her a great deal—she came upstairs every day to see me. And she did other things. It's indelicate to tell you this, but it will give you an idea of what the times were like. For a man in hiding there is always a problem— he cannot go downstairs to the toilet. One used a newspaper. So each day, Zofia would take a package on her bicycle as she rode to school, and each day put it in a different trash can along her route. For four years, the little packages. This long-haired blond girl on her bicycle with her books.

"Back to the guitar lesson. Zofia is playing. I am correcting her mistakes. We are laughing, I am singing the notes for her to follow. Then—a horrendous banging at the door downstairs. Germans shouting. *Where is the Jew?* Zofia's father and I had made a hiding place between the partitions of the wall. No other Jew in Poland could have fitted into this tiny space, but for Sasha Kirnov it was all right. 'Keep playing. Don't be afraid of the Germans. Don't look at the hiding place,' I told Zofia. I got into the space between the walls. Under my feet was a carpet of rat droppings. A strong smell of rats. I had a pistol, just a small one—not for the Germans but for myself. I held it against my temple, standing between the walls, ready to shoot myself if I was discovered. I heard Zofia playing her guitar. Then the boots of the Germans on the stairs. They burst into the attic and found a little girl playing the guitar, but no Jew. Naturally we hid all traces of my presence during the day—blankets into the trunk, cups and saucers downstairs, and so on. For an hour they searched, pounding on the walls, trying to find a secret hiding place. They failed, as you can see. They had never heard of a man hiding *between* the walls. After they went away, I came out. I was shaking, I can tell you. Little Zofia took the gun out of my hand. I remember just what she said: 'Sasha, look at you! You have dirt all over your face, even right on top.' I always told her that a bald man was lucky because his face never stopped like other people's—it went right over the top of his head."

Kirnov, chuckling, relit his cigar. Zofia's face was wreathed in a smile. "Sasha," she said. "I had never seen you dirty before."

They were as cheerful over this memory of fifteen-year-old danger as they seemed to be concerning the hazards of crossing the frontier a few hours hence. They were proud of each other, a sly old fellow and a beautiful young girl who between them could outwit the world. They had done it in Warsaw and they could do it again. These two knew each other better than anyone else could know either of them. Whatever Sasha may be—KGB agent or part of a plot to do murder in the Sudan—he is a very good godfather to Zofia Miernik. He has raised her to live by her wits, and in her kind of life that is a more valuable training than religion.

No one who was in that cottage with them could have doubted that the current of love and trust that passed between them was real. I looked at Kirnov, who once again had his feet tucked under him like a tailor, and made a decision that I knew was not rational. I decided to trust him absolutely for the rest of the time I was in Czechoslovakia.

At a few minutes before ten, Kirnov began to tidy up the cottage. He removed all traces of our presence, wiping every surface we might have touched with a damp cloth; he even took the plates Zofia had washed out of the cupboard and polished them. "Now," he said, "hands in pockets until we go. It's always wise to leave the nest clean." Zofia returned from the bedroom, wearing slacks and heavy shoes and a kerchief knotted under her chin. She carried a small red rucksack.

Inside the car, Kirnov turned to me. "Paul, I don't for a moment think you are such a romantic as to carry a gun, much less use it. But I like to anticipate everything I can."

"I won't be doing any shooting," I said. Absolute trust does not extend to telling an opposition agent whether you're armed—especially when you're not. Kirnov nodded in a satisfied way and started the Citroën. The ride was sedate, compared to our trip out from Bratislava. Kirnov seemed to be keeping to a close schedule; he looked at his watch often, and twice stopped the car to wait. Once, after checking the time and the landmarks, he pulled into a side road and turned off the lights and the motor. Through the open window I heard a couple of bicycles whir by on the highway. "Patrol," Kirnov explained. We drove from there with the lights off and once nearly ran over an old woman in black who leaped out of the way with a yelp of fright.

We were driving north. On our left were the white fingers of the frontier searchlights along the Morava River. At Kúty we left the main highway and turned northwest over a series of dirt roads. Kirnov, still running without lights, put his head out the window. We crossed two rivers on wooden bridges; these must have been the Morava and the Dyje. Turning south, we passed under a railroad embankment, and Kirnov asked me to get out and walk ahead of the car. "You'll see a grass path on your left in a few minutes," Kirnov said. "Guide me into it, please."

Searchlights were visible again, only a few hundred yards to the south. I found the path Kirnov wanted, and he drove in and parked the car. We walked on for another half mile, through a grove of straight young trees. We were directly between two towers. I caught Kirnov's sleeve and asked him where we were. "Twelve kilometers east of Drasenhofen," Kirnov whispered. I snorted: Kirnov's greedy officer of frontier guards was also *our* greedy officer of frontier guards. Sasha had led me to the crossing point I had been going to use in case I missed the river steamer.

It seemed unlikely that any amount of greed would persuade this officer to permit two crossings at the same point in one night. The escape Kirnov had arranged was scheduled to take place fifty minutes before the one Vienna had arranged for me. I fervently wished I had been told how much *we* had paid: any figure over five thousand dollars would have given me confidence that the officer planned to open fire at 11:30 P.M. instead of midnight. But I didn't know.

Zofia was busy, pinning a white handkerchief to the back of Kirnov's coat. "No more talking from here," Kirnov whispered. "I'll lead on." He moved off, feeling his way among the slender trees. It was a shallow woods, and as we approached the edge of it there was some light from the backwash of the sweeping searchlights. These now lay only a few hundred feet ahead of us. Kirnov stopped, then straightened up with a large green bottle in his hand. "All is well," he whispered. "Lie down. Ten minutes." Zofia handed me the rake; I hadn't noticed that she was carrying it, and in fact had forgotten all about it. Zofia and Sasha forget nothing. She unpinned the handkerchief from his coat and stuffed it into his pocket. Her teeth shone as she lay looking into Kirnov's face; she was sprawled on her side, her head propped on her elbow. She kissed the little man.

The nearest watchtower was clearly visible above the trees to our right. Its searchlight swept the ground to either side in a W pattern, meeting the light from the adjoining towers at the points of the W. Anything moving across the plowed ground while both lights were working would certainly be seen at once. There were no dark spots. It was perfectly quiet; not even a cricket sang.

I found myself smiling broadly at the back of Kirnov's nude scalp. If he had set up a trap to have me killed or arrested, I would just have to walk into it with his garden rake in my hand. The time Vienna had arranged for my crossing was fifty minutes too late. If I refused to go across at 11:10, Kirnov's time, he had only to whistle up the guards. I could hardly dodge around in the woods for an hour, get back to the jumping-off point, and sprint across the border alone. Even if I wasn't shot on the spot, I was carrying enough forged papers to spend the rest of my life in Pankrac.* The idea of overpowering Kirnov did not seem realistic. I could not have done it quickly enough to prevent Zofia from giving the alarm. Breaking Zofia's neck was not an appealing prospect. I have never been sure that all that deadly stuff we had in training would work in real life. I could imagine Kirnov slipping out of my judo grip like an eel instead of dying with a twitch and a sigh. The truth of the matter is that Kirnov's story about the Warsaw attic kept me from getting too bloodthirsty: who could strangle a Jew who had come that close to being killed by the SS?

Kirnov reached over and took my hand. He tapped my watch with his forefinger and then gave my hand a squeeze. It was 11:09. All three of us rose to our knees. We were in a pocket of silence (one does hear one's own heart at such moments), and then we heard the sound of a man talking loudly in Czech.

The searchlight wavered, then stopped sweeping, its beam

---

*A Czech prison, equivalent to the Russian Lubiyanka.

pointed away from us at an acute angle. The light on the left kept tracking its own perfect W. There was a corridor of darkness about 50 yards wide directly ahead of us. "Go," Kirnov said. Zofia stood up and strode out of the woods and into the plowed ground. Before I turned around to begin raking away our footprints, I looked up and saw the light in the window of the farmhouse in Austria. Zofia reached behind her and grabbed the tail of my coat.

It was a very slow trip. I had difficulty seeing our footprints, and the dirt was slick with dew. It stuck to the teeth of the rake. I had to tell Zofia to go slower. She immediately obeyed. Behind us I could hear the officer berating his men. The watchtower was a distinct outline, a skeleton of planks with the light mounted on a pedestal behind the front railing. To the right of the tower, about a hundred yards away, I saw a group of soldiers with slung rifles. They had their backs to us, and they were staring upward at the tower. Zofia walked on, exerting a steady pull on my coattails. "Twenty meters more, fifteen meters more, ten meters more,' she said in a low, steady voice as we went. Finally she said, "The meadow."

I felt grass under my feet and turned around. The woods lay before us. Zofia began to run and I loped along behind her, carrying my rake at port arms. We entered the trees and kept going until we were well inside them. When we turned around, the searchlight on the tower had resumed sweeping. It was 11:14. The silence had descended again, and I heard a small noise from Zofia. She was pressing her fist against her cheek and biting her lip. I touched her face. It was wet with tears. She sniffed loudly and moved her head away from my hand.

We climbed up a bank onto the highway. Zofia removed her kerchief and shook out her hair. I was surprised to see that it fell to her shoulder blades. Tears were still shining on her cheeks when Miernik arrived seconds later to meet us.

He had come out from Vienna in a taxicab.

39. REPORT BY CHRISTOPHER'S CASE OFFICER.

1. This officer proceeded to Point Zebra (on the Austrian-Czech frontier) at 2340 hours on 16 June to await the arrival of Christopher and Zofia Miernik. Position was assumed in a wooded area overlooking the border, and surveillance was maintained continuously by this officer and one other officer from the Vienna station until 0005 hours on 17 June.

2. At 2400 hours, the time at which Christopher was supposed to cross the frontier, searchlights on the two watchtowers adjoining the crossing point were extinguished.

3. At 2402 hours, both searchlights were lighted again, and a detachment of troops came into the cleared strip on the Czech side of the frontier. Approximately twenty men were involved. They carried out a thorough search of the area, including a wooded strip on the Czech side of the frontier.

4. It was assumed at the time that this search was directed toward the capture of Christopher and Zofia Miernik. No effective action to prevent this outcome was possible in the circumstances, and none was attempted by this officer.

5. This officer strongly recommends that the Vienna station undertake a reexamination of its relationship with the Czech officer commanding this sector of the frontier.

40. DISPATCH FROM THE AMERICAN STATION IN VIENNA.

1. The Czech officer commanding the frontier sector that includes Point Zebra has explained that he was aware that Christopher and Zofia Miernik had crossed the frontier earlier than the time arranged between him and the Vienna station.

2. His action in ordering a search of the area around Point Zebra therefore presented no danger to Christopher. The U.S. officers who had planned to meet Christopher on the Austrian

side of the frontier had no knowledge of this at the time of the incident, and it is natural that they feared for Christopher's safety.

3. In our opinion, there is reason for a continuation of the normal operational caution that this station has always exercised in its dealing with subject Czech officer. But we have no grounds for disillusion. His action had the effect of protecting his reputation with his superiors and also obliterated any traces of Christopher's crossing over the plowed ground along the frontier. On balance we regard the futile search action ordered by the Czech as an intelligent *ad hoc* operation that protected his interests as well as our own.

41. FROM MIERNIK'S DIARY.

Reunion! There by the roadside were Zofia and Paul when I arrived in my taxi. The picture of them, and especially of Zofia with tears on her sweet face, rises out of the green ink with which I am covering this page. Until the moment I saw them I did not believe in my heart that they would be there. Even now, while Zofia sleeps in a room just down the corridor, I am not quite convinced that everything is as I know it to be—my sister safe at last and my friend out of danger. Of course I should have realized that Sasha would arrange everything perfectly. How many persons have had the gift of such a friend? He sent me no messages by Zofia. She *was* the message.

After the perfection of Sasha's plan, my arrival on the dark road in a Viennese taxi seemed humorous to Zofia and Paul. The more I explained that I could not drive with my arm in a sling (and with no Austrian driver's permit), the more they giggled. The taxi driver was befuddled by my instructions, but very glad to have the enormous fare. I gave him a very large tip in addition, so he went away as happy in his way as we were in ours. No doubt he put two and two together, but what does that matter? We will be out of Austria tomorrow, and we need never return.

Zofia has not changed at all. She is the same willful girl. It was my plan that she should go at once to Geneva and stay in my flat. I believe that Léon and Ilona would care for her until I am able to find a place for us to be together. But as soon as she heard of our trip to Sudan, Geneva was out. She insists on coming along. Paul merely shrugs when I discuss this with him. He agrees to discuss it with Kalash.

I have already made the mistake of mentioning the possibility to Nigel. Naturally he is opposed; I think perhaps he will change his mind when he meets Zofia. "This is not supposed to be an expedition on which one brings along one's sister," Nigel says. He points out the danger in the desert. He reminds me that Kalash speaks often of bandits. "You are putting your sister in danger of rape." Actually I think he is just opposed to having to deal with another Miernik. I annoy him. It is more than his natural impatience now. . . . Ilona. Poor Nigel has found that he is not so nonchalant about this girl as he thought. It is impossible to regret what happened between Ilona and myself. I am shocked that I should feel such indifference to my betrayal of a friend, but there it is—a truth to be faced.

Tonight I thought nothing could intrude on my happiness. I have not felt such emotion or known such serenity since I was a child. On my way to collect Zofia, all my life flowed by in my memory. She is the last link to that short interval of happiness that I knew (and Zofia was too young to know) between my birth and the war and Mother's death. Zofia suffered more from Father's death than I. All capacity for sorrow was lost to me when Mother was killed. I have never until now been able to think about the details of that death. I mean think in words. The picture is in my mind at all times, and I push it down a hundred times a day.

We are walking across the field. The earth is still cold after the winter. It is muddy—streaks of wet earth slimy under our feet. The daisies have opened, and also some yellow flowers that must have been jonquils. There are cattle in the next field. We walk into the woods and suddenly we are surrounded by a group of Polish soldiers—ragged and filthy. They call themselves partisans but in fact they are stragglers, semi-criminals who have seized on the war as an excuse for banditry. Father had explained this to me and now I see that what he said was true.

They are bold with Mother. One of them touches her on the breast and she leaps away and, holding my hand, begins to run. Behind us I hear the hard breathing of running men. Mother slips on a patch of mud and falls. There is a long brown streak on her skirt, like filth. I try to help her up. I feel a blow on the back of my head. They are all around us. Mother lies on the ground, panting, her eyes filled with—not fear but contempt. "Tadeusz," she says, "go home. I'll be along." I am pulled to my feet and kicked on the tail of my spine. The pain is nauseating. I run into the woods and hide, covering my eyes with my hands.

I hear a burst of machine gun fire. I creep back and find my mother's naked body. They have pulled her dress upward over her head, so her face is hidden. On her stomach are five tiny blue holes, and under her body a pool of red blood. Her legs are pulled apart as if they wanted to break them from her body. I find her underclothes and pull the torn cloth over her legs, to cover her. I lift her body and pull down her dress. Her hair is loose and stained with the blood she coughed into it.

I knew what had happened to her. I did not want Father to know that Poles had done this. So I told him a German airplane strafed us. I was in such a state of shock I could hardly talk. But I could lie. Father never believed it. Never. But it was better that I could let him blame the Germans: he had sent us into the countryside so that we would be safe.

Nigel does not know what he does when he speaks to me of Zofia being raped by bandits in the desert.

42. REPORT BY COLLINS.

My attempts to elicit details of Christopher's adventure in Czechoslovakia have so far come to nothing. Christopher himself is uncommunicative, and Prince Kalash seems already to have forgotten the incident. It was, he says, a boring day spent in a boring country. Miernik will say nothing. He sits up much of the night, writing in his diary. He carries this journal with him in the small briefcase that he has in his possession at all times.

2. Last night (18th June) Miernik gave a celebratory dinner at the Hochhaus Restaurant to introduce us to his sister. Zofia Miernik is a beautiful and intelligent girl and she would have been the feature of the evening if Miernik himself had not turned up in evening clothes. He went ahead of us to the restaurant to supervise arrangements. He had booked the best table on the terrace, which has a marvellous view of Vienna. By the time we arrived, champagne (German variety) was chilling in ice buckets and a squadron of waiters was bowing and flourishing napkins. Miernik, in his double-breasted dinner jacket and old-fashioned starched collar (with *white* tie), looked rather like a trained bear. (Christopher's description.) But as usual he had got exactly what he wanted: just the right table, just the right degree of obsequious service, just the right tunes from the orchestra. His helpless air is an illusion. He is a tyrannical stage manager.

3. Zofia Miernik arrived with Christopher. She was wearing a blue frock cut very low at the neck, which certainly was not purchased in Warsaw. She speaks fluent German with almost no accent. On meeting Prince Kalash, she revealed that her English is excellent as well. Whatever else they may be, the Mierniks (assuming that Zofia is in fact a Miernik) are an educated family. Once we were seated, Miernik had the champagne opened and stood for a toast. "Gentlemen," he said, "I present to you my sister, Zofia, in the hope that your friendship for her will be as steadfast as your friendship for me." We all drank, though I did so with understandable mental reservations. Miernik then began snapping his fingers at the waiters, and a meal was served that actually began with caviar and ended with baked Alaska. Obviously it cost a fortune, but one assumes that Miernik has adequate sources of money.

4. I attempted to interrogate Zofia. A look of amusement crept over Christopher's face. Miernik apparently had less confidence in his "sister's" discretion; he was distinctly nervous. I asked Zofia how long she planned to remain in Vienna before returning to Poland.

"I plan to travel for some time," she said. How exactly did she travel to Vienna? Was it not inconvenient to leave Poland? "Friends were very kind," Zofia said, "it was a very enjoyable journey—so much to see I had never seen before." Yes, but how did she come—by air? by railway through Berlin? "By car, mostly. You've no idea how bad the roads are in the people's democracies—but even that is preferable to flying; one is likely to land in a meadow or on a strip of country road." She told of a friend who had flown to Bulgaria. Every hour or so, the old Dakota nosed over and bumped down in a field. Peasants came scrambling out of the woods carrying cages with chickens in them and blanket rolls, elbowing each other away from the door of the aircraft in a free-for-all rush for the seats. Some sat on the floor, eating sausages. Fifteen years under Communism has not deprived Zofia of her sense of class consciousness; as she mimicked the Bulgarian peasants she might have been a duke's poor relation trying to talk in Cockney. If all this was produced by the Polish secret service they have a right to be pleased with their methods. Prince Kalash asked Zofia to dance and she rose and followed him onto the floor (H.R.H. does not let females walk ahead of him, of course). The Viennese were frozen in the middle of their fox-trots by the sight of this towering black holding a perfect Aryan specimen in his arms. As they danced it was plain that Prince Kalash would be raising no objection to Zofia's joining our expedition. After they returned to the table, Zofia excused herself. Prince Kalash, lifting his wineglass and giving Miernik a friendly glance, observed: "Your sister has beautiful breasts. That is rare in a white woman." Miernik has learnt that Khatar's style of speech is never meant to be insulting. "I'm very happy you think so, Kalash," he said. "Since childhood Zofia has been quite beautiful." But when we returned to the hotel, Miernik was careful to escort his sister to her room himself, and I'm sure he advised her to lock the door.

5. After Zofia Miernik had retired, and her brother had gone out for his usual midnight walk, Christopher rang me up and invited me to the bar. Over a cognac he told me that Miernik was determined to take Zofia along on the remainder of the trip. Prince Kalash is, as

I predicted, more than willing. "Miernik is afraid you'll be disagreeable about it," Christopher said. "I am to use my influence with you to persuade you to accept the inevitable." There was no basis on which I could openly object to her coming along. I said I thought it was a bad idea to introduce a girl into the situation, especially such a good-looking one. Christopher refuses to see a problem. No doubt his instructions as well as his instincts tell him to keep an eye on Zofia. Once again I tried to implant the idea that Zofia cannot possibly be Miernik's sister. "I don't see why not," Christopher said. "I don't look anything like my brothers and sisters. Besides, what difference does it make?" There is between us a sort of cousinship; he sees that I am an agent like himself, and he understands. Each of us takes it for granted that the other is under discipline, though nothing has ever been stated in the open about this. There are limits to this kind of a relationship: I cannot cross the boundary to ask him what precisely he was doing in Czechoslovakia. He cannot come over to my side to volunteer any information. The conversation dwindled down to an hour of good-natured chaff about the Mierniks. "If they do have the same father," Christopher said, "the old man must have been under an enchantment. He got old Tadeusz while he was still a frog, and Zofia after he was turned into a prince." That's as good a theory as any I've been able to put forward.

43. REPORT FROM THE FILES OF THE VIENNA CRIMINAL POLICE.

The body of a well-dressed male was discovered at approximately 1015 hours on 19 June in the Prater, in shrubbery between the Hauptallee and the Trotting Course. Discovery was made by Fräulein Hilde Schenker, who had entered the park with the purpose of bird-watching.

There was no identification on the body. Through comparison of fingerprints taken from the cadaver with those in the central police files, it was established that the dead man was one Heinz

Tanner, aged about forty, domiciled at III. Vienna, Baumgasse 17.

The body showed no marks of violence. The preliminary ruling of the ambulance physician was that Tanner had died of natural causes, probably of a heart attack.

An autopsy was ordered after the identity of the dead man was established. Time of death was approximately 0130 hours 19 June. Examination of the mucus of the nose and throat, of the lung tissues, and of the other internal organs revealed traces of cyanide. Forensic investigation suggests that cyanide was introduced into the body in the form of a spray.

This leads to the conclusion that the victim was murdered, probably by an assailant who approached and sprayed cyanide into Tanner's face from extremely close range.

A similar method has been used twice in the past year. The victims were the leader of a Polish émigré group in Munich (18 October) and a young woman in Berlin (11 January) who was suspected of being engaged in espionage activities.

Tanner's dossier shows a history of contacts with known representatives of foreign intelligence services. (See secret files.)

It is assumed that this crime was politically motivated. No information of any kind relating to this crime is to be made available to the press, which has already reported that an unidentified man died of natural causes in the Prater on the relevant date.

44. NOTATION BY THE AMERICAN STATION IN GENEVA.

Records of the Swiss federal police indicate that Tadeusz Miernik was absent from Switzerland last October 17—18 and on January 11. In both cases he reentered the country by train.

Christopher reports Miernik was absent from his hotel from midnight until at least 0130 on 19 June, the date of Tanner's death.

Vienna is asked to withhold this information from its Austrian police liaison for the time being.

45. REPORT BY CHRISTOPHER.

21 June. Journal of the Miernik Expedition (cont'd): We rose at five and were on the road by six. Through most of the morning it was a silent ride, partly because of the gray weather, partly because of the strain created by Zofia's presence. Collins does not like having her along, and he is not one to conceal his emotions. He is now barely civil to any of us.

We arrived in Innsbruck in time for lunch. After the meal, Kalash and Miernik went off to find a cuckoo clock for some relative of Kalash's, and Zofia and I went for a walk through the town while Collins stayed with the car. Zofia was subdued; I don't know whether it's a reaction to the excitement of the other night, or whether she's disturbed by Collins' hostility. We passed a music shop and I took her inside and bought her a guitar. She was delighted by the gift and kept the instrument with her when we got back in the car. As we climbed toward the Brenner, she played a little and the Polish songs brought a smile to Miernik's lips. Even Collins softened a little and asked for a couple of songs.

There was still a lot of snow beside the road at the top of the pass. We stopped at the summit and walked around shivering in our summer clothes. It was a brilliant day at that altitude, with the Dolomites rising through the clouds to the south. Kalash got out his camera and posed us all against the snowy backdrop. Miernik moved as the shutter clicked, then volunteered to take a shot of all of us with Kalash. Collins said, "Miernik, why do you always jump about when your picture is being taken? Kalash has a whole roll of film showing one American, one Englishman, and a Polish blur."

There was difficulty at the Italian frontier over Miernik's passport. The *commandante* of the border post was puzzled that Miernik should have been given a thirty-day visa on a passport that expires in eleven days' time. Moreover, he does not like Polish passports. He examined every page of the little brown book and subjected Miernik to an hour of questions. It was all very polite, but Miernik was in that state of acute distress which any contact with men in uniform seems to produce in him. It was hard to blame the Italian for being suspicious. Zofia, it turns out, is traveling on an Ecuadorian passport. (This document may well be genuine; it shows her true name and actual date and place of birth; no doubt Kirnov has an obliging friend in some Ecuadorian consulate.) Kalash, too, is a rare bird to appear at an Alpine outpost, and both Collins' passport and mine are filled with suspicious visas and stamps. By any standards, we are a peculiar group.

Kalash saved the situation in the end. He did not mind the wait (he has told me that he has no sense of time, a quality he regards as one more proof that he is a wiser and happier man than any white who grew up surrounded by clocks) but he saw that the rest of us were getting impatient. He strode into the customs post and we saw him through the window, talking to the Italian while Miernik fidgeted in the background. I thought he might try bribery, and I had a picture of all of us languishing in some damp jail in Bolzano.

Then we saw the *commandante* smile, nod, and sit down at his desk. He scribbled for a moment in Miernik's passport and banged away at it with his rubber stamps. Miernik and Kalash emerged. "That man is a bureaucrat," Kalash explained. "He needed a way to cover his tracks, but of course he hasn't the imagination to invent a solution. I told him to cancel Miernik's thirty-day visa and substitute one that expires when the passport expires. A great light broke in his brain, as perhaps you saw through the window. So we can go, taking this dangerous Communist along with us. I think I have a great future in diplomacy. Ambassador to some Christian country. It's good for the mind to deal with the Catholics, they are so eager to be honorable. If that man had been an Arab, we could have given him some money and avoided all this bother. But where would the intellectual challenge have been?" He patted the roof of the car, as if rewarding a willing beast. "The Cadillac had a good deal to do with it as well," he said. "Had we arrived on motorcycles, old Miernik would be in chains. A policeman always reckons that if one has money enough to buy a big car, one has money enough to buy a bigger policeman. He hesitates to trifle with a Cadillac. A Rolls-Royce would have been just as frightening in your palmy days, Nigel. No more, alas."

"Such foolishness," Miernik said, stamping around in the road, flourishing his passport. "If I were a spy I would not be coming into Italy on a Polish passport. Spies have American passports. He actually searched my sling for concealed weapons or maybe micro-film. I could not reason with him."

Kalash pushed Miernik into the car and shut the door. "You really must speak to Miernik," he said. "I found him talking Latin to that Italian. The man speaks perfectly good English. He asked me why Miernik was speaking Romanian if he was a Pole. Really, I'm surprised Miernik didn't unpack his rosaries and wave them about. *Latin.* I ask you, Paul. He suffers from intellectual egoma-nia." As is his habit when he is overcome by disgust, Kalash went promptly to sleep in the back seat. I drove down the mountain, a good deal slower than Kalash had driven up the other side.

We arrived in Verona in the late afternoon. Miernik, of course, had all the Baedeker details. He took us on a walking tour of the city, ending in a grubby little courtyard in which is located, accord-ing to the tourist guides, the balcony of Juliet. Miernik denounced it as a fake. Kalash picked up Zofia and tossed her onto the bal-cony, which is not far above ground level. Then, standing with one hand on his heart, he recited Othello's death speech.

"That's the wrong play, Kalash," Miernik said.

"I know it is, you bloody pedant. I never played Romeo at Oxford, at least not on stage. It's a foolish play in any case, all Shakespeare's plays are very foolish. People killing themselves for sex—an Italian might, I suppose. But a Moor? I rather like that line about taking the circumcised dog by the throat, though. My ancestors were certainly put off by all that English foreskin. Made the fairies among 'em shudder. *Autre pays, autres mœurs.*"

We walked on to the Albergo Due Torre for supper. The atmos-phere seemed gay enough when we entered—music, dancing; eager waiters: Italy is the last outpost of cordiality. We ordered food and wine and sat back to enjoy the scene. At the next table was a party of Germans. One of them, a blond type in a coat with a belted back, rose and bowed to an Italian female child at the adjoining table. He called for a waltz and danced with the little girl, who must have been about eight years old. His companions, another man and two middle-aged women, laughed in delight. The German took the child back to her parents and thanked her with another deep bow. Then he sent her a big pink drink full of fruit, and bowed again, clicking his heels. Miernik watched coldly (as did all of us except Kalash), and Zofia stared fixedly at her wineglass. The Germans wore that air of racial superiority which some of them seem to think is the correct attitude for a traveler south of the Alps. It was apparent that they had been officers at one time, and they spoke Italian. *"Waffen* SS," Collins murmured, "returning to the happy scenes of wartime duty."

The violinist, a small, shriveled man wearing round smoked glasses (not sunglasses—old-fashioned smoked lenses, almost black), scuttled across the floor to the Germans' table. He smiled and asked in broken German if he could play a German song for them. The man who had danced with the child gave him a cursory glance and named a song. The violinist played it. The other German requested a different song. None of the Germans paid any attention to the musician as he played; they went on with their conversation, laughing across the table at one another.

The Germans began by asking for songs everyone knows: *Röslein, Die Lorelei,* and so on. Then they changed to a long list of obscure German drinking songs. They gave the violinist no rest between tunes. As soon as he completed one they asked for another and demanded that he play each faster than the one before. "I want to see your fingers dance, Maestro," said one of the Germans with a guffaw. He and his friends began giving the instruction in unison: *"Più rapido!"* The violinist obeyed them. He tap-danced around the table, pointing the neck of his violin at the ceiling and floor, wiggling his hips, smiling in a crazed desire to please. It was Pavlovian. Zofia said, "That man must have been in one of their camps." I believe she was right. The skin of his face was drawn back in a desperate grin, his body jerked. It was like watching a skeleton dance out of the gates of Dachau.

In the middle of a tune, the Germans rose. The violinist continued his jig, the grin fixed on his face. He was running with sweat. The Germans dropped money on the table to pay their bill. Then the one who had danced with the child gave his companions a humorous wink. He took a thousand-lira note out of his pocket, spat on it, and slapped it on the violinist's sweaty forehead. It stuck there. The violinist gave a high giggle and kept on playing with his head thrown back so the bill would not fall off.

Miernik's chair went over backwards. He was standing and speaking to the Germans. He held a table knife in his hand. The Germans stood their ground, either astonished by this display of bad manners or unfrightened by a one-armed man with a dull knife. One of the German women carried a Pekingese in her arm; throughout the meal and the violin concert she had been feeding it and talking to it.

"One moment," Miernik said. "I want to kill your dog." The woman shrieked, and a look of real horror came into her eyes. Her husband stepped between the dog and Miernik. "You are drunk," he said.

"Quite sober," Miernik said. "Hand over the dog. We have been watching you and we have our orders. The dog must die."

The German turned on his heel and began to herd his friends toward the door. "Halt!" Miernik shouted. "Come back or I shoot." The Germans stopped and turned around again—all except the woman with the dog. She now had both arms around the animal. She stared at Miernik over her hunched shoulder. "You are insane," she cried.

"How long have you been hiding this dog?" Miernik asked in the loud German he was speaking. "Speak up—and remember there are witnesses present."

"Who are you?" asked the German. "You are not a German."

"My name does not matter. It is enough that you know that I am an officer in the Dog Death Brigade. You have forgotten that dogs are not human beings. They are dogs. *Dogs.* Dogs who are shitting on our sacred soil, taking food from the mouths of good human children."

The violinist looked from Miernik to the Germans, and his giggle changed to a spasmodic, snorting laugh. He had heard this sort of talk somewhere else. With his hand over his mouth, he scuttled away, the thousand-lira note fluttering to the floor behind him.

"If you did not have that arm in a sling," the German said, "I would slap your face for you."

"I don't doubt it for a moment," Miernik said. "Your late leader, Reichsführer Himmler, would do practically anything to protect a dog. He may be dead, but the kingdom of his ideas lives on. Take your dog and go. But remember: one day soon the gutters will run red with the blood of dogs."

The German put his arm around his wife, who by this time was sobbing as she reassured her Pekingese in baby talk. They left. Miernik poured wine for all of us, and sat down.

For the remainder of the meal we talked about Puccini. Miernik believes that romantic composers prepared the ground for totalitarian politicians: both deal in illusions, knowing that the illusions people have about themselves as individuals and as nations are stronger than reality.

Miernik and Zofia retired early. Kalash, walking around the silent town with Collins and me, chuckled over our translation of Miernik's confrontation with the Germans. "It's nice to see him show a little wit," Kalash said. "But you Europeans really are tribalistic. No hope for you, I'm afraid, until you pass out of this primitive stage and learn to be more cool-headed about all these enmities and superstitions."

Later, passing Zofia's room, I stopped, meaning to knock. Through the door I heard her voice and Miernik's, speaking in Polish. I have to report that I felt no curiosity at all about what they might be saying; I was, instead, happy that Miernik at last had someone besides me to talk to late at night.

22 June. Uneventful day, except for what sounded like a raging argument between Zofia and Miernik in Polish as we sped down the *autostrada* toward Naples. Thinking that there might be some substance in what they were saying, I used my dandy Zippo for the first time. This is not, incidentally, the least conspicuous device you could have given me. I don't smoke, so I have to manipulate it inside my pocket. I leave you to struggle with the tapes. The car will be in the garage of the Albergo Commodore tonight. It will be loaded on the ship at eight o'clock tomorrow morning.

46. TRANSCRIPT OF A CONVERSATION BETWEEN MIERNIK AND ZOFIA MIERNIK, 22 JUNE, "CADILLAC LOG" (TRANSLATION FROM POLISH).

ZOFIA: . . . not going to be a very pleasant ride if you go on like this. We went over all this last night.

MIERNIK : Zofia, you never change. You do something horrid and then put the blame on those who want to help you.

ZOFIA : Horrid? How horrid? I am an adult, Tadeusz, and I made the decision as an adult. There was nothing for me where I was. I was learning nothing.

MIERNIK : But simply to quit without telling me. It was unfair— not to say dishonest. I should think you could have trusted me. And poor Sasha. When he couldn't find you, think how he must have felt.

ZOFIA : Sasha found me. He understood perfectly.

MIERNIK : *I* don't understand perfectly. You throw away your university degree, you go to live with a lot of scruffy people who call themselves artists, who are under constant surveillance by the police. It's unbelievable. You might have put everything in danger. Suppose the whole group had been arrested? How would Sasha have found you then?

ZOFIA : But all those things did not happen, Tadeusz. Sasha found me, I am here, all is well. And I have no use for a degree from Warsaw University that means nothing.

MIERNIK : Nothing? It means the difference between a life as a professional, a teacher perhaps, and life as an outcast. Even in the West they attach some importance to education.

ZOFIA : Tadeusz, I don't want to teach. I am not a professional type. You are. I'm not. Also, I'm capable of taking care of myself.

MIERNIK : Living five in a room with men and girls together, with no bath, with no proper papers? If that's how you take care of yourself . . . We spent years building up a certain picture of you, and you tear it up on a whim.

ZOFIA : Tadeusz, I wasn't in any danger. I was quite happy, in fact. That's something, isn't it? To be happy in Warsaw while one is young? It was nothing terrible. Now, thanks to you and Sasha, it's done with. If I ever want to go back to a university I can do it.

MIERNIK : Irresponsible. When I think that I asked Sasha to help you, thinking the danger was so much less than it was . . . The danger was your fault.

ZOFIA : There was no danger to Sasha. He can do anything.

MIERNIK : Perhaps he can. But to *ask* him to take extra chances as you did. I don't know how I can apologize to him.

ZOFIA : If you do, he'll laugh at you. It was a lark for Sasha.

MIERNIK: You think everything is a lark. Life is not a lark. You have never been asked to do an ugly thing in your life. You could have ruined everything.

(Remainder of Polish conversation consists of remarks by female voice on landmarks. Both voices change to English before tape ends.)

47. REPORT OF AN AMERICAN SURVEILLANCE TEAM IN PARIS (EXCERPT).

18 *June, 1737 hours.* Routine surveillance of Vasily Kutosov continues. In Luxembourg Gardens he approaches a female, aged approximately twenty-five, long dark hair, blue dress, medium height, exceptionally attractive. Kutosov, removing hat, speaks to young woman, who is feeding pigeons.

Conversation between two subjects ensues. Duration 7 minutes, 45 seconds. Forrest approaches subjects at approximately 1740 hours and ascertains that they are speaking Russian.

Kutosov is overheard to say: "It is a simple assignment. You have only to watch him and remember what he does. If he goes out alone, be sure he carries the little device that you will be given. You needn't worry that he'll come to any harm."

Kutosov and female subject, after more conversation that was not overheard (audio surveillance was impractical because of lack of cover for the technician), continue feeding corn to the pigeons. Subject female has never before been seen with Kutosov. Her photograph is attached.

48. NOTATION BY HEADQUARTERS.

Female subject positively identified as Ilona Bentley, British subject, DOB 11 May 35 Berlin, now resident Geneva, Switzerland. Cross-files: Geneva (info): Christopher: N. Collins: T. Miernik. Action (London): Request biographical data British liaison.

49. REPORT BY COLLINS.

Though it is of no probable operational importance, I report to you that Ilona Bentley has turned up in Naples. She appeared at the door of my hotel room this evening (22nd June), explaining that she had arrived in Naples two days before.

2. Miss Bentley joined our group for dinner and evidenced no particular curiosity about the presence of Zofia Miernik. Later she asked where the Miernik girl had joined us, and I told her Vienna. The subject was dropped.

3. I have to report that Miss Bentley wishes to join our group as well. As you may know, she and I have been friends for some time, and there has recently been some trouble between us of a personal nature. I have attempted to persuade Miss Bentley to return to Geneva, but I cannot be certain that she will do so. The ship on which we are travelling to Egypt is fully booked, and it is therefore unlikely that she will accompany us. However, Miss Bentley is an impulsive young woman who at the moment seems determined to renew her friendship with me, and she is certainly resourceful enough to find her way to Egypt by other means of transport. I realize that this unexpected event is awkward, and I shall do my best to sort it out.

50. FROM MIERNIK'S DIARY.

The appearance of Ilona is most disturbing. She came down to dinner with Nigel and sat among us as if we had all met by accident in the Brasserie Centrale in Geneva. This is still her world, it seems natural to her to be among friends. But the world of Geneva seems far behind me, and I do not wish to be reminded of it. Especially it is painful to be reminded of it by an Ilona who comes downstairs with Nigel, her face bearing every sign that they have just made love. Ilona attaches no importance to her body apart from the pleasure it gives her; that the memory of it should cause suffering for her lovers does not trouble her. I doubt that it even occurs to her.

Automatic emotion: Why has she followed us? What is her secret purpose? From whom does she take instructions? All this is nonsense. I will never get away from the beating of my rabbit's heart. Obviously she has come to make it up with Nigel. It will not be easy. He sat morosely through the whole meal, avoiding my eyes. There can be no question that he *knows*. Were I in his place (and of course I am: if he shares Ilona's body with me, I share it with him) I would accept things for what they are: a whim of Ilona's, an indulgence of her sexual curiosity that will never happen again. "Bad luck, Tadeusz!"

Christopher watched the byplay with his usual amusement. There is something about him that Zofia likes. After the adventures they've had together, this is natural. It is to Paul that she always talks (they lapse into German when the rest of us are talking about something else: I wonder why?). The contrast between Zofia and Ilona is extraordinary. One cannot judge a sister's sexuality, but there is something withheld in Zofia, whereas Ilona is so accessible. It is more than manners, more than coloring—the one girl pale and blond, the other olive and black. The girls do not like each other. Ilona's attitude: "I permit you to talk to the American, but the others are mine—and so would he be mine if I wanted it that way." Zofia's attitude: "I see what you mean, and I understand perfectly how you achieve your results." They have an inborn talent for insult, women.

Tomorrow we sail. All this with Ilona will be behind me. It is a shock, seeing her when I never expected to see her again. After tomorrow, this will finally be true. Regret makes a cold supper. The fact of the matter is, I would abandon the journey, abandon all I have promised myself to do at the end of the journey, abandon my friends—if Ilona were to come to me instead of Nigel. A few doors away, they are together. I know what it is to be sore with love: with sex, as Kalash would say. Even sex is more than I hoped for. It would be enough for me; love is for the beautiful. What is more ludicrous than jealousy in an ugly man? And yet. And yet. And yet. And *yet!*

51. REPORT BY CHRISTOPHER.

23 June. Our ship's sailing has been postponed for at least two days. Engine trouble, says the purser. Egyptian stupidity, says Kalash. She is an oily old freighter called, of all things, the S.S. *Nefertiti.* Her registry is Egyptian. The purser was evidently afraid of losing our passage money, as he loaded the Cadillac, had our baggage taken aboard, and collected our tickets before giving us the news about the delay. He tells us that we are welcome to stay aboard while repairs are made. "Better view of Naples Bay from the deck than any luxury hotel," the purser said. He's right about that, but we'll move back to the Commodore anyway.

The delay is serious for Miernik. The voyage takes six days, so his passport would expire before he reached Alexandria. (I'm beginning to wish that his people *had* fixed him up with an American passport, or at least an Ecuadorian one.) You will have further cause to suspect him, despite all his dilemmas, when I tell you that he burst into Arabic during the discussion with the purser; Kalash says he speaks it well, with a Syrian intonation. Miernik was too upset by the change in the sailing schedule to bother to explain how he happens to speak this language so much better than he told me he did.

Once Miernik is inside Egypt, he can at last throw away his Polish passport; the Sudanese laisser-passer Kalash obtained for him will get him out of the country. (But not into it: his visa is stamped on the Polish passport.) Interminable discussion: what to do about Miernik? Kalash, of course, was in favor of ignoring the entire situation; he has no doubt that he can get Miernik ashore in Alexandria even without a passport. "There will be a certain amount of shouting," Kalash explains. "The Egyptians are a nation of crazed louts. But in the end I will find someone who knows my name and who will take old Miernik's money. All will be well." Miernik is not willing to accept the 10 percent chance that Kalash is wrong. He thinks that Kalash would leave him on the docks, chained to a couple of Egyptian cops, if the plan failed.

"Kalash is a wonderful man," says Miernik, "but you know how he is—he'd have forgotten my existence in half an hour."

In the end it was decided that Miernik will go back to Rome and fly to Cairo. Money does not seem to be a problem for him. Of course he has his final pay from WRO, and I suppose he has been able to save some of his salary. It's possible, too, that Kirnov packed a few thousand dollars into Zofia's rucksack along with the Ecuadorian passport. Then again, if you're right about his auspices, he has no worry about funds.

The rest of us, including Zofia, will wait for the ship. Kalash will not leave his father's Cadillac in the care of an Egyptian crew on the high seas: "The governor would be most unsympathetic if I turned up to tell him that I'd let some Egyptian halfwit put the car ashore in Libya. These coasts are teeming with people looking for bargains in big American automobiles."

The presence of Ilona Bentley in Naples adds a certain drama to the proceedings. Both Miernik and Collins have been looking pretty feverish since she arrived, and the notion of leaving Ilona behind in Miernik's care does not appeal to the Englishman. Ilona added to the tension by taking Kalash with her in her rented two-seater Fiat when we left the pier, leaving the rest of us to follow by taxi. They did not reappear until dinner time. Kalash told me they had driven to Positano for lunch.

"She ordered some disgusting mess of noodles and began shoveling away," Kalash said. "Ilona is a very coarse feeder, as you know—must have something to do with all that starvation as a child. She says she saw the value of appetite very early in life, watching her fellow prisoners scuffling around the soup pot in the concentration camp. She's been indulging all her appetites ever since, so she'll have something to look back on if ever she's locked up again. Odd sort of girl. It's rather appealing, her ignorance of modesty.

"We were lying on the bed a little later. Ilona was messing about with her tongue and I was quite sleepy. She crawled up my body and prised open my eyelids with her fingers. Most annoying, but you know what she is—sex jolts her wide awake. 'Kalash,' she said, 'you are a god.' I thought that rather nice of her, as I hadn't put forth any special effort after such a heavy lunch. 'Kalash,' she said, 'take me with you.' It appears that she wants to join us in our journey down the Nile. Copulation in the desert has a great appeal for English girls. Ilona has always dreamed of ecstasy under the desert stars. She hears the babble of exotic marketplaces in her imagination. She is in love with all of us, including poor Miernik, it seems. She lay there on top of me, murmuring all these secrets, licking my eyes and rolling my member between her knees. Impossible to refuse under the circumstances, although I must say I wonder about the morale of our little group if she decides to do the same for all of us, all at the same time instead of separately."

So do I. Miernik and Collins do not have Kalash's sexual insouciance. (Perhaps they would have if they were sharing a black girl instead of a white one; Kalash regards European females as part of the fauna and beds them as casually as an English prince would shoot grouse driven into his gun.) We will at least be spared an orgy aboard the *Nefertiti*. Ilona plans to fly to Cairo with Miernik. Miernik does not as yet know this. Neither does Nigel Collins.

I don't altogether believe that Ilona's only motive is sexual adventure, though she certainly gives every indication that this is important to her. I suppose that it would be a good idea to get a rundown on her so that I'll know whether I'm dealing with a nymphomaniac or something else. You can assume that your man Christopher will be staying on the bench: Ilona is awfully pretty, and as your investigations have doubtless shown, I am normal. But the potential mess is bad enough without my adding to it.

52. FROM THE FILES OF A BRITISH INTELLIGENCE SERVICE.

Bentley, Ilona Maria. Born at Berlin on 11th May, 1935, the daughter of a Hungarian national named Hanne Szemle (born at Budapest on 21st December, 1905) and of Bentley, John Brian

Thomas, a British subject born at St. Petersburg, Russia, on 9th February, 1899, the elder son of Roger Alan Arthur Bentley, C.M.G. (q.v.), and of Lucy Anne Wyndham. For fifty years before the Russian Revolution, the Bentley family operated an export-import business at St. Petersburg; John Bentley's father and grandfather served as H.M. Consul in that city for brief interims in the nineteenth century. John Bentley was educated privately in St. Petersburg by English and German tutors; he spoke both these languages, as well as Russian, perfectly. He witnessed the Bolshevik uprisings in St. Petersburg and afterwards claimed personal acquaintance with a number of the leading Bolsheviks, including Trotsky himself. Bentley hinted throughout his life that he had actually taken part in street fighting in St. Petersburg in 1917. In 1919, the family returned to England, and the following year Bentley went up to Magdalen College, Oxford; he took a third in Oriental Languages. In 1926 he published a book about the British expedition to Russia in 1918–19, *The Death Rattle of Imperialism.* It is believed (though not confirmed by documentary evidence) that he became a member of the British Communist Party in 1928. From 1927 to 1931 he frequently published articles in a variety of British periodicals on political and literary subjects. In 1932 he went to Berlin as a correspondent, accredited by a number of British publications including the *Daily Star.* Bentley wrote frequently for the *Daily Worker* under a variety of pseudonyms.

Ilona Maria Bentley, who is Bentley's only child, was illegitimate. The marriage between Bentley and Hanne Szemle did not take place until 23rd September, 1938, in Berlin. At that time Bentley claimed paternity, and the child was afterwards granted British nationality on the basis of her father's claim. Bentley had left Miss Szemle and their daughter in Berlin in 1937, when he went to Spain to cover the Civil War from the Nationalist side. Three weeks after his marriage to Miss Szemle, he returned to Spain, where he was killed on Christmas Day, 1938, while covering the Nationalist assault on Barcelona. Bentley's wife was half Jewish, the daughter of a German-born Jewess. The German government refused to recog-

nize the British nationality of Mrs. Bentley and her child, owing to
the German parentage of the mother, and to the disparity between
the child's date of birth and the date of her parents' marriage. It was
believed that the authorities were influenced also by Bentley's out-
spoken Communist sympathies. In refusing permission to Mrs.
Bentley and her child to leave Germany in 1939, the German
authorities referred to an undissolved previous marriage between
Bentley and a German woman, but the existence of the earlier marriage was never established to the satisfaction of H.M. Consul.

In 1942 (date probable) Hanne Szemle Bentley and her child were
arrested by the German authorities and sent to Bergen-Belsen concentration camp. The mother died there on 18th April, 1943. Ilona
Bentley was liberated with other surviving inmates in 1945. She was
at that time barely ten years old, and she was unaware of her own
identity. She was not identified as Ilona Bentley, and therefore as a
British subject, until February, 1946, when an examination of the
files at Bergen-Belsen brought forth her British passport and that of
her mother. In June, 1946, investigators succeeded in locating the
child in a refugee centre in the British Zone of Occupation, and in
establishing her identity through a comparison of the number tattooed on her forearm and the one entered by a German clerk on her
British passport, which formed part of her file at Bergen-Belsen.

The child was given into the custody of her paternal grandparents
on 15th July, 1946. The grandmother died the following year, and the
grandfather in 1952. Ilona Bentley, as her grandfather's only heir (her
father's brother died in action in Crete), inherited an estate valued at
£175,000 after death duties. This included substantial amounts in
Swiss franc accounts in the Union de Banques Suisses, Geneva.

During summer holidays, and after leaving school, Ilona Bentley
travelled extensively in Europe, and in 1956 visited Hungary as a
tourist. The Hungarian rebellion took place during her visit. On
30th October, 1966, she arrived at the Austro-Hungarian frontier
in the company of a young Hungarian named Feriz Kárdos, whom
she attempted to smuggle into Austria. Kárdos was arrested and
subsequently sentenced to life imprisonment on charges of subver-

sion and murder arising out of his activities in the Budapest uprising. Ilona Bentley attempted to persuade the British Embassy at Budapest to intervene in behalf of Kárdos, whom she described as her fiancé. No intervention was possible. Ilona Bentley, in an interview with an officer of the embassy, claimed to be pregnant by Kárdos; if this was true, she never bore the child.

Ilona Bentley has a certain reputation for sexual looseness. Throughout her adolescence she created disciplinary problems at a variety of schools, and she was sent home on one occasion for misbehaviour with a boy from a neighbouring town. (According to the records of the psychiatrist who interviewed her after her release from Bergen-Belsen, she claimed to have been sexually abused by adult inmates of the camp.)

On coming of age, Ilona Bentley took up residence in Geneva, Switzerland, where she enrolled as a student at the university. At this time she relieved the solicitors who had been appointed as her guardians under her grandfather's will of their responsibility for management of her affairs. The Swiss police, who have exercised their ordinary controls over Miss Bentley as a foreign resident, have noted no activity on her part that they construe as harmful to Swiss interests. Our own enquiries have yielded nothing of political interest. Miss Bentley was taught Russian by her grandfather.

53. LETTER FROM ILONA BENTLEY TO AN ACCOMMODATION ADDRESS USED BY SOVIET INTELLIGENCE IN PARIS (TRANSLATION FROM FRENCH).

Rome, 25 June

Darling Marie-Dominique,

By the time you receive this I shall have taken wing for the Nile! A wonderful two days in Naples, marred only by your failure to join me as you had half promised to do. I waited for you (leaving a darling young man sulking alone) at the station on the night you said you might come, but alas, the train contained nothing but strangers. I did so want to tell you all my news (and I have such a lot of it!) in person. Perhaps you'll get in touch with me before the thirtieth at the address I gave you.

Everything went perfectly. I astonished my little friend by popping into his room no more than five minutes after he had arrived. He is still annoyed with me—but not *that* annoyed! We had quite a lovely time together—I mean *all* of us at dinner that evening and in a long walk round this noisy city. (It's awfully friendly of the natives to fondle one as they do—if I had magic skin that photographed all that touched it I should be quite covered with fine Italian hand-prints!)

I suppose you will not be surprised to know that M.'s sister has joined the party. They collected her in Vienna. I was not so much surprised to see her as to see what she looks like. She is quite beautiful in a placid way—blond hair, cornflower eyes, nice figure—*but* a rather mean mouth. She certainly does not resemble her brother. I'm sending you a roll of snaps to keep for me. If you're curious you can have them developed.

She and all the rest except M. are sailing today. There was some delay with the ship, an awful old tub that smells of machine oil and greasy shish kebab. M. and I fly down this afternoon from Rome. He is positively quaking—afraid of airplanes, I suspect. Afraid of the unknown, too. He is a timid chap. On the way from Naples in the car he held on for dear life, saying, "Here you are a little less frightening, darling—you fit right in with the Italians, who drive as madly as you do!"

He has been awfully sweet to me. In Rome we could not use our day and two nights to relax—we had to see the sights. Most methodical he is. I know a great deal more about the Forum, the Pantheon, the dates on which the city walls were built, the relationship between Berini and the Barberii pope than I ever expected to know. Marvelous food! *Awful* wine! M. runs around talking *Latin* to everyone. It's most amusing, but they seem to understand him. At the Vatican, of course, he was a great hit with the chaps in petticoats.

The plan is this: we will all meet on the thirtieth in Cairo and then continue on by car. I've no idea how long the trip will take but it should be thrilling, so I don't care really about the time element. I do hope you'll ask your friends there to look me up. It's so much more fun to see a strange city with one who knows it. And giving my news to someone you love will be almost as good as giving it to you.

Ever with love,
Annelise

54. FROM OUR DEBRIEFING OF ZOFIA MIERNIK (TRANSCRIBED SIX MONTHS AFTER THE EVENTS DESCRIBED IN THIS FILE).

You must understand that I was uncomfortable from the beginning. First of all, I had hardly ever seen any foreigners except for German soldiers when I was a child and the occasional Russian later on. Here I was, out of Poland for the first time in my life, and surrounded by a lot of my brother's friends who spoke languages I had only used in school. I did not always understand exactly what they were saying—the talk went back and forth so quickly, they were all so clever and sardonic. My friends in Warsaw were artists, serious people who suffered all the time and talked only of themselves and their painting and sculpture—which, incidentally, no one would ever be able to see because it was decadent. I am not a melancholy person and I used to long for gaiety.

Now I had more gaiety than I knew what to do with. I found all of them charming. Paul I liked at once. He seemed so kind and so free of envy and sadness—exactly as I had always imagined an American to be. Of course he did a generous thing for me at the very beginning, so I was grateful to him. Nigel was another matter. As things went on I realized that he was nothing like as cold and sarcastic as he seemed at first. As for Prince Kalash, I ask you to imagine the impression he made upon me, this enormously tall, absolutely black man with the manners of a king. He frightened and fascinated me.

I did not like Ilona at all, at the start or afterward. I liked her less when I saw the state Tadeusz was in when we got to Cairo. All his life my brother had been a morose person. He was easy to hurt. Ilona had hurt him badly. *He* thought she had made him happy, but she is not the sort to make anyone happy for very long. When first I saw her I realized the sort of girl she was. I am no puritan. I have nothing against sex. But there should be, if not actually love, then some feeling between people. Ilona was in-capable of feeling. Her aim in life was only sensation. Nigel was already her lover. Nigel was my brother's friend. She used them against each other to increase her own pleasure. She would have used Paul as well but he was too strong for her.

Back to Cairo. Ilona and Tadeusz met us when we drove up to the hotel. They had been together for five days. My brother, following along behind her, had been transformed into a lapdog. He cringed with love for her. The change in him was nauseating. From a man with a brilliant mind and the very best instincts he had changed into a character out of a pornographic novel. His eyes never left her. *Her* eyes never touched him—except in amusement. When Nigel got out of the car, Ilona embraced him, pushing her whole body against his, and kissed him passionately. With her tongue. On the steps of the hotel, surrounded by strangers and servants. Tadeusz actually staggered at the sight. I looked at Tadeusz, looked at Ilona—and *knew* what the situation was. It was a shock. Perhaps it seems comical, but I had always assumed that my brother was a virgin. He has always been more like a priest than anything else. In fact, that's what he wanted to be when he was a boy and I don't think he ever entirely got over the idea. He was super-religious. To get mixed up with someone as carnal as Ilona must have torn him apart. His suffering was pathetic.

Q. We'd like to know a little more about the boat trip. Did anything happen that you thought was important?

A. No, nothing. It was a dreadful trip from the viewpoint of the food and the surroundings. A dirty ship, awful food. Kalash was sick most of the time. He complained about the bunk, which of course was too short for him. I believe he had to sleep on the floor. Nigel kept to himself a great deal. He was very moody, even short-tempered. When we got to Cairo I understood why. Paul and I were together a lot—most of the time. I played the guitar he had given me. He told me about his home in America. He comes from the mountains. Also, he wrote me a poem every night. He writes lovely poetry, but only when he has been drinking. It's odd how sad his poems can be, when on the surface he is such a happy person.

Q. Was it on the ship that you and he . . . ?

A. That's not really your affair, is it? The answer is no. Everything happened much later. On the ship I knew what would happen eventually. We were young and together. From the start there was feeling between us. The details belong to Paul and to me.

Q. Of course they do. Our interest is not salacious. We are trying to understand the relationships, that's all. Now, can we talk about Cairo? What happened there?

A. Not a great deal. There was the situation with Ilona. Nigel and Tadeusz began at that time to feel like friends again, I think. They realized neither of them was to blame. Ilona loved every minute of it. I make her sound cruel. It's not that. She is amoral. What others feel does not affect her. I stopped detesting her when I learned about her past. How could she be a whole person after Belsen? But whatever the reasons, she is what she is, and she causes great, great pain. Things went on more or less as before—it was a holiday. It started out as a holiday. We had jolly times.

We went to the museum and saw the mummies. We found restaurants—life for these people takes place mainly in restaurants. We swam in the hotel pool. We drank big glasses of alcohol, various kinds of gin drinks. Except for Kalash, who is a strict Moslem. He drank lemonade.

We stayed only two days. On the first morning, Kalash and Nigel went off together somewhere in the car. Ilona left the hotel before any of us were awake and did not come back for breakfast. Nigel and Tadeusz were in a state. Where could she be? Nigel asked Kalash at breakfast if he had spent the night with Ilona. He made it into a joke, but it was no joke. Kalash said no, he had not seen her since the night before. When she came back she had a beautiful amber necklace she said she had bought in a bazaar. She tried it on for us; it was a necklace for a queen. She told a very amusing story about her bargaining with the Egyptian who sold her the necklace. She mimicked him, she mimicked herself. All the time I knew she was lying. I had seen the very same necklace in a shop in the hotel. Later I went by and asked if they still had it. "Ah, miss! Your dark-haired friend, the beautiful girl, bought it last night!" Why tell such a story? Paul too went off by himself and was gone for a long time. Everyone scattered, it was noticeable.

Tadeusz and I were left by ourselves. I bought a bathing costume and sat by the pool in the sun. Tadeusz sat with me, writing in his diary. He kept watching the door for Ilona. For once he had no brotherly advice to give me. He asked me a few questions about Paul. When I said I liked him Tadeusz beamed. He *loved* Paul Christopher. He kept telling me what a kind and honest boy Paul was. The others he liked—he was loyal to his friends. Paul he loved. A man can love a man, you know. Their friendships, when they are deep as Tadeusz's and Paul's seemed to be, are almost love affairs. They forgive each other and trust each other much more easily than they can do with any woman. A great romantic, Tadeusz. He was born into the wrong age. He was the ugly knight, Paul the beautiful knight. The ugly always think they owe something to the beautiful. Hence Ilona. And Paul.

Q. You never found out where everyone went?

A. I never asked.

Q. And the next day you left in the car? That was July second.

A. The next day we left in the car. We started down the Nile. After we had driven out to the Pyramids and the Sphinx. We all had our pictures taken on a camel in front of the pyramids. All except Tadeusz, of course.

Q. Why not Tadeusz?

A. He always hated being photographed. It amounted to a psychosis. He believed himself to be the ugliest man alive. Even now I have no picture of him. Once he told me, "If you have no photograph of me, you'll remember my actions instead of my face. I don't want you to be reminded each time you look at a photograph what a poor piece of work God made of me."

55. AMERICAN SURVEILLANCE REPORT FROM CAIRO (EXCERPT).

1 July, 0745: Subject (Ilona Bentley) emerged from Nile Hilton Hotel and entered taxi at curb. I followed by car. Because of light traffic, pursuit presented no difficulty, but there was relatively high risk of detection. Subject kept watch through rear window of taxi. I used other vehicles in line of traffic as shield whenever possible.

0810: Subject left taxi in Khalili Bazaar. She carried a hand purse and a camera equipment bag on a shoulder strap. Until 0820 subject moved casually through bazaar area, taking photographs.

0823: Subject, after looking around her, presumably to spot possible surveillance, entered a curio shop (Akhbal's: the red-fronted shop at the top of the steps at the entrance to the bazaar).

0827: Second European female entered curio shop. She carried a camera equipment case identical to first subject's (i.e., Bentley).

0828: As view was impossible from outside the shop, I entered and observed Bentley and second female exchanging camera cases.

0832: Subjects broke contact. Bentley continued to saunter through the bazaar to no apparent purpose until 0945, when she returned to the Nile Hilton in a taxi.

(Note: From photo files I subsequently made tentative identification of second female subject. She is believed to be Olga Borosova,

a clerk in the Soviet Embassy, Cairo, and a known operative of the Soviet intelligence service.

Throughout remainder of surveillance, which terminated at 0645 hours 2 July when Bentley departed Nile Hilton in a Cadillac limousine (Swiss license X—3675), Bentley carried her camera on her person at all times. Lack of necessary manpower precluded any attempt to enter her hotel room for a search of her personal effects.

56. REPORT BY CHRISTOPHER'S CASE OFFICER (FROM CAIRO).

1. Christopher reported to this officer at 0820 on 1 July at the safe house provided by the Cairo station. He observed no surveillance en route to our meeting. I found the agent in good condition, but in only fair spirits. He delivered written reports (attached) and a lengthy verbal report, which is summarized below.

2. Christopher reports that Miernik has made no move to take him into his confidence concerning the latter's assumed mission in Sudan. Christopher expressed reservations about Headquarters' theory that Miernik is in fact a Soviet/Polish agent with any specific mission in Sudan. Christopher stated: "I think you guys ought to consider the one possibility you haven't considered—that Miernik is not telling an elaborate cover story, but the truth." I assured Christopher that this possibility had been thoroughly considered and had not yet, in fact, been rejected.

3. Christopher bases his doubts on his observation of Miernik in the course of the journey. Miernik seems, in Christopher's words, a much less suspicious character outside of Geneva than in it. He is given to emotional outbursts (see Christopher's report on the incident with a group of German tourists in Verona, Italy) and to a general carelessness of behavior that is not, in Christopher's view, characteristic of a professional agent. Christopher now has almost no doubt that Zofia Miernik is, in fact, Miernik's sister: "No one could fake the affection he obviously has for her."

Christopher was advised to bear in mind that Miernik's seemingly uncontrolled behavior may in fact be a device to divert suspicion. This would be consistent with the weakness of Polish operatives for elaborate role-playing.

4. In this officer's opinion Christopher's judgment has to some extent been impaired by an apparent attraction to Zofia Miernik. Nothing in Christopher's report made specific reference to this point, but he reports on the activities of this girl with less than his usual objectivity.

5. Christopher was, in addition, very favorably impressed by Sasha Kirnov. His attitude seems to be a mixture of professional admiration for the manner in which Kirnov conducted the border-crossing operation, and what must be regarded as personal liking for Kirnov. Christopher has by no means abandoned his caution with respect to Kirnov the KGB man. But he states openly that he found Kirnov the human being quite admirable. (Christopher is more than usually sympathetic to Jews who suffered under the Nazi regime, and this is not the first time Christopher's operational effectiveness has been compromised by his inability to be objective about the Jewish victims of World War II.)

6. As an indication of Christopher's considerable intuitive equipment, this officer mentions that Christopher expressed a caveat about Ilona Bentley before I had briefed him on our suspicions concerning this woman. He found her appearance in Naples questionable and had already begun to regard her as a potential opposition agent. Christopher cites Bentley's sexual relationship with Miernik and presumably with Collins as a classic Soviet tactic to compromise and control these individuals. His mind is open as to whether Bentley is in place as an independent reporting asset for the Soviets, with instructions to monitor Miernik's performance of his assignment. He thinks it possible also that Bentley has been assigned to influence, and report upon, Prince Kalash el Khatar. (See Christopher's reporting for a claim by Khatar that he too had sexual relations with Bentley on 23 June.) If this is the case, Bentley merits the closest possible surveillance by Christopher.

7. In accordance with instructions, this officer refrained from giving Christopher a full briefing on the situation in Sudan concerning the Anointed Liberation Front. Khartoum should note that Christopher knows nothing of (a) interception of Soviet radio traffic; (b) the existence of Firecracker; or (c) the proposal to co-opt symbolic leadership of the ALF through the use of Prince Kalash as an *agent provocateur.*

57. REPORT BY COLLINS.

As arranged, Prince Kalash el Khatar and I went on the morning of 1st July to the Splendid Garage in Heliopolis to take delivery of the weapons. I should have preferred to make this journey in a hired car, but Prince Kalash insisted on travelling in his Cadillac, which attracted a great deal of attention. While waiting to be admitted to the garage the car was surrounded by a troop of boys begging for money. Even Prince Kalash was unable to disperse them, and they hung about peering through the dirty windows of the garage even after we had driven inside. I have no doubt they were able to see the loading of the weapons, *which were not wrapped,* and the ammunition boxes. It was altogether a sloppy operation. I found your man still asleep and unshaven; he gave off a distinct odor of *arak.* The weapons, three Sten guns, two Walther pistols, and several hundred rounds of ammunition, were lying loose under his bed. There were traces of rust on all the weapons, and the bores of two of the Sten guns were clogged with grease. We took delivery of the weapons and ammunition and concealed them in the Cadillac. This motorcar is equipped with a "secret" compartment behind the rear seat, a fact I had not hitherto been aware of. Prince Kalash, at least, is delighted with the firearms transaction. The exact amount I paid over to the gun dealer was 800 United States dollars. We returned to the hotel and joined our companions without further incident.

2. Prince Kalash has informed me that he has invited Ilona

Bentley to accompany us to the Sudan. He says that he admires Miss Bentley's pluck in following us all the way to Cairo. I had not been aware that this was her intention when we parted in Naples, but I cannot say that I am surprised that she turned up. She travelled by air in company with Miernik. This turn of events is at worst an inconvenience, and although I would prefer that no passengers be added, I am unable to prevent Prince Kalash from carrying whomever he pleases in his own car.

3. We depart early on 2nd July. There is some dispute over the route. Prince Kalash wishes to take the shorter coastal road along the Gulf of Suez. Miernik argues in favor of the highway along the Nile, which would take us through the Valley of the Kings. He desires to see the tombs and funerary temples there. I expect that this controversy will not be resolved until we are under way, but in any case I will make contact as arranged on arrival in Khartoum, probably on 6th or 7th July.

4. In our conversations I have given you as many details as are known to me concerning the actions of Miernik and his "sister." There has been nothing in their behaviour that would lead one to think that they are along on this journey for any reason other than pleasure. They have not so far responded to my questioning on any matter of substance. I shall take your advice and abandon my attempts to reach them through the methods I have been using. For the balance of the journey I shall be as matey as possible with a view towards establishing an atmosphere in which confidences can be exchanged.

58. REPORT BY CHRISTOPHER.

2 July. Ilona Bentley is a natural mimic. She does a very funny Winston Churchill, and as she emerged from the Hilton this morning to see the Cadillac groaning under the camping gear Kalash has lashed on its roof, she paused and puffed up her body like a fat man's. In Churchill's voice she asked, "Is this the end of the beginning, or the beginning of the end?"

A good question. We started for the desert in a spirit of amity, if not of gaiety, and arrived at the Pyramids only a few minutes after dawn. Much wonderment on everyone's part: how did they *do* it without pulleys and geometry? Miernik, of course, turns out to be an amateur Egyptologist able to quote dimensions, angles, and the exact number of dressed stones in Cheops's Pyramid. In the shadow of the Sphinx, Kalash gave us more Shakespeare; he played Antony as well as Othello for the drama society before he was expelled from Oxford. "I was found by a languid don with three unclothed English girls in my college room," says Kalash, explaining his dismissal. "Poor fellow never imagined that heterosexuality existed on such a scale."

Miernik's wishes prevailed, as they usually do, and we followed the road along the west bank of the Nile to the Valley of the Kings, and afterward went to Karnak (Thebes, you know). These ruins have no operational importance, so I won't linger over a description. Even Miernik was struck dumb by the Temple of Amen Ra at Karnak and broke silence only to decipher a few of the enormous hieroglyphs on the broken columns and on Thotmes's obelisk. Even when these buildings were whole, five thousand years ago, they must have known the stealthy footfall of spies; some Hittite Miernik undoubtedly was watched through peepholes by agents of the pharaoh. *(He cannot be what he seems. . . . He seems to be what he is not. The knife!* says one. *Not until we know his purpose,* says another.) It's a very old profession.

We were all in favor of staying at a hotel in Luxor, but Kalash was anxious to camp out. He shipped an elaborate outfit from Geneva—tents, sleeping bags, folding tables and chairs, stoves, and so on. "As for me, I need nothing but a burnoose and a gun," says Kalash. "But I wanted you white explorers to have some of the comforts you're used to." Kalash does not believe in maps, but I am keeping track of our route as best I can on a big Michelin map. We turned east just south of El Kab and in a few minutes were passing through the empty desert. This is fairly hilly country; the land is the color of old bones.

Night comes very quickly in the desert, as you've no doubt heard, but Kalash seems to know exactly when this is going to happen. He stopped near a place called Soukari (before we got to the town: "If the Egyptians don't know we're here they won't come creeping out to steal our shoes") and we made camp about an hour before the sun disappeared. Kalash has barred all alcohol while we are in the desert, but he has laid in a huge supply of oranges, lemons, and limes. Zofia squeezed some of the fruit and made drinks with the last of the ice from the Hilton. Kalash fished the ice cubes out of his tin cup and threw them into the sand. "You'll be less thirsty if you learn to drink tepid fluids," he said. He issued warnings about deadly six-inch scorpions and imparted other desert lore. He is dressed as a sheik for the trip, and his warnings, issuing out of a white headdress, are very believable.

We dined on canned goods heated by Ilona on an alcohol stove and afterward sat around in the light of a gasoline lantern, listening to Zofia's guitar. She was well taught by Sasha Kirnov—she can play almost any tune after it's hummed to her. Ilona knows a great many Russian songs, learned from her grandfather. The language suits her well; she looked wild and melancholy in the lamplight with her black hair falling over her breasts. Her hair was the color of the night behind her, so her white face seemed suspended in air, like the face of a girl in a dream. Miernik was hypnotized. So were we all.

It grew very cold shortly after nightfall, and we put on jackets. There were three small tents, each big enough for two persons. The girls decided to share one of these, and Miernik and Collins paired off in another—they want to keep an eye on each other because of Ilona, I suppose. Kalash, after the guitar had been put away, walked beyond the edge of the lamplight and lay down on the ground, drawing an end of his costume across his face. That left me alone in the third tent.

I couldn't sleep, but it was too cold to get up, so I lay on my stomach in the sleeping bag, looking out at the stars through the open flap of the tent. Kalash was an unmoving white shape a few feet away. At about midnight I heard a slithering sound next door, and then I saw Miernik sliding out of the mouth of his tent. He stood upright, looked around, and then walked straight for the Cadillac. He opened the door softly and the interior light went on briefly. There was a pause before light showed again, this time in thin streaks around the edges of the window shades. There are blinds on all the windows. Of course there is no way to cover the windshield, but the car was pointed away from camp, so the pool of light on its hood was unlikely to disturb anyone.

I got up and put on my boots. Kalash, still not moving a muscle, said, "What is that imbecile doing in the car at this time of night?"

"I'll ask him," I said. "Maybe his wounds are bothering him." (Miernik has removed his sling, but he still moves rather stiffly.)

Kalash said nothing more, and I assumed he went back to sleep at once. I walked to the car and looked in through the windshield. Miernik was sitting in the back seat with his thick Mont Blanc fountain pen in one hand and a smallish book in the other. He turned the pages of the book, ran his finger down the edge of the page, counted the lines to the point where his finger stopped, and then wrote a number on a sheet of paper. Then he repeated the process.

I guess I don't have to tell you folks that he was writing a message, using a book code. I moved back out of the light but kept watching. Miernik was absorbed in his work. He went at it rapidly, with none of the fussiness and hesitation he usually displays. He'd find a word, note the number of its line on the pages, and enter it with the page number in a five-digit group. Judging by the place at which he'd opened the book, he was using three-digit pages. Therefore the first three digits are the page number and the last two the line number. I suppose he uses the first word on the line cited. The book had a gray cover with red lettering.

After five minutes or so, I started back to my tent. "What is he doing?" Kalash asked from the floor of the desert.

"He's reading," I replied.

Miernik came creeping back about ten minutes later. Kalash did not speak to him, and I was glad I didn't have to. Catching him red-handed bothered me less than I might have expected. There is a certain satisfaction in being a successful Peeping Tom; otherwise no one would do this sort of work. But Miernik's damn foolishness annoyed me. Why did he choose this time and this place to mess around with a book code? Where would he get rid of it? Not even the Soviets use natives with cleft sticks as moving dead-drops, and in the desert Miernik would certainly find no other way to get rid of his clandestine message. It would be typical of the man to entrust it to the Egyptian mails in the next small town we come to. The whole scene—sneaking out to the car at night, pulling down the shades, scribbling away in circumstances that offered a 99 percent chance for detection—was so amateurish. It made me angry that Miernik could be such a fool.

3 July. Two things to record in connection with the events of last night:

1. Miernik's book is Tocqueville's *Democracy in America,* World's Classics edition No. 496 (Oxford University Press, 1959). He left it lying on his sleeping bag when he came out for breakfast.
2. This morning, in Marsa Alam, he did mail a letter at the post office.

59. DECODED VERSION OF MIERNIK'S MESSAGE.*

JOURNEY IN FINAL STAGE. MUCH TROUBLED YOUR FAILURE COMMUNI-
CATE. GREATLY HOPE THIS MEANS NO CHANGE IN PLANS OR DIMINUTION

---

*This message was intercepted on 11 July in Buenos Aires in a routine check on correspondence addressed to a box number known to be used by Sasha Kirnov. After Christopher delivered his report in Khartoum (6 July) a round-robin cable was sent to all stations in the world, instructing them to give priority to intercepted letters bearing Egyptian postmarks. Christopher provided certain other helpful details, e.g., that the envelope was addressed in green ink in a large hand. It is conceded that the interception of this message was more a matter of luck than of efficiency. Once it was in our hands, decoding presented no problem because we knew, as a result of our agent's alert work, the title of the book used to write the code. Without this information, a book code is, of course, indecipherable.

HOPES FOR SUCCESS. COMPANIONS AMIABLE. HAVE ADDED ENGLISH GIRL *(B)*ALTIMORE *(E)*XCELLENCE *(N)*OWHERE *(T)*RIUMPHANT *(L)*OVE *(E)*XCELLENCE *(Y)*OUNG. EXPECT REACH DESTINATION TWELFTH OR THEREABOUTS. MONEY GIVEN COURIER VERY GENEROUS. HER PAPERS SUPERB. MY HOPE IS FOR SAME AFTER PRESENT VENTURE. TRUSTING FRIENDS TO PROVIDE AS FINAL FAVOR. NEXT MESSAGE FROM CAPITAL OF DESTINATION COUNTRY. AFTER THAT SILENCE UNTIL WE MEET AGAIN.

60. REPORT BY A POLISH NATIONAL CONTROLLED BY A WESTERN INTELLIGENCE SERVICE (EXCERPT).

. . . Colonel Puszinsky of the Intelligence Service reported to the deputy foreign minister on 26 June that the requirements laid down for a joint Polish-Soviet operation in Africa had been fulfilled. The deputy foreign minister declined to be told full details of the operation and asked for an outline report only. Colonel Puszinsky assured him that a suitable Polish citizen, trained in intelligence work, had been assigned as a liaison between the Soviet Embassy in an East African country and an organization of freedom fighters in a different but neighboring country. The agent was en route to his assignment and on arrival would fall under control of the responsible Soviet officials. An official expression of gratitude on the part of the Soviets had been received by Colonel Puszinsky for communication to the deputy foreign minister.

61. DISPATCH FROM THE AMERICAN STATION IN VIENNA (EXCERPT).

In the hope of allaying Geneva's anxiety over the apparent confusion surrounding Christopher's border-crossing operation, we have conducted a full debriefing of the Czech officer in command of Point

Zebra. He states that the crossing by Christopher and Zofia Miernik was authorized by the Czech counterintelligence arm. The Czech CI officer who made the authorization was accompanied by a Russian known to our source as "Major Shigalov." Our source believes that Shigalov is an officer of the KGB. It was Shigalov who instructed our source to create a diversion and permit the crossing by Christopher and the Miernik woman. There were no instructions to hold fire if Christopher and Zofia Miernik were discovered by the troops. Chances of that happening were regarded as minimal by Shigalov. Our source assumes that the crossing was a KGB operation designed to infiltrate personnel into the West with the credibility that accrues from a hazardous escape across the frontier. He has taken part in a number of other episodes that followed a similar operational script. We tend to agree with his judgment, assuming that his version of events is accurate. He has in the past been highly reliable.

62. INTERCEPTED TRAFFIC FROM SOVIET TRANSMITTER IN DAR ES SALAAM (DECODED 5 JULY).

1. Initiate Golgotha 7 July.

2. Rendezvous 0147 15 July [map coordinates for a point 48 miles west-northwest of El Fasher] with Richard. Recognition code: Heaven is far away. Reply: Allah awaits us near at hand.

3. Long live the brave fighters of the Anointed Liberation Front and the great cause of the workers.

63. CABLE FROM THE AMERICAN STATION IN KHARTOUM.

1. AT DAWN ON 7 JULY THE BODIES OF THREE OFFICIALS OF CENTRAL GOVERNMENT WERE FOUND IN MARKETPLACES OF EL OBEID, OTBARA, AND KASSALA, THREE IMPORTANT TOWNS LYING IN A CRESCENT AROUND KHARTOUM AT AN AVERAGE DISTANCE OF 200 MILES.

2. IN ALL CASES VICTIMS WERE MUTILATED INCLUDING CASTRATION AND CRUCIFIED HEAD DOWNWARDS ON X-SHAPED CROSSES.

3. FIRECRACKER CONFIRMS ALL THREE MURDERS WERE CARRIED OUT BY CELLS OF ANOINTED LIBERATION FRONT AS FIRST STAGE OF "OPERATION GOLGOTHA."

4. "OPERATION GOLGOTHA" IS TERROR CAMPAIGN LONG PLANNED BY ALF. MURDERS, WITH MUTILATION AND CRUCIFIXION OF VICTIMS, ARE INTENDED TO DEMONSTRATE THAT ALF CAN STRIKE ANYWHERE AND ANYTIME IT PLEASES AGAINST CENTRAL GOVERNMENT AND ITS OFFICIALS.

5. MURDERS WILL CONTINUE WITH CRUCIFIED VICTIMS BEING DISPLAYED PROGRESSIVELY CLOSER TO KHARTOUM. OPERATIONAL PLAN OF "GOLGOTHA" CALLS FOR CRUCIFIXION OF NEXT VICTIMS TEN DAYS HENCE AT POINTS 20 MILES CLOSER TO KHARTOUM ON MAIN ROADS EAST NORTH AND WEST OF THE CAPITAL.

6. FIRECRACKER WAS UNABLE FOREWARN US OF THIS ACTION AS ITS LEADER IS "AHMED" (TRUE NAME UNKNOWN), THE OTHER PRINCIPAL ALF FIGURE TRAINED IN THE USSR. DETAILS OF "GOLGOTHA" WERE COMMUNICATED TO "AHMED" BY A SOVIET CASE OFFICER WHOM HE MET IN LATE JUNE (DATE UNCERTAIN) IN KHARTOUM. INSTRUCTIONS TO INITIATE "GOLGOTHA" WERE SIGNALED BY SOVIET CLANDESTINE RADIO ON 5 JULY. (WE INTERCEPTED AND DECODED BUT WERE UNABLE DETERMINE DETAILS "GOLGOTHA" UNTIL AFTER IT WAS LAUNCHED.)

7. WE EMPHASIZE TO FIRECRACKER IMPORTANCE OF LEARNING AND COMMUNICATING DETAILS NEXT PHASE "GOLGOTHA" BEFORE THIS TAKES PLACE.

8. REQUEST HEADQUARTERS CLEARANCE TO BRIEF SUDANESE POLICE LIAISON ON DETAILS KNOWN TO US INCLUDING SOVIET INVOLVEMENT BUT NOT REPEAT NOT INCLUDING DISCLOSURE OUR CONTROL OF FIRECRACKER.

9. FOLLOWING IS TEXT OF ALF HANDBILL POSTED AFTER ASSASSINA-
TIONS IN MARKETPLACES PRINCIPAL SUDANESE TOWNS (TRANSLATION
FROM ARABIC):

BELOVED BELIEVERS!

O BELOVED OF ALLAH! TODAY THREE CURSED LICKSPITTLES OF THE
KHARTOUM CLIQUE THAT OFFENDS GOD AND THE TEACHING OF HIS
PROPHET HAVE BEEN SENT TO ETERNAL PUNISHMENT. GOD IS GREAT.
YOU WILL FIND THEM IN YOUR MARKETPLACE WITH THEIR FACES IN
THE DUST. OTHERS WILL DIE AS THEY HAVE DIED. O BELOVED OF
ALLAH! IT IS WE THE ANOINTED LIBERATION FRONT WHO HAVE TAKEN
GOD'S VENGEANCE ON THESE MEN WHO SELL OUR BIRTHRIGHT TO
THE IMPERIALISTS! THE HOUR COMES NEARER WHEN ALL THESE
VICTIMS IN KHARTOUM SHALL DIE OR FLEE OUR VENGEANCE! NEXT
TIME WE STRIKE CLOSER. WE SHALL STRIKE EVER CLOSER!

64. DISPATCH FROM WASHINGTON TO THE AMERICAN STATIONS
    IN KHARTOUM AND GENEVA (8 JULY).

1. Khartoum is instructed to inform the Sudanese authorities of
the details of "Operation Golgotha," and to brief the head of the
Sudanese Special Branch on the activities, membership, and plans
of the Anointed Liberation Front.

2. No operation is authorized that involves any risk to the life of
Prince Kalash el Khatar. Khartoum may suggest the infiltration
of Prince Kalash into the ALF to Special Branch and to the Amir of
Khatar. Any decision to utilize Prince Kalash in this manner must,
however, be made by the Amir and by the appropriate Sudanese officials. Khartoum may assure all parties of its cooperation, but it may
not assume operational responsibility, which belongs to the
Sudanese. Not only the appearance but also the reality of noninter-
ference in the internal affairs of Sudan must be preserved.

3. Surveillance and reporting by Christopher with regard to the

activities of the party traveling with Prince Kalash will be continued. Christopher will be handled by [his case officer from Geneva], who is assigned to temporary duty in Khartoum for the duration of Christopher's activity within Sudan. Control of all U.S. aspects of this operation remains the responsibility of Khartoum.

4. In addition to his reporting function, Christopher is authorized to involve himself in covert action against all opposition elements, short of the use of violence. Khartoum will fully brief Christopher on all operational aspects of which he does not already have knowledge.

5. Khartoum's briefing of Christopher should include the information that Headquarters has tentatively concluded that Tadeusz Miernik and Ilona Bentley are agents of the Soviet intelligence service. We believe Miernik is probably an asset of the Polish intelligence service on loan to the Soviets as principal agent in charge of their operations with regard to the ALF. Bentley is believed to be a Soviet agent assigned to monitor the performance of Miernik. These conclusions are based on evaluation of information from a variety of sources,* all of which tend to confirm that Miernik is the key to Soviet control and exploitation of the ALF in its terrorist phase. (The role of Zofia Miernik cannot at this time be determined. It is possible that she was employed as a courier to supply funds to Miernik, although her use in this role would not conform to normal Soviet funding techniques. It is somewhat less possible that she was defected as a payment to Miernik in order to assure his optimum operational performance. The entire scenario of double

---

*The sources referred to here are Christopher's reporting, particularly his discovery that Miernik was communicating with a third person through use of a book code; the reports by a Polish agent that a Pole was being sent into Africa under Soviet control; and the account by the Czech frontier guards officer relating the peculiar circumstances surrounding the border crossing by Zofia Miernik. Other scraps of information, seemingly minor, also aided in fastening suspicion on Miernik. In regard to Bentley, her correspondence with Soviet letter-drops under a cover name and her meeting in Cairo with a Russian intelligence officer were sufficient to remove any but the most marginal doubts about her role. Miernik's presence in Vienna, and in West Germany at the time of the cyanide murders in Munich and Berlin, was given some weight, but we regarded it as unlikely that he had been used as an assassin.

defection of a brother and sister is typical of the elaborate cover mechanisms of the Poles, and the anomalies in the Miernik situation may well be explained by the involvement of the Polish intelligence service in what is essentially a Soviet operation.)

6. Headquarters is hopeful that Christopher will be able to remove any doubts that Miernik and Bentley are under Soviet discipline. Khartoum may use its discretion to invent an operational device that will permit Christopher to confirm that these two operatives are, in fact, what we suspect them to be.

7. Our objective is the neutralization of Miernik and maximum embarrassment of the Soviets through public exposure of their role in the operations of the ALF. The prerequisite for attainment of our objective is the neutralization of the ALF. Headquarters is confident that the Sudanese security forces, aided by the information we are able to provide to them, will be able to deal effectively with the threat presented by the ALF.

8. Headquarters, in consideration of British sensitivity to operations in one of their former colonial areas, has instructed London to brief its liaisons with the British intelligence services on "Golgotha" and the situation concerning Miernik and Bentley. It is considered that the British may have information that is not at this time available to us. The pooling of information and of operational resources can work to mutual advantage. Christopher's cover will be protected.

65. REPORT BY CHRISTOPHER.

4 July. Apart from ten or twelve hairbreadth escapes from death, the trip continues uneventfully. The peril comes from Kalash, who believes that cars are meant to be driven at their maximum speed. The road along the coast is fairly good until Ras Banas, about a hundred miles north of the Sudanese border, where it turns into a goat path. With the Red Sea on our left and a range of bleak hills on our right, we hurtled down the coast, one rear wheel often spinning in empty air over the edge of a precipice. Pedestrians and camels, and cars when we met them, scattered before the Cadillac like flocks of ducks. One terrified nomad went over the edge of a low cliff in a swan dive; if he landed on his head he must certainly have been killed. Kalash drives on, muttering in Arabic, with no hint of expression on his face, while the girls shriek and Miernik covers his eyes.

The Cadillac is not designed for this kind of travel. It overheated several times and twice got stuck in the sand when the wheels slid off the harder surface of the dirt road. It is obvious that we are going to have to have a second vehicle, a Land Rover or a Jeep, if we are going to make it to El Fasher. Kalash agrees and tells us that we'll have no trouble buying what we need in Port Sudan. If we live, we'll arrive there tomorrow morning. I've no doubt that Kalash can accomplish anything in Sudan. When we arrived at the frontier, he stopped the car, spoke one sentence in Arabic, received a smart salute from the guard, and drove right on through. "Now, Miernik, you can stop worrying about clerks and passports," Kalash said. "In Sudan, my name is your passport."

We camped last night by the sea on a cliff a few miles above the town of Dunqunab. Kalash chose the spot carefully. It is, he says, exactly opposite Mecca across the Red Sea. He prayed for quite a long time at sunset and sunrise, facing in the holy direction, while the rest of us shuffled around in embarrassment. There is something incongruous about Kalash, of all people, prostrating himself and banging his head on the ground. But his religiousness is obviously genuine, while it lasts. As soon as he says his final "amen" and slaps the dirt off his robes he is the Kalash we have always known and loved: bitter tongue, sardonic eye, stiff pecker. "I have gone forty-eight full hours without a woman," he told me tonight as he turned away from Mecca; "we really must do something about this monastic arrangement of tents." Kalash has only one tone of voice: distinct. His words were clearly audible to the girls; Ilona flashed a joyful smile at Zofia. It was not returned.

While the girls made supper, Kalash and Collins opened the secret compartment of the Cadillac and extracted an armload of weapons: three Sten guns and a couple of German automatics. The two of them bought these firearms in Cairo. Kalash thinks we may need them when we get into bandit country. While Kalash and Collins sat at the camp table, loading clips from a pile of cartridges, Miernik pulled me aside. "Paul, you must protest! We must get rid of these guns. We were not consulted about this at all. It's dangerous merely to carry these things! Suppose we are stopped by the police?" I told him I didn't think the Sudanese police would present much of a problem to Kalash. Moreover, if there were bandits along the route, we'd need something to scare them off with. "Bandits? *Bandits?* Nigel spoke of bandits, but I thought it was a joke," said Miernik. "I cannot take Zofia where there are bandits." He was in a state of great agitation, and even now, when I have all but concluded that he is straight from the KGB, I feel a little sorry for him. Even if he's acting all the time, letting his emotions crawl all over the surface of his skin must be bad for his nerves. Dealing with him is certainly bad for mine.

Finally he consented to shoot at a target with the rest of us. Collins turned out to be competent with the submachine gun and the pistol: he shoots fast, without sighting, a pretty certain sign that he's had training. Kalash is not too bad for an amateur. I shot as awkwardly as I could, still building cover. (Collins grinned at me, absolutely sure that I was faking it.) Collins had been goading Miernik all through the shooting, apologizing for the noise, telling him to stand well back, warning him about shooting himself in the foot. By the time Miernik's turn came, he was angry. His lips were set, his eyes were turned aside, and he looked (as he usually does when he is disturbed) as if the sweat was ready to burst through the pores of his face. He took the Sten gun out of Kalash's hand, slapped a clip into the receiver, and stepped up to the mark. He was as steady as a rock and the picture of perfect shooting technique. Every round in the bull's-eye with the Sten. Every round in the bull's-eye with the pistol. He stared at Collins contemptuously, tossed him the empty Walther, and stalked away.

It was a remarkable display of shooting. And a remarkable breakdown in self-control. "Well," said Collins. "Isn't *that* interesting?" Kalash took off his sunglasses and watched Miernik's thick figure tramping up the little hill that separated us from the camp. "If I were you, Nigel," he said, "I'd be very careful about creeping into Ilona's bed while that Communist is about."

We have been eating well out of the cans. Ilona is an inventive cook and a very efficient one, a circumstance that gives me one more opportunity to mention that appearances can be deceiving. Zofia, who shines with domesticity, exhausted her kitchen lore when she made tea in the Czech farmhouse and sliced all that bread and cheese and salami for Kirnov and me: she cannot open an egg without breaking the yolk. Whereas Ilona, whom the Marquis de Sade would have picked out of the crowd across a football stadium (if Ilona didn't spot him first), is a treasure. "I like to wife about," Ilona will say, stirring up a *sauce béchamel* over the camp stove, or sewing on buttons for Miernik. She complains, as we all do, that Kalash will allow us no wine. "How can I make sauces without Chablis?" Ilona demands.

"I won't have you ruining the desert with your filthy Christian ways," says Kalash. "Once your liver is cleaned out, your disposition will improve, Ilona. You've always been a most agreeable girl, but your thoughts are muddy. You stumble in your speech. Wine, my dear, wine is what does it."

After dinner, while Ilona sat on the ground, scratching Kalash's feet (his father, the Amir, has a concubine who is the most accomplished foot-scratcher in Islam), Miernik got out a notebook and interviewed Kalash about his ancestry. What was his exact relationship to the Prophet? "One doesn't go about reciting these pedigrees, Miernik. Put away your pen and enjoy the evening." Miernik persisted. "Very well," said Kalash. "I am of the sons of Mohammed and his wife Kadija, who was the Prophet's first convert, and who died after the Prophet was besieged in Mecca."

Miernik was impressed. "I had no idea," he said, scribbling on his pad. "Well," Kalash said, "no one else has, either. The family has scrolls with the genealogy all marked down. But is it true? What is true at the point where the Holy Koran leaves off? The Khatar family always had a lot of weak blood, younger sons who didn't like to lop off heads and testicles as the line of the elder sons to which I belong always enjoyed doing. They sat about in our mountain strongholds, watering the family tree. Not exactly objective scholarship, but good enough for my ancestors. From what the Koran says I think the Prophet must have been a good deal like my father—a big strong fellow who knew how to enjoy this world while waiting for the ineffable pleasures of the next. He started the custom of using the sword on those who were reluctant to believe in the heaven of Islam. Showed the beggars how wrong they'd been. Before their heads had rolled to a stop they found themselves in outer darkness, regretting they hadn't listened to one of my forebears. My family have always been enthusiastic missionaries. I learned how to handle a sword before I could talk. Very important skill in a world teeming with infidels. Can you handle a sword, Miernik?"

A full moon was shining. The air over the desert was so clear that you could see the lunar craters and mountains and seas with the naked eye. Zofia and I went for a walk; the sea was not far away and I thought she'd enjoy a stroll along the beach. (She had never seen salt water until we got to Naples.) About a hundred yards from the camp I heard running footsteps behind us: Miernik. He handed me a loaded pistol. "What is that for?" I asked. "Better to have it and not need it than the other way around," Miernik said. Zofia giggled. I took the clip out of the gun, putting the ammunition in one jacket pocket and the weapon in the other.

We scrambled down a bank and walked along the beach. White sand, white surf, pale girl in the white moonlight. Zofia has a way of walking with her head down and her hands behind her, just like Miernik. She said, "Tadeusz thinks he startled you today, with the guns."

"Well, he shoots a lot better than one would expect. Where did he learn that, in the army?" (Trap! Miernik was never in the army!)

"No," said Zofia, "he was never in the army. He had asthma. But he was trained to shoot when he was a youth. Everyone had to learn a sport, the authorities wanted to do well in the Olympics. Tadeusz couldn't run because of his asthma. He was a very good wrestler and boxer, but he always lost to boys who were less good because he ran out of breath. They said, all right, you don't need to breathe to be a marksman. They discovered he was a kind of genius with firearms. My father said it was because Tedeusz is wholly lacking in aggression—when he shot, there was no emotion. The target was just a target, not an enemy. So he was very cool. It was an intellectual problem—trigonometry with noise. But Tadeusz hated it, and as soon as he got out of school he stopped competing. The authorities were very upset. Tadeusz managed to lose several competitions and they finally let him go. They realized he was losing on purpose. I suppose the Americans won the gold medals in shooting as a result. I'm sure Tadeusz's lack of patriotic fervor is noted down in his dossier."

For everything Miernik does there is a simple explanation.

Zofia and I walked on until we came to a rock formation that blocked the way. We walked back barefooted through the fringe of the tide; the water of the Red Sea was warmer than the air. We encountered no bandits. When we reached the camp everyone had gone to bed. I put the Walther in one of my boots and fell asleep with the sharp smell of the pistol in my nostrils. I dreamed in great detail of a Miernik. Not Tadeusz.

66. FROM MIERNIK'S DIARY.

*Kennst du das Land wo die Zitronen blühn?** What fragrance can be smelled through a mask? I carry the curse of a witness. I do not live, I observe life. I thought that Ilona would carry me into the

---

*"Do you know the country where the lemon trees bloom?" (Goethe)

center of experience. With this girl I would see only the dark of my eyelids, I would smell, touch, hear—*feel*. But who stood beside the bed in Rome, looking down on the hairy body and the silken body joined together? Who heard the groans and the whispers? Who observed the fluids dripping down to stain the sheets? Miernik. The real Miernik, the true. As the hairy one ejaculated into the tight purse of Ilona's belly, he was more a part of the cold witness than of Ilona. Life has no power over me. I have been trained by experts not to live. Death itself does not interest me: it is the final act of life: only that. *Life is not enough.*

Still in all, I am not yet perfect. I know remorse. I am as wracked by guilt as a drunkard. I go to sleep with a groan, awake with a cry. "Filthy bastard!" I mutter, conversing with myself. These interior dialogues I have with the true Miernik are my last form of prayer: "God damn you!" Since childhood I have wished to summon a force more powerful than the real Miernik. "Loathe him!" I instruct the saints, with a finger pointed at my heart. If Kalash is among the sons of Mohammed, I was begotten by Augustine. "O Lord, make me pure—but not yet."

Here in the desert I have lost all desire for Ilona. Even if she put her mouth on me I would not change. She does not know this: that flagrant kiss for Nigel in Cairo was designed to show her power. I realized, watching his hands on her body, that even she means nothing to me. The knowledge filled me with guilt: I had cuckolded my friend, brought this girl to a hundred orgasms, walked with her through the streets of Rome with my secretions swimming in her womb. And for nothing. The jealousy that I felt in Naples (and before, and even while Ilona whimpered under me) would never come again. Yet it gave me a moment of life before I subsided into my coma.

So, on with the sleepwalking. Kalash cuts a magnificent figure in his robes. In the desert he becomes a fragment of nature absolutely at peace, walking on the bones of his ancestors. He says it will take ten days to reach El Fasher. It is almost fifteen hundred miles over awful roads, through desert. The Cadillac will be worn out by the time we get there. Or perhaps before. Kalash is quite prepared to walk if necessary. I am not; I have promises to keep. In Port Sudan we bought a Land Rover from some cousin of Kalash. We had a mechanic check it over, and it seems to be all right. We have a chain to pull the Cadillac if necessary. The Land Rover cost five thousand dollars; I do not like to think what the price might have been if we had bought it from someone to whom Kalash was not related. Kalash, of course, carries no money: what king does? Christopher and Collins between them contributed three thousand. That meant that I had to make up the balance from Zofia's rucksack. It was a painful moment. Nigel :"Come, come, Miernik, we all know you've got a lot of money on you. Give." How could he know? He could not. It's part of his tactic to penetrate me: he is like a clumsy window washer, hanging above the street, smearing the pane with a dirty rag. When at last he can see inside he will mistake the scene for something it is not. In many ways Nigel is a stupid man: he mistakes harassment for domination, and cheap curiosity for imagination. But it was better to pay than to be marooned in the desert.

That prospect pleases me less all the time, because of Zofia. Where she is concerned I am alive. She is a dull pain for me; worry has coiled around my stomach for her ever since I was left with responsibility for her. She looks like Mother—slimmer, and her gaiety has not yet turned into kindness—but otherwise she is very like her. Mother found me comical too, but with the same forgiveness.

Kalash's machine guns awakened my anxiety. He really does believe in the possibility of bandits. That aspect of this country was not covered by my research: I know the language, the history, the religion. Knowing the names of everything does not equal knowledge. Knowledge is what I gained in that grove of trees in Poland, dressing Mother's corpse. Hearing the Sten guns go off, smelling the cordite, I listened for a woman's shriek.

This time, Zofia. I did not want to leave her alone out of sight beyond that hill. Prey: my sister might be prey to some band of animals. (I never have sex that I do not smell the woods where Mother died: ferns rotting in the damp earth: Ilona said the first time that I smelled of ferns: I was startled into another passion when I thought myself empty.) As I got ready to shoot, Nigel once again tried to annoy me, and he succeeded. I knew what the look on his face would be after he saw me shoot. Miernik? *A marksman?* He was suitably astonished.

It is not just the desert that is a threat. Where is Sasha? When there was no letter in Cairo I was in a panic. Did this mean that he had lost at last? He never fails to keep a promise. He told Zofia that a letter would await us in Cairo. There was no letter. Zofia found an explanation: the Egyptian mails. For me, that is not an explanation. It is a threat that Zofia may be alone, absolutely alone. Besides me, there is only Sasha. By now he should be back in Brazil, reading my message. Shaking his little head, sighing over my asininity. So I tell myself. Weeks of silence ahead. Zofia carefree for the first time in her life. I say nothing about Sasha, nothing about his letter, nothing about my message.

Beside me, under the sky, Zofia plays her guitar. Polish music—how rich it seems to me, how thin it must sound in the ear of an Arab. Ilona, sitting between Nigel and Kalash, lifts their hands to her lips and kisses them, first the black hand, then the white.

67. DISPATCH FROM THE AMERICAN STATION IN KHARTOUM.

1. In accordance with Headquarters' instructions, we have briefed Chief Inspector Aly Qasim of the Sudanese Special Branch with regard to "Golgotha" and the broader question of the sponsorship, membership, and objectives of the Anointed Liberation Front. As we expected, Qasim already had in his possession a good deal of information, but he expressed appreciation for the facts this station made available to him.

2. The Sudanese security authorities are anxious to move against the ALF in a shorter time frame than the one we had envisaged. Qasim is under orders from his superiors to prevent any additional kidnappings, executions, and/or public crucifixions of government officials. He is determined to carry out this order, and he made it obvious that the value of any future relationship between Special Branch and this station will depend on how effectively the two are able to cooperate during the next few days.

3. Qasim considers that the only feasible way to prevent the success of "Golgotha" and other terrorist activities on the part of the ALF is to destroy the leadership of that organization, together with as much of the membership as possible. We pressed the view that the capture of leading ALF figures, and their subsequent trial, would be of great value in terms of the political education of the citizenry, but Qasim was only marginally interested in this point. "I am not a lawyer or a propagandist," Qasim stated. "I am a policeman, and it is my duty to kill this ALF as I would kill a poisonous snake in my garden."

4. Qasim, who is a fervent Muslim and a loyal servant of the Prime Minister, is particularly incensed that the ALF should style itself as a Mahdist movement. He regards this manipulation of the religious faith of the country by the Soviets as particularly reprehensible. "We will show them what a *real* holy war is," Qasim stated. He is particularly anxious to lay hands on Miernik, after the latter has made contact with the leadership of the ALF and is proved to be a Soviet agent. We expressed an interest in having access to Miernik for debriefing purposes following his arrest, and Qasim assured us that this would be possible.

5. Qasim suggested the use of Prince Kalash el Khatar as an *agent provocateur* before we could lay this possibility on the table. He flew to El Fasher immediately and obtained the permission of the Amir of Khatar to employ Prince Kalash in this capacity. Qasim shares Headquarters' reluctance to expose the prince to personal danger, and we are confident that he will find a formula that will produce the desired operational results with a minimum of risk to

young Khatar. (Qasim, incidentally, is a nephew of the Amir, so he has family as well as professional reasons for caution and concern.)

6. Qasim is hopeful that Prince Kalash will be able to learn the identity of the next set of victims before the date of their murder. Once in possession of this knowledge, he believes that he can protect the lives of the government officials involved, and either capture or kill their would-be assassins. We are putting pressure on Firecracker to report the names of the next group of victims, but he has not as yet succeeded. "Ahmed," the ALF leader in charge of the terror campaign, refuses to divulge details on security grounds. We are hopeful that Firecracker will be able to break down Ahmed's reluctance. If in fact he does so, we will hand over the information to Qasim without delay.

68. REPORT BY CHRISTOPHER'S CASE OFFICER (FROM KHARTOUM).

1. Christopher reported to me at 0300, 6 July, in my room at the Grand Hotel. He arrived in Khartoum at approximately midnight—July. Christopher's condition and morale are excellent.

2. Christopher was fully briefed in accordance with Headquarters' instructions. The information imparted to him seemed to stimulate his competitive instincts, and I was left in no doubt that he will carry out his assignment with efficiency and enthusiasm.

3. Christopher has come around to the view that Miernik is an opposition agent. Lacking Headquarters' distance from the subject (and lacking also some of the information available to Headquarters) he was understandably less quick to fit the puzzle together. The briefing given to him by this officer, combined with his own observation of Miernik's use of a book code and his display of expert marksmanship, enabled Christopher to reconcile his personal regard for Miernik with intelligent suspicion about Miernik's auspices and probable purposes.

4. Christopher expressed a willingness to reveal himself to Prince Kalash el Khatar for the purpose of providing a direct channel to the prince during the remainder of this operation. I support Khartoum's veto of this proposal. However, I endorse Christopher's recommendation that Prince Kalash be advised to use extreme caution in his contacts with the ALF. Christopher suggests that Prince Kalash hold no meetings with ALF personnel on their own ground, but that he meet them at all times in the palace of the Amir, where he can be properly protected.

5. Christopher has proposed an ingenious plan to confirm the identities of Miernik and Ilona Bentley as opposition agents. Before departing Khartoum he will confide to Bentley that a friend of his in the American Embassy has told him that an ALF leader called "Ahmed" is in fact an agent of the U.S. intelligence. If Bentley is an agent, she will certainly communicate this information to the Soviets, and any action they take with respect to "Alamed" will constitute confirmation that Bentley is reporting to them. Secondly, Christopher suggests that we pass the word on Miernik's arrival in Sudan, together with the exact route of the Cadillac in the days ahead, to Firecracker, with instructions that this information be communicated by radio to Soviet control in Dar es Salaam. The Soviet response can then be read for reactions that may confirm opposition interest in Miernik. At a minimum, this device will win points for Firecracker with the Soviets, who ought to be impressed by his ability to locate and identify Miernik before they have made Firecracker aware of his existence.

6. Christopher and his traveling companions depart Khartoum shortly after dawn 7 July. They will follow the White Nile south to Kosti, then turn west on the main highway to El Obeid. From El Obeid they will take the road through En Nahud to El Fasher. Estimated date of arrival: 12 July.

7. This officer will proceed to El Fasher on 11 July to provide support to Christopher after his arrival there.

69. REPORT BY CHRISTOPHER.

6 July. This situation certainly has a tendency to unravel. This afternoon Kalash phoned and asked me to come to his room. When I arrived he told me that he had just been visited by Chief Inspector Qasim ("a cousin of mine who is some sort of policeman") who had asked him to get in contact with the Anointed Liberation Front as an *agent provocateur*. This man wants me to play spy to a lot of Communist cutthroats," said Kalash. "He told me it was my duty to Sudan. He has already taken the liberty of getting my father's permission. I suppose my father thought it would be a good substitute for war. He certainly doesn't have much interest in the fate of Sudan. I'm too old now to go out and kill lions with a spear as I was made to do when I was a boy. Really, Paul, these people never tire of their games."

I asked if he had agreed to help Qasim. "Agreement doesn't enter into it. He handed me a letter from my father. I am ordered to go through with this nonsense. It's most inconvenient."

Then Kalash dropped the following bombshell: "I think it will be better if you and the others go back to Europe at once. Have a sail on the Nile if you like, but then get a plane to London. I shall be occupied with plots and disguises, I expect. There will be no time for hospitality, and my father is certain to be in a mood over this. I can't think what he might say if I showed up with a Cadillac full of foreigners at a time when he's arranged for me to help kill these Communists. Best for you to leave."

I told him I wanted to stay. Maybe I can be of some help to you, I said. "After all, I owe you something for that wonderful ride you gave me across the Czech frontier."

Kalash stared at me and laughed. "I suppose you do," he said. "We both seem to be the playthings of fools. Has it not struck you how very odd our friendship has become? We have progressed from a weekly luncheon to an hourly mystery. I was raised in the belief that white men are amateurs of intrigue—my father used to

go to the Governor General's mansion on the Queen's birthday
and talk loudly in dialect about slitting the throats of all the
Englishmen there. They would smile at him through their sweat
and talk about building a school in some benighted village.
Because they didn't understand our language, he thought they
didn't understand our intentions. They understood that we had no
power to carry out our intentions; you can't slit a throat without a
knife. Now they've hardly gone and we're back where we were
before Gordon was beheaded—slicing up each other. One of the
bigwigs of this Communist band—they call themselves the
Anointed Liberation Front, if you can imagine that—is a bastard
brother of mine. I don't know him, my father got him on some
woman someone gave him. But my father wants him dead. He's
an insult to the blood, you know, throwing in with a lot of
Russians in order to kill his relations. Father should have sent *him*
to Oxford. I'm afraid I've lost stomach for all this medieval nonsense.

Since the matter was out in the open, I advised Kalash to be
very careful in his dealings with the ALF. The thought that he
might be harmed had not occurred to him. Kalash has the idea
that his person is untouchable in Sudan. Of course he may be
right. But I don't think that his half brother is likely to have much
respect left for the old traditions after his training in Moscow, not
to mention the fact that Kalash and the Amir are the principal
obstacles between him and whatever his notions of power and self-
esteem may be. "I suppose he may have some idea that he can take
over the family," Kalash said. "It's happened before. Illegitimate
sons are the curse of our system."

It took a great deal of persuasion, but in the end Kalash agreed
that we can finish the journey to El Fasher with him. Unless his
cousin the chief inspector is as indiscreet as Kalash, there should
be no trouble. "It will be rather interesting to see which way old
Miernik shoots if the Communist camel corps falls on us along the
way," says Kalash. So it will.

Kalash has agreed not to discuss his conversation with Qasim with any of the other members of our group. He seemed mildly insulted that I thought he might do so: "It's not the sort of thing one would discuss with Miernik or the girls, you know. One merely tells such people to go when the time comes. One is less ready to be rude where you are concerned, Paul. It's a great convenience having you about—you're so willing to be kind to Miernik. That gives the rest of us the freedom to be annoyed all the time, which is the only natural response to such a man. In the end, you know, it will all burst out. You'll be the one to strangle him."

Kalash gave me one of the notices posted by the ALF after they carried out their crucifixions. When we met for drinks this afternoon, I had Miernik translate it in Ilona's hearing. (Kalash did not join us in the bar.)

Later I invited Ilona to go shopping with me on the pretext that I wanted to buy some amber for my mother. In the taxi I told her that a classmate of mine, now some sort of official in our embassy in Khartoum, had told me a story about the ALF. Its leader, a Sudanese named Ahmed, was in fact working for the Americans. "It's shocking as hell to me," I told Ilona, "that the United States should be mixed up in such a thing. My friend said that diplomacy is more interesting than most people imagine. He's always been an ass. I don't suppose the story is true, but all the same . . ."

Ilona showed no special interest in the information. She advised me not to disturb myself over what governments do. "They have nothing to do with us, Paul," she remarked. "They won't abolish themselves as they should—but we can ignore them."

She held her forearm in front of my eyes so that I could read the blue numbers from Belsen tattooed on her skin. "Of course," she said, "ignoring them is not always easy. They have ways of getting one's attention."

70. FROM THE DEBRIEFING OF ZOFIA MIERNIK.

By the time we reached Khartoum all of us, I think, wanted a few minutes alone. One gets incredibly dirty in the desert. In camp, Kalash allowed us only a little water in the morning for washing—enough to clean the teeth and the corners of the eyes. So when we got to the Grand Hotel (which is not so very grand, by the way) we all went in our own directions and took baths and so forth. I didn't see anyone from midnight one night until just before dinner the next. Not even Tadeusz. All of these people were tremendous diarists—they were always writing down the day's events, like explorers or journalists. I don't know why. I supposed when I didn't see anyone that that was what they were doing—writing. I was glad to take a hot bath and be left alone. I read an American book Paul had given me. I closed the blinds and didn't go outside at all. I had had enough of the sun. I wanted a cool dark place.

Q. Was there any more byplay between Collins and your brother over Ilona?

A. No. After we left Cairo they both became surprisingly uninterested in Ilona, and she in them, for that matter. We all became comrades. There was no more sexual banter. I must say Ilona behaved very well. She did most of the work around the camp—the cooking and sewing and so on. She behaved like a chum instead of a tart. She really was very fond of all the men. I never liked her, as I've told you, not even after she had undergone this change in personality. But I could see her charm. Really, she gave one no cause to condemn her. She accepted everyone else exactly as she found them. I suppose I should have done the same for her. As for Tadeusz, he was more like his old self. That peculiar cringing behavior I saw in Cairo disappeared once we got into the desert.

Q. We'd like as many details of the trip out of Khartoum as you can remember. Can you just take it day by day for us?

A. I don't remember each day equally well, of course.

We left on a Friday and went down the White Nile. Kalash drove the Cadillac, with Ilona and Collins and Tadeusz as passengers. I rode with Paul in the Land Rover. Kalash had to go more slowly because the Land Rover couldn't keep up. After we left the paved roads, the Land Rover led, because of the dust. We stopped a few times to look at the scenery. It was rather thrilling to see the boats on the Nile—dhows, with those sharp sails like the wings of swallows. Once we saw a whole group of them together and Paul said, "Look, the sails are like a line of Arabic script." That's just what they looked like.

Actually, nothing much happened until Sunday night. By that time we were in a routine—start off very early, drive until just before dark, make camp, have supper, talk awhile. Usually I played the guitar. Ilona would sing. It was a happy atmosphere.

Q. What did you talk about?

A. Anything but ourselves. I found this strange at first. For a Pole it was disconcerting—we are always discussing our souls. Westerners do not speak of their inner lives—at least not Paul and Nigel and Ilona. Kalash, of course, is a black Englishman. On the trip we talked about literature, the theater. All of them had a great store of information. One of them was bound to know all about almost anything that came up in conversation. Nigel, for example, seemed to know the names of all the butterflies and birds in the world. No one ever mentioned politics. The subject did not seem to interest them.

Q. There were no arguments, no conflicts?

A. No. The only possible friction would have come over Ilona, between Nigel and Tadeusz. As I said, that didn't happen. It was all very civilized, from beginning to end.

Q. Let's talk about Sunday night.

A. Yes. Well, it had been a serene day. We camped somewhere near El Obeid. Kalash had led us off the main road. He wanted to show Nigel the place where the army of the Mahdi had wiped out the English and the Egyptians seventy-five years ago. Kashgil was the name of the place where the battle took place. Kalash told us where the armies had been and described the massacre in great detail. He knew exactly how many rifles and cannon had been captured, how many foreigners had been killed. He was amusing. "On this spot an English officer, a rather fat one with an angry red face, Nigel, charged into a group of native horsemen, waving his sword and shouting insults. He was killed more quickly than the others because we rather admired his bravery." Nigel was not amused. These English don't much like the memory of defeat, especially when they lost to natives. Paul stood by smiling; he always found Kalash delightful.

We camped not far away, between some hills. There was a big moon; for the whole trip we had wonderful moonlight. There was no reason to expect what happened. We went to bed as usual about nine o'clock. Ilona always stripped completely before going to sleep, and hung her clothes on the rope of the tent. We perspired a great deal during the day, of course, and the night air took away some of the odor. I wore an American T-shirt Paul had given me as a nightgown. But Ilona slept naked. She was a restless sleeper, turning and muttering all night. Since we had left civilization, Kalash had made us sleep with the guns. He and Tadeusz and Paul had the sub-machine guns, Nigel a pistol. Ilona and I had a pistol, too, hanging on a hook from the ridgepole of the tent.

I was asleep when the noise started. I was not confused at all. As soon as I woke, even before I opened my eyes, I knew that shooting was going on. I thought: bandits. Kalash had said all along that there might be bandits. The first shots were not very loud. Then there was a tremendous amount of firing. The flap of our tent was open and I looked out. All up and down the hillside were muzzle flashes, flickering in the darkpink and blue, like the flame of a gas stove. Also yellow, all mixed together. Kalash was running in his white robes with a gun in his hands. He fell full length and I thought he was killed. But then he began to shoot again. Nigel and Tadeusz came out of their tent on their hands and knees, also shooting. Beside me, Ilona kicked away her sleeping bag and reached up for the pistol. "We have to get out of the tent," she said. "They'll shoot into the tents." She was a quick thinker— she stopped me from crawling out the front of the tent. She ripped open the back and we crawled out that way. She was naked and I might as well have been, in my T-shirt. It was terribly frightening for a woman to lie there with her body exposed. We huddled on the ground together, in a little depression in the dirt. Ilona held the pistol in both hands.

Up to now I had not seen Paul. I wondered if he had been shot. Bullets were flying all through the camp. Sparks flew off the cars as the bullets hit. It seemed quite impossible that any of us would live through all this. Nigel and Kalash were under the Land Rover, firing. Now Tadeusz had vanished as well. I was filled with a peculiar feeling—I don't know how to describe it. That my brother should have gone through all he had gone through in order to be murdered in the middle of nowhere by a bunch of illiterate tribesmen. Oddly enough, I thought of that English officer Kalash told us about, the fat one. I understood his rage. How dared these savages kill *us*, who were so intelligent, so cultured, so civilized?

Kalash and Nigel kept shooting. All of a sudden, there was much more firing on the hill, machine guns. The bandits began to yell to each other, Kalash and Nigel got on their feet and ran out toward the hill. They fell down side by side and shot again.

Then the firing stopped. It was very sudden. The sound persisted. There was a kind of ringing in the air—the memory of the guns going off. Kalash leaped into the Land Rover and started it up. Nigel got in, too, holding Kalash's machine gun. They went tearing off into the desert with the lights blazing, and pretty soon, a few hundred meters away perhaps, I heard them shooting again. While they were gone, Paul and Tadeusz came running into the camp. They were wearing only their shorts, carrying their guns.

Paul's face was covered with blood. The lower half of his face. They were calling our names. Ilona and I stood up, and although Paul and my brother were only a few feet away from us, we both *waved.* Ilona and I stood up on our tiptoes, as if we were standing in a crowd on a train platform, and waved. Remember, she was completely naked and I was wearing only that shirt that came down to my hips. Paul stopped in his tracks and laughed. He roared with laughter. Of course, it was a funny sight—Ilona with that big pistol in her hand and me beside her, waving. Paul just thought it was awfully funny. It was the tension, and the relief.

All I could see was Paul's blood. I thought he'd been shot, naturally. So—this will seem strange, perhaps, but at the time it seemed so obvious—I pulled off the T-shirt and pressed it against his face, to try to stop the bleeding. He let me do it. All he had was a nosebleed—he fell or something and hit his nose and it gushed blood all over him.

So when Kalash and Nigel came back with the Land Rover they found us like that—two nude girls and their friends standing by with hot machine guns. They hardly glanced at us. Kalash had gathered up the bodies of the bandits they had killed. They had thrown three of them into the back of the Land Rover. A fourth was only wounded, but very badly. All were dressed in white robes, with great stains of blood on them. Kalash tried to question the wounded one. He was not gentle about it. He pulled the man into a sitting position and shouted at him in Arabic. The man's head kept rolling onto his shoulder. Kalash gripped his chin and held the head upright. The man was breathing very loudly and blood was pumping out of his body. Spurting. Nigel wanted to put a tourniquet on him, but Kalash kept shouting at the dying man. He was very young. I don't think he heard what Kalash was saying to him. Certainly he never answered. His eyes rolled back in his head and he died. I suppose you know that the bowels and the bladder empty at that moment. I didn't. What I remember is the sudden, rotten stink. Kalash stood up and held his hands in front of him, fingers rigid and spread out wide, in a gesture of disgust.

While this was going on, my brother crawled into one of the tents and came back with two blankets for Ilona and me. We wrapped up in them and Ilona—this will show what people will do under stress—lit the camp stove *and made tea.* We stood about drinking tea with sugar and tinned milk in it with four dead bodies on the ground at our feet. Kalash and Paul searched the bodies. They found something that interested them, but I don't know what it was. They didn't discuss it with the rest of us.

It was a miracle none of us was even hurt, except for Paul's bloody nose. The bandits had attacked too soon. Kalash couldn't understand why the bandits had been so stupid. He seemed offended that they had opened fire from such a distance instead of sneaking into the camp and executing us in our sleep. Paul said the bandits probably did not realize we had firearms. Perhaps they thought we would surrender, or run into the desert. Maybe all they wanted was to steal the cars and the equipment.

There were five or six bullet holes in the Cadillac, and one of the windows was smashed. I don't think the Land Rover was damaged at all. Both cars ran all right. When I went back to the tent to get my clothes I saw that there were several holes in the canvas. Ilona was right about that, and so it's true that she saved my life, just as Nigel said to me later on.

We didn't sleep anymore that night. The men went out into the desert a little way and waited with their guns—set up a perimeter, as Paul said. Ilona and I lay near them in our sleeping bags. The bandits didn't come back.

The next morning, when we went away in the cars, we left the dead men where they were, lying in the sun. Kalash walked from one body to the other just before he got in the car. He spat on the face of each corpse. For just a moment, while he did that, one could see that his people had not always been gentlemen from Oxford.

71. REPORT BY CHRISTOPHER.

I was still awake when I heard Kalash speaking to me through the wall of the tent. He said, in his ordinary penetrating tone of voice, that he had spotted a half-dozen men moving toward the camp from the hill that lay to the west of us. "Silly fellows are crawling along on their stomachs in the moonlight and dashing from shadow to shadow," he said. "They have guns."

I pulled on my boots and picked up the Sten gun and the extra magazines. The camp could not have been in a worse defensive position. The tents were pitched in a shallow canyon, with four low hills lying all around it and only a narrow track of firm ground leading out. There was no cover, except for the vehicles. It was obvious that somebody would have to get around behind the attackers, and I told Kalash that I'd try it. The moon was full, but fairly low on the horizon, so that there was a strip of shadow behind my tent. I cut the canvas and crawled out. Kalash stuck his head around the end of the tent and gave me what I believe is called a wolfish grin. He seemed to be looking forward to whatever was coming.

I heard him waking Miernik and Nigel as I crawled off to the right as fast as possible. The ground was flinty and I was sorry I hadn't taken time to put on my clothes. I could feel the skin peeling off my knees and elbows and the blood oozing. It was about twenty yards to the shoulder of the hill, which was really just a hillock. Fair-sized boulders, the color of sand in daylight but now as white as eggshell in the moonlight, were scattered over the face of the hill. Each rock threw a puddle of shadow big enough to conceal a man. As soon as I got under cover of the hill I stood up and ran along its base until I thought I was due north of the attackers and a little behind them. Then, crawling again, I went up the hill.

When I got to the top I found a rock to hide behind and looked around. There was no sign of movement in the camp. Kalash lay on his back in full view in front of the tents. About ten yards below me, lying behind rocks, were the bandits, six of them abreast. The light was very good and I could see them plainly. They were wearing white robes with U.S. Army rifle ammunition belts around their waists. Five had M-1 rifles and the other, probably the leader, had a submachine gun slung across his back. They were about fifty yards from the edge of the camp. I thought they'd try to get closer before attacking.

I decided to move off to the right and downhill a little, so as to be out of the line of fire from the camp, and also to get into an enfilading position. I backed away from my rock, stood up in a crouching position—and fell over a walkie-talkie radio. When I went down I smashed my nose with my own Sten gun. By some miracle, the fellows down below didn't hear anything. I got around on their flank with no trouble, except that blood was running off my chin. I pinched my nostrils but I couldn't get the blood to clot. My vision was slightly blurred, though it cleared in a minute or two.

The bandits were exactly where they had been before. The leader got up on his knees, unslung his machine pistol, and gave a hand signal. His troops unlocked their M-1's: I heard the safety catches clicking. The bolt on a Sten gun is very noisy. I figured if I pulled mine to put a round in the chamber I'd have five M-1's shooting at me from a range of ten yards in about four seconds. In less time than that, they opened fire on the camp. At the first shot, Kalash stood up in the moonlight in the middle of the open ground and began firing at the hillside with his Sten gun. He certainly was a lovely target. I lost a little time watching this scene. As Nigel and Miernik came rolling out of their tent, I began to fire.

No one but the leader, whom Kalash apparently inspired to stand upright and match testicles, was a very good target. He fell almost at once. It took the others several moments to realize that I was behind them.

When they did, they all turned around and started shooting in my direction. There was no way to move from behind my rock: rounds were slamming into it and throwing dirt all around it. There was a lot of fire coming from the camp, but it was doing the attackers no damage as they were all in the prone position behind boulders of their own. I fired a few bursts around the sides of my rock, but I'm sure I got no results. The bandits were firing whole clips at me. I could hear the M-1's bang out eight shots as fast as the trigger could be pulled, and then the clang of the empty clips being ejected.

I thought I was a dead man. Then I heard another Sten gun and, looking up the hill, I saw Miernik. He was down in the kneeling position, firing just as he had done at the paper target a few days before—methodical bursts of two and three rounds. The bandits, screaming in panic, began shooting at him. I was able to start firing again. Almost as soon as I did, they began to run. The only way for them to go was straight into the rising moon. They were perfect silhouettes. I stood up and fired a burst. One of them fell. Miernik came down the hill, reaching me as I was putting another magazine in the Sten gun. He put his hand on my arm and said, "Let them go. We've done enough."

Miernik walked over to the men we had shot and turned them over. Idiocy," he said. "Idiocy." He uttered a loud sob. He picked up their weapons by the barrels and flung them into the darkness. Then, without another word, he began to run down the hill toward the camp. I followed. The Land Rover, with Kalash at the wheel and Nigel standing up in the front seat with a Sten gun in his hands, went tearing out of the camp. Ilona and Zofia were unhurt, and very calm. For some reason neither of them had any clothes on. The sight of them filled me with joy. I was, after all, alive against all my expectations of a few minutes before. But I felt not even a fficker of sexual desire. Zofia tried to do something about my bloody nose. Both girls stood there, completely unself-conscious, making no effort to cover themselves, until Miernik went and got them a couple of blankets.

Kalash brought back the three men Miernik and I had killed, as well as one who was still alive. He sorted through the bodies and pulled the wounded man out of the Land Rover by the feet. Kalash tried to question him, but the man was too badly shot up to speak before he died. There was blood all over the place. Miernik moved away while Kalash worked on the wounded man, but the girls did not flinch.

Kalash and I searched the bodies. In a wallet carried by the leader we found a thick wad of Sudanese money and a photograph of Kalash. It was a perfect likeness. Kalash was wearing European clothes, and he was seated at a table in an outdoor café that I rec-ognized as the one on the Ile Rousseau in Geneva. Kalash handed me his picture without a word, then took it back and tucked it away in his robe. The money he scattered over the ground. Kalash gazed thoughtfully at the hills for a few moments, then took my arm and walked me out of earshot of the others. "What do you make of all this?" he asked.

"I don't like their having your picture," I said.

"No. I wonder where they got it. I've never seen it before, and I didn't notice anyone creeping about the Île Rousseau with a cam-era while I drank my lemonade. Ilona's always clicking away, but one wouldn't think any of these corpses ever knew her."

"Did she ever photograph you on the Île Rousseau?"

"My dear Paul, she has photographed me everywhere except in bed. A lot of people have taken pictures of me. Total strangers snap me on the streets of Geneva—Germans and Japanese, usu-ally. I find this whole episode very annoying. No sooner am I approached to be a spy by Qasim than a lot of buffoons begin shooting at me. If it weren't for you I might well be dead."

"The man to thank is Miernik," I said. I told him about the firefight on the hillside.

"He's a peculiar type, Miernik," Kalash said. "I found him vomiting up his tea a few moments ago, over behind the tents. When I tried to speak to him he muttered something about being a murderer. 'I have just done murder,' he said, 'murder!' Better to do it than have it done, I should have thought. When he went floundering out of the camp I thought he must be running away. So did Nigel—he very nearly shot him. That's what British officers do to cowardly privates, you know."

I tried to leave the girls with the idea that the bandits had been only bandits. Zofia and Ilona seemed to believe that the attackers were interested in the cars (and possibly in white females). Neither Collins nor Miernik made any effort to contradict my theory. Neither of them believes it for a moment.

Kalash decided that we should post guards for the rest of the night. In the morning we will move out, and drive nonstop to El Fasher. It's about 450 miles. At the rate we've been moving over these roads—which get worse from here onward—we should cover the distance in about twenty-four hours. We have four drivers, counting Ilona. (Miernik cannot drive, but we could hardly have a better man riding shotgun.)

I'd like to think about the events of this evening before trying to interpret them. Finding Kalash's photograph on that body is a serious matter. If I were in charge of this operation, I'd lock him up in his father's palace with armed men on all the doors. His value as a double agent, leading the ALF to destruction, is now questionable, to put it mildly.

There are so many possible explanations for Miernik's behavior that I hardly know where to start listing them. Did he kill a couple of his own agents in order to protect his cover? Was his reaction after the shooting revulsion over the betrayal of his own people? Was it genuine horror over having to kill anyone at all? Was he really trying to save my skin—and, more likely, his sister's?

Everything he does muddies the water. At this point I'm content to let you figure the whole thing out.

72. INTERCEPTED RADIO TRAFFIC FROM SOVIET TRANSMITTER IN DAR ES SALAAM (DECODED 8 JULY).

1. Message for Qemal's (i.e., "Firecracker's") ears only. Qemal acknowledge with recognition sign.
(Qemal acknowledges.)
2. Message for Qemal follows. Ahmed is suspected enemy agent. Repeat. Ahmed is suspected enemy agent. Take standard action personally. Report results. Message for Qemal ends.

73. REPORT FROM FIRECRACKER TO THE AMERICAN STATION IN KHARTOUM.

Last night I received a personal message by radio from Dar es Salaam. They informed me that Ahmed is an enemy agent and instructed me to kill him. I carried out the execution personally, using one .45 caliber bullet in the head, about one hour after receiving the above message.

I have searched Ahmed's body and his personal effects, but I have not found the names of those to be executed. I believe he had memorized the list. I do not know if he has passed on the names to the execution teams. It is possible the list will now be changed, owing to the treason of Ahmed. Any new list would come to me, as I am now in sole command of our headquarters.

I had much difficulty explaining Ahmed's death to our followers. They do not believe him capable of treason. I explained that a traitor is always clever, and often is able to deceive his friends for a long time. They resent the fact that I killed Ahmed on the order of foreigners, without a trial, etc. My position is difficult. I do not know what hazards lie ahead. If there are any messages, I will leave them in the usual place.

(9 July)

74. INTERCEPTED RADIO TRAFFIC FROM SOVIET TRANSMITTER (10 JULY).

Message for Qemal follows. Standard action in case of suspicion is arrest and interrogation not repeat not summary execution. Most disturbed Ahmed's death. You should have held Ahmed for Richard. You will explain your action to Richard on his arrival. Meanwhile recall assault teams white, green, yellow, blue. Golgotha suspended. Richard brings you new orders. Message for Qemal ends.

75. REPORT BY COLLINS.

We arrived at the palace of the Amir of Khatar shortly before dawn on 11th July after a twenty-four-hour drive through the desert. It was a nervous journey, but there were no incidents. After the events at Kashgil we kept weapons at hand, and during our one stop (at En Nahud to take on water and petrol) we attracted a certain amount of attention. A small crowd gathered to inspect the bullet holes in the cars and to gaze upon Ilona Bentley and Zofia Miernik in their shorts. We had submachine guns slung round our necks and I expected the local police to make inquiries (after all, there were four dead bodies behind us in that dry wadi). But none was forthcoming. Prince Kalash was recognized by all who passed by, and he spent a good deal of time exchanging blessings in Arabic.

2. The Amir's palace lies some distance from El Fasher, on a high hill above the Wadi el Ku. It has rained recently in the mountains and the wadi is more or less full of water. I mention this because we had to tow the Cadillac across several brackish streams, using the Land Rover and a cable. The motor got wet and we lost an hour drying off the wiring and the sparking-plugs with bits of cloth. Even though we were stopped in territory controlled by his father, Prince Kalash insisted on working in the dark while Miernik and Christopher stood guard with Sten guns. He has become altogether less careless since the attack. We travelled without headlamps, steering by moonlight. Since the last stage of the journey was made along steep mountainsides on narrow rubble roads, there was a certain amount of risk. I was interested that even this did not rouse Miernik from his torpor. Since the shooting affair he has been very subdued. He sat silently in a corner of the rear seat, fingering his Sten gun and staring into the night; ordinarily he would have been gasping and giving warnings to the driver.

3. The palace is a vast structure; portions of it appear to have been cut from the living rock of the mountainside. We arrived in the gray false light of five o'clock. The cold air stung the bare skin. All round were the outlines of the mountains, like a drawing in ink. Kalash shattered the quiet by pounding on a thick door. A voice issued from a window and Prince Kalash answered with his name. A yellow light was carried past a whole row of windows and the door swung open. In the doorway, with a lamp in his upraised hand, was a very large man down on his knees. I suppose he was a slave. He said something in Arabic in a peculiar singsong voice, and Prince Kalash responded. The big man shuffled away, still on his knees, and came back a few moments later with a veiled woman. She stood upright in Prince Kalash's presence, but recoiled at her first sight of Ilona and Zofia, whose bare legs shone in the lamplight. To the girls Prince Kalash said, "This woman will show you to your rooms. She'll bring you food and arrange for a bath before you sleep. I recommend you to put on ordinary

clothes before you come down tomorrow. We aren't used to bare legs in this house. I'm afraid we won't see a great deal of you. You'll be expected to remain in your end of the house and to eat with the women, unless of course you want to dine alone. Don't wander about. I'll send someone for you tomorrow and perhaps we can see a bit of the country." Ilona grinned. "Kalash," she said, "are you locking us up in the harem? Has all this been a plot to lure us into Arab slavery?" Prince Kalash waved her away with no hint of his usual good humour. "My dear Ilona," he said, "just go with the woman and try to behave yourself. You can keep your pistol if you fear for your virtue." Ilona removed the pistol from her camera case and handed it to Kalash. She and Zofia, with their faces looking back at us over their shoulders, followed the Sudanese woman into the dark interior of the palace.

4. Miernik, Christopher, and I were shown into apartments fitted with Western furniture. Apparently one of the amirs had had a shipload of beds, chairs, etc., sent down by Harrod's around 1910. There were hunting prints on the walls in heavy frames, and several lamps with fringed shades: these were gas-mantle lamps, connected to nothing. The actual light was provided by an oil lamp. In a bookcase were a matched set of Sir Walter Scott, the essays of Macaulay, and several bound volumes of *Punch* for 1898 through 1903. It was all rather touching and quite comfortable. The slave who had opened the door for us came in with my baggage. I found him gazing curiously at me and realized that I still wore the Sten gun. I smiled, removed the magazine, cleared the action, and pulled the trigger on the empty chamber, smiling to show that my weapon was unloaded and I meant him no harm. He grinned in return and backed out of the room: I don't know whether this was a sign of respect or an act of caution. When I inspected my baggage I noticed that Ilona's camera case had been brought into my room by mistake. There was no way to return it to her, as she had vanished into the seraglio, so I put it aside and went gratefully to sleep.

5. When I woke I found a black child of about twelve sitting

cross-legged beside my bed. As I opened my eyes he poured a cup of tea and thrust it into my hands. He hopped out of the room, returning with a tin bathtub, which he carried upside down over his head. The tub was soon filled with water, and the boy stood by as I bathed, taking the soap out of my hand and giving it back as necessity required. He offered in dumb show to shave me, but I did it myself while he held a mirror over the steamy tub. He gave me a breakfast of fried eggs and what seemed to be peppered mutton, watching brightly while I manipulated the knife and fork. I found that he had unpacked my bags; my clothes, freshly pressed, were neatly arranged in a tall armoire. The whole experience was like a description by Thackeray of the beginning of a weekend in an English country house a century ago. There was even a large pile of writing paper with the arms of the amirate embossed in one corner.

6. After breakfast the boy left me for a few moments, staggering out under a load of crockery. Ilona's camera case, newly shined, with all the scratches on the leather filled with boot polish, stood on a table. I opened it. Inside the case I found the Lefca with which Ilona takes her innumerable photographs, a lot of film, and the usual extra lenses and filters. There was, also, an Exakta 35.millimetre reflex camera that I had never seen before. This is an East German camera. It contained no film. With no special curiosity, I opened the back of the camera, cocked it, and tripped the shutter. I saw no light through the lens. The opening was set at f2.8, so I should have seen a spot of light the size of a sixpence. I tried again a couple of times, then unscrewed the lens. At the back of the lens, inside the housing of the viewfinder, was a round metal object approximately the size of a half-crown. It was something more than half an inch thick. It took me some time to realize what it was. It was a short-range radio homing device of the kind that is attached to cars. Once activated, it emits a steady signal on a fixed frequency. Anyone knowing the frequency, and having suitable receiving equipment, can locate the homing device, estimate its distance, and follow the car in which it has been planted.

As the device in Ilona's camera was enclosed in a sealed plastic packet, I assumed that it had not been activated. I put it back where I had found it and replaced the other items I had taken out of the camera case.

7. Soon after I made this discovery, Prince Kalash appeared at the door with Christopher and Miernik in tow. We went along to the Arnir's apartment, a series of very large rooms full of rugs; fantastic geometric designs covered the walls in a continuous *coup d'oeil.* The Amir awaited us at the end of a long room where he sat on a divan with papers covered in Arabic script scattered over the cushions. He is a long bony old man with the face of an eagle; Prince Kalash looks just like him. The Amir's hair is white, and a close-cropped beard like a strip of bleached felt covers his black cheeks and chin. He looked us over with hard dark eyes and with such an expression of ferocity that I thought we had offended him in some way. None of us had bowed or fallen prostrate, but Prince Kalash would, I suppose, have told us had this been expected. The Amir, after inspecting each of us in turn, began to speak in the perfect English he learned at Winchester and Oxford. "I welcome you to my house," he said. "I hope that you are comfortable. Your quarters are perhaps less picturesque than you anticipated. My father had the idea, entirely correct I think, that Europeans like to sleep in beds and sit on chairs. In this room you will have to crouch like a native." He indicated a row of cushions and we sat down. "My son has told me of the great service you rendered him on the journey here. I am very grateful. There have always been fools in our desert, and that at least does not change. I am happy that none of you was injured. I hope to meet the young ladies who accompanied you. I hope they are comfortable too, but of course you wouldn't know whether they are or not. I believe they are happy enough. As for the Cadillac, it is shot full of holes. I can't think why that American wanted to give it to me, but it was kind of him. Perhaps he thinks I am an oil sheik. I rather wish I was." (Prince Kalash afterwards explained that the Cadillac was a gift of "a rich

friend of Paul's.") He stopped speaking and once again stared at each of us in turn. When his eyes fell on me I said: "We are most comfortable, Your Highness. Everyone has been very kind." He nodded. To Christopher he said: "You are an American. Your country interests me." Christopher looked expectant, but the Amir did not elaborate on his statement. Instead, he turned to Miernik and spoke in what sounded to be slow, careful Arabic. Miernik replied. The Amir nodded. "Remarkable that a Pole should speak Arabic," he said. "What was your purpose in learning the language?" Miernik muttered something about scholarly interest. The Amir glared at him. "In the past we have had very few scholarly foreigners," he said. "Usually if they spoke Arabic they were worldly indeed. Perhaps you are the herald of a new era in Africa. One hopes so. We have been through a very tiring time with the Egyptians and the Turks and the British." He sank into another silence, unmoving on his divan. At length he looked directly at Prince Kalash, who stood up at once and led us out of the presence.

8. In an anteroom we found a Sudanese wearing European clothes. He stood idly by a window, smoking a cigarette. Prince Kalash, on catching sight of this man, changed the direction of his stride and seized him by the shoulder. He said something to the man in rapid Arabic and was answered in the same language. The man put a hand on Prince Kalash's forearm and looked across the room at us, raising his eyebrows. Prince Kalash spoke another sentence in Arabic and then turned away. Miernik had followed the conversation with evident interest, but he made no comment as we walked through the house. I asked Prince Kalash who the man was. "Nobody," he replied. "One of my horde of cousins. His name is Aly Qasim. He's an irritating chap." Miernik gazed silently at Prince Kalash during this explanation, then wagged his head in a gesture of disbelief. He went into his room without a word. If Prince Kalash noticed this behaviour, he made no mention of it.

9. At about five o'clock, we met the girls on neutral territory, in

another room furnished in the Victorian style. They had been scrubbed and perfumed by young girls, much as we had been tended by boys. Apparently the household possesses any number of tin bathtubs and enslaved children. I gave Ilona her camera case. She put it carelessly on the floor beside her. "I thought they must have mixed up the bags," she said. "I ought to get some wonderful colour pictures of this house. I only wish I had lights. What walls! The eye is absolutely caressed everywhere it looks." She may well assume that I am too much the gentleman to have searched her case. In that she is wrong, as I seem to have been wrong in her. No innocent person carries the sort of thing I found concealed in her extra camera. I wondered if she had used the bug to guide the ALF to our camp at Kashgil, but I now think that unlikely. No doubt she is looking forward to using it in some future situation. *What* situation? I shall keep a close eye on the Exakta. And on Ilona, my newest and least likely enemy.

76. FROM THE FILES OF CHIEF INSPECTOR ALY QASIM.

On the morning of 11th July I flew in a police aircraft to El Fasher and thence by helicopter to the palace of the Amir of Khatar. My departure from Khartoum was precipitate. At five-thirty in the morning I received a telephone call from the prime minister. He was in a state of alarm. The Amir had wakened him ten minutes earlier with a radio-telephone call. Prince Kalash had been attacked near Kashgil by a band of six armed men. He had killed four of his attackers and was unhurt himself. Both the Amir and Prince Kalash connected this attack to my plan to infiltrate the prince into the Anointed Liberation Front. They demanded an explanation. I was instructed to satisfy the Amir that the prime minister was taking measures to ensure the safety of Prince Kalash.

Within fifteen minutes I was dressed and en route to the airport, where the aircraft was standing by. As my car travelled through Khartoum the muezzins were making the call to prayer. My driver looked anxiously in the rear-view mirror, anticipating an order to stop by the mosque, but I had no time even for that. I told him to drive on.

I had left instructions for a detail from Special Branch to proceed to the scene of the attack on Prince Kalash to carry out an investigation. I ordered the pilot to overfly Kashgil, and after some searching we located the site. There were four bodies scattered over the floor of a wadi. They had been abused by the jackals. The clothing was strewn about. As we flew over the scene at low altitude, vultures rose from the corpses. It was apparent that my men would find very little evidence, but I radioed the location of the dead and gave instructions for the investigating team to travel by helicopter so as to reduce the time element.

I arrived at the palace at approximately ten o'clock. It was not until three o'clock that my uncle, the Amir, received me. I had in the meantime been offered no refreshment. These signs of the Amir's displeasure were underscored when I happened to encounter Prince Kalash in an anteroom. He was accompanied by the three male foreigners who have been travelling with him. With no regard for their presence, he immediately began to berate me. "I will tell you, since the collection of the simplest information seems to be beyond your capacities, that you very nearly got all of us killed," Prince Kalash said. "Your Communists are very bad shots. Otherwise I and my friends here would be dead." I made a ritualistic reply, as I knew that the man Miernik understood Arabic. "God is great," I said, attempting to give Prince Kalash a warning glance. One does not warn princes; they say what they like. "I shall be interested to hear from you how these Communists knew precisely where to find me in a thousand square miles of desert," Prince Kalash went on. Finally I managed to quieten him. He went away with his friends.

My interview with the Amir began on a painful note. I had, of course, anticipated his anger. Prince Kalash, after all, is his eldest legitimate son. The Amir has trained him since birth for the succession, and he is pleased with the result as only a father can be who sees in his son a version of himself. That this son had nearly met a meaningless death was most upsetting. The Amir himself had put Prince Kalash in death's way by agreeing so casually to let him be used against the Communists. He was responsible for the prince and he had very nearly lost him. The Amir now needed someone to blame for his own mistake. So it is when things go wrong for the powerful.

The Amir is modern to the extent that he does not require educated men to prostrate themselves on approaching him. Ordinarily I should have stood upright in his presence; on this occasion I lay face down at his feet. "Get up, get up," the Amir said. "I want to see your face." He handed me a photograph of Prince Kalash. It was soiled and cracked as if from much handling. "This was found by my son on the body of one of the assassins," the Amir said. "Explain."

"I can speculate, Highness," I said. "But I cannot explain. Who knows what thoughts such men have? We know that these terrorists are looking for a figurehead, some great figure to give respectability to their activities. That is why Prince Kalash was approached, with your gracious consent, to assist us in destroying this so-called Anointed Liberation Front."

"Their purpose was to kill Prince Kalash," the Amir said. "That much should be plain even to a civil servant like yourself."

"With respect, Highness, that is not plain at all." Here I was able to play the card that in the end saved the situation. "We have laid hands on one of the assassins who escaped. He is in fact under my control. Unfortunately he was unable to inform me in advance of this attack upon the prince's camp—I say 'on the prince's *camp*' advisedly, for such was the nature of the enterprise. There was no intention to harm Prince Kalash. The intention of the terrorists was quite different. Nevertheless, had I known beforehand of this plan I should have taken steps to prevent it. There was too much risk in it for the prince. I blame myself most severely that he was subjected to the smallest danger.

"Prince Kalash has no doubt omitted to tell you of his extraordinary courage in the face of this attempt. While the assassins were shooting into the camp, Prince Kalash stood upright, faced them, and returned their fire. The terrorists were less than fifty yards away. Surely they could have killed him easily had that been their intention. But I believe they had orders that forbade any harm to the prince; had they injured him, much less killed him, they would have answered with their own lives.

"No, Highness. These murderers did not intend to kill Prince Kalash. They had instructions to *capture* him. Undoubtedly their plan was this: to take the prince to their headquarters, use the name of el Khatar as a blessing on their organisation and their activities, and perhaps in the end collect a ransom if they failed. They wanted to kill the Europeans. I know for certain that they were under orders from their masters, the Russian espionage apparatus, to kill all but one of Prince Kalash's friends. We have not been able to learn which of the Europeans was to be spared. But the prince himself they wanted alive."

All of this was quite true. The man who furnished the information was a constable of Special Branch named Mahjoub Mirghani. On my orders Mirghani had insinuated himself into the ALF; on fleeing the scene of the attack he had abandoned his companion and made his way to our headquarters at El Obeid. I was in possession of his report only a few hours after the shooting affray. The Amir received my information in his usual way; his blood and his life school him never to show surprise. He sat impassive while I spoke, no muscle of his body or face betraying the slightest movement.

"Do you believe they could have succeeded?" he asked. "With better planning and more skill, and in the absence of my Constable Mirghani, who opened fire before the order was given in order to warn Prince Kalash—yes. But they did not in fact succeed."

"Then you believe that Prince Kalash, even with his friends dead at his feet, would have surrendered to these fools?"

"That, of course, was the unknown factor."

"You do not know my son. He would have died before submitting to capture. I admire your police work. It is impressive that you have all this information. But if a prince is murdered no good comes out of knowing who killed him. Prince Kalash would certainly have died along with his friends if the fight had gone the other way. Then what would you have told me? That his death was a mistake? I should not have been comforted."

At this point Prince Kalash entered. I repeated to him what I had just told the Amir. The prince received my report with more animation than his father had done. He was curious about the origins of the photograph he had found. "Find out where it comes from," he said; "that information is very important." I explained that the photograph had likely been supplied by the Soviet intelligence people. Tracing the photographer was not only an impossible job, but a meaningless one. Prince Kalash did not accept this line of argument; he wanted to know who in Geneva had betrayed him. I told him I would pursue the matter.

It was apparent that the Amir would not again be anxious to risk Prince Kalash. I therefore presented to him an alternative plan. This involved his illegitimate son who is in a position of leadership in the ALF.

"Highness, may I speak to you of this man Qemal who claims to be your child?" I asked.

"He *is* my child," the Amir said. "I remember his mother very well. She died young. The boy grew up here. I treated him as a son. One assumes that one's sons will not become Communists."

All this I knew. The Amir must be permitted to speak rhetorically.

"A son is a son," I said. "The son of an Amir is always the son of an Amir. Not even Communists can change that. They can manipulate Qemal's pride in his birth, but they cannot change that pride in its essentials. I know the boy. The fact that he is your son is the central fact of his life."

"Of course it is," said the Amir. "Get to the point, Aly." If he called me by my name I knew the storm had passed. "Highness, I ask you to treat Qemal as a son. I can get a message to him. I should like to tell him that he is welcome in this household. Bring him here on your word. Once he is here, let me speak to him—not as the head of the Special Branch but as your nephew and as his cousin. Let me tell him that if he delivers his Communist comrades to us, you will forgive him this foolishness."

"What good is that to him?" the Amir asked. "He wants more than my fatherly embrace. Look at what he's done already. He wants power. He cannot help that, it's in his blood. He has gone beyond forgiveness."

"The forgiveness need not be genuine."

The Amir's eyes bored into the flesh of my face. "I do not," he said, "betray my own son."

"The alternative is the death of many innocent men. I have told you of their plan to assassinate the leading figures of the government. Do you owe these men nothing, Highness? They have their positions because you do not object to them. All are honourable men. Many are members of this family. With the greatest respect, Highness, to do nothing is to betray *them*. We do not know what names are on the killing list of the ALF. God knows who we might send to his death."

The Amir closed his eyes and fell into one of his silences. This lasted for some time; it is uncanny how long he is able to remain still. As a child I believed that my uncle, when he closed his eyes and sat like a statue, was hearing the advice of the Prophet. Now, apparently, he was guided to a means of betraying Qemal without being himself obliged to play the traitor.

"You may send your message to Qemal," he said, opening his eyes. "But he must deal with Prince Kalash, who can make whatever promises he likes; Prince Kalash has no power to keep promises now. When he sits here as Amir he will not be bound by anything Prince Kalash has guaranteed."

Prince Kalash looked at me. He was as impassive as his father. I took my leave and began my preparations.

77. NOTE BY THE KHARTOUM STATION.

The information contained in the above memorandum did not come into our possession until 20 July, when Qasim returned to Khartoum. Qasim gave us no advance notice of his plan concerning Qemal—who was, of course, the agent we called "Firecracker." It was therefore impossible to inform Qasim of Firecracker's value to us, not to mention the considerable service he had already rendered to his country.

It is our impression that Qasim's proposals to the Amir were in the nature of a spur-of-the-moment attempt to salvage his operation to destroy the ALF and to rescue his own credit with the Amir. This turn of events could not have been anticipated except through advance briefing of Qasim on Firecracker's role and identity. This would have constituted a breach of security that at the time was considered unacceptable.

78. FROM MIERNIK'S DIARY.

By last night I had regained control of myself. The killing unnerved me. As my own psychiatrist I know why only too well; the machine gun will never be my weapon. I see Mother's face in every muzzle flash. How could I know those men would choose to attack us? Once they had done so, instinct took command. Some mystical force, occupying a place on the spectrum of emotion somewhere between rage and ecstasy, flooded into the cavity of my body. It is the primitive brain, not the mind, that controls men in all important matters. I did not consciously think of protecting Zofia, much less Ilona and the other males. One does not operate rationally at such moments. I ran into the darkness, meaning to kill, knowing that only murder would release me from the force that seized me. I had no thought for the lives of those men, no thought for the future, no thought for anything except the Sten gun that was dearer than any part of my own body.

I do not dramatize; if anything, I fail to find language gorgeous enough to describe what I felt and what I did. The death-giver is beyond language, beyond thought, he enters another region of experience. No wonder the Society of Assassins, the SS, the Cheka took on the character of religious brotherhoods. They knew secrets other men dared not seize. It was only afterward, looking at those ragged blood-stained bodies, that I realized what I had done, and what my act meant in terms of the future. The dead men, in themselves, still had no reality for me. Only the act of killing had meaning. I realized that I had loved killing them. The after-emotion was similar, I think, to that which must be felt by a man who acts out an obsessive sexual fantasy. He dreams for years, lurks about schoolyards, reads in the newspaper of more courageous maniacs. At last he rapes a child. Joy is what he feels in fact; horror and remorse is what he knows he must feel in theory. He instructs his mind to repel the memory of ecstasy. The mind obeys, but the primitive brain lies down for a little happy sleep: he knows it will awake again, overpower the mind, and insist on a repetition of the crime. He watches over its cot with tenderness.

Of course I knew who the victims were. Pathetic dolls manipulated by men like me. We plant the germ of an idea in them and send them out to die of their infection. Perhaps they were as happy when the bullets ripped into them as their ancestors would have been to receive the spear-blade that sent them to Allah. As they died in the moonlight did visions of Marx pass before them? Did an incantation by V. I. Lenin echo in their ears? The wretched will always find something they do not understand to die for. Death itself is their reward: Christ, Mohammed, and Beria must all have expired with a final little shiver of spiritual avarice, knowing that they had been the brokers of so much joy.

Tonight—life! Or Kalash's vision of it. He has himself been rather glum, but for different reasons from mine. To be the object of murder is not, for Kalash, a religious mystery but an insult to his position at the apex of the human species. Apparently he and his father have worked out some suitable revenge, for today he was cheerful again. Late in the afternoon he had Paul and Nigel and me summoned to one of the gardens inside the walls of this astonishing palace. We found him sitting under a baobab tree whose branches provide a canopy above the little courtyard. A lion slept under a stone table a few feet away. (These beasts are household pets of the Khatar; slaves are specially trained to capture them as cubs and to acquaint them with human customs. They seem to be decorative rather than functional; I don't believe they act as watchdogs, for example. Kalash in his blunt way had told Zofia and Ilona to be careful of them. "Girls who go near lions when they are menstruating often are killed. The beast smells blood and attacks. No amount of training can remedy this behavior. Otherwise they are quite harmless." Kalash pays less attention to the lions than an Englishman to a dozing terrier. He is magnificent in his lack of sentimentality.)

Kalash told us that he had arranged a party for us. Since Geneva he has talked about Somali girls, who are much valued here for their beauty and sexual ingenuity. From somewhere (probably the same corner of the palace where my sister and Ilona are sleeping) he had collected eight Somali girls—two for each of us. He had laid on a supper. Suitable clothing would be supplied to us by our servant boys. "Miernik," he said, "I shouldn't want your fastidiousness to interfere with your pleasure. I give you my word you have no disease to fear from these girls." He set a time for the commencement of the party and left us.

I had brought my diary with me and I remained in the garden after the others left with the lion snoring gently beside me. As I was writing a few moments later, Kalash reappeared. "Tomorrow morning," he said, "I have to go out into the mountains on an errand. There are some rather interesting ruins along the way, and

it occurred to me you might like to see them. I can only take one
of you as I will be accompanied by a couple of my father's men.
You are the obvious companion. Paul and Nigel haven't your interest in archaeology." It developed that he was talking about the
stone relics of the Darfur dynasties, so of course I agreed to go.
He assured me that he expected to spend a peaceful day. "I should-
n't think you'll need your Sten gun this time," he said. On some
of these ruins are paintings of Christian saints on horseback. It is
an interesting cultural puzzle that no one will ever solve. I suspect
that Kalash is as much descended from these wild kings as from
the Prophet.

Just after dark my boy appeared and helped me into the regalia
Kalash had provided—robes and a turban, which the child, giggling, wound around my head, walking in circles with the end of
the cloth in his hand while I sat on a stool; Going before me with
a lamp, he guided me through the passageways of the palace and
into a square room hung with mirrors. The mirrors were placed at
floor level—sensible enough, since one sits on cushions laid on the
carpets. Kalash and the others were already on hand, reclining
behind low tables laid with platters of food. I joined them and was
given a glass of tea by the boy, who then withdrew. We were quite
alone, the first time I had been out of sight of servants since we
arrived at the palace. Nigel gazed frankly at his reflection in the
mirrors. "I rather like the look of myself in this outfit," he said. "I
think I have the figure for it. As for you, Miernik . . ." I did look
odd, but if one is going to wear fancy dress it's good to wear it in
a place where masculine beauty is meaningless.

Music began to play, filtering through a screened door. I suppose the musicians were in the next room. With the first notes, the
Somali girls entered. Not one of them could have been more than
fifteen. Their faces were gentle, unmarked by experience, and
wreathed in smiles. They approached Kalash on their knees. In
Arabic he said to them, "You are late and we are hungry." They
rose with a collective giggle and two of them joined each of us.
One immediately unbuckled my sandals and began to rub my

feet. The other sat beside me and put bits of food into my mouth with her fingers. After each mouthful she would wipe my lips with a cloth. Variations of this went on with Kalash and Paul and Nigel and their girls. I tried to speak to them in Arabic but discovered that they did not understand the language. It was not a verbal experience that Kalash had arranged for us.

After a time the girls danced. They were not particularly graceful, but they believed that they were, and that was rather charming. One or the other of them from time to time would sing. There was much giggling. The girls neither ate nor drank. Kalash lay back, utterly relaxed, and accepted the food and the caresses. Paul and Nigel seemed able to approximate his nonchalance. As for me, I gradually lost the excruciating self-consciousness I had felt on entering the room in Arab clothing. The girls were so eager to please, and so obviously unable to imagine any life but the one they led, that inhibitions were irrelevant. In Europe what we were doing would have been an orgy which could only have taken place in a pornographic novel; in the Amir's palace it was as ordinary as prayer.

At length I was no longer hungry. The girls kept trying to feed me until I refused three or four times. (I suppose this is part of the etiquette.) Then they led me to an alcove, where we lay down again. They arranged my limbs, glancing and nodding at me until I indicated that I was in a position of perfect comfort. They then removed their clothes and lay down beside me. Their bodies were remarkably beautiful: perfect breasts, long tapered rib cages, round buttocks carried high at the back, and the straight-calved long legs of their race. The only flaw, to my Central European eye, were the navels, which were protuberant and about the size of a walnut. One girl knelt and stroked my face with her breasts. The other rubbed my legs. I was still fully clothed; she reached under the skirts of my robe. Soon she left off this massage, which was intensely pleasurable (she seemed to know the location of all the nerve centers in the joints of the toes, ankles, and knees).

Biting, kissing, stroking, and tickling, one from the direction of the head and the other from the feet, the two girls met at the center of my body. As four hands and two mouths moved over my skin, I touched theirs. It was soft and smooth like a pelt, as if lacking pores; I have never felt such skin on a white woman. The girls were extremely inventive—though I suppose "inventive" is the wrong word. They had been trained in skills developed over generations by these desert people who look on appetite as a Slav looks on painting, as something which exalts and instructs each time it is experienced. One of the icons that will hang in my mind henceforth is this: a supple black girl gazing intently into my face with a look of great kindness, little lines of effort between her large eyes; she opens my lips and, counting my spasms, spits delicately into my open mouth in perfect rhythm with me.

The girls cleaned themselves like cats and went to sleep. I rose quietly and stepped out of the alcove. In other alcoves, Paul and Nigel slept with their black girls twined around them. I saw nothing of Kalash, who doubtless copulated in some other more regal place. Outside the door, asleep on the bare stones, was my servant boy. He awoke, fetched his lamp, and led me back to my room. Even as I write this the odor of the Somali girls (pepper and musk) still clings to my nostrils and my skin tingles. I understand why sheiks and amirs fear revolution: who would want to live without Somali girls once he has had them?

Miernik must. I think of what lies ahead. I know what I must do, which means taking myself out of the world for a time. What a queer successor to the desert saints is Miernik! What I have just done with the Somali girls is what those wild believers fought with prayer, hair shirt, and a diet of excrement. How they must have disgusted God. He was preparing temptations that make sex pale. In my desert, it is not pleasure and indulgence that provide the occasions of sin, but the opposite. In this desert, I plan meticulously to do what my nature tells me *not* to do: suffer, deny, betray. That is my assignment on earth; I sought it myself, and now—ten thousand kilometers from Warsaw—it is within my grasp. As ear-lier explorers passed through this continent looking for the source of the Nile, I trudge toward my rendezvous, seeking the very spot, the X on the map of political idealism, where the long river of futility empties into an ocean of sand.

O poetic! I wonder if God anticipated that Christianity (and all its branches that are the various forms of civilized politics) would prove to be the means by which men concealed their own nature from themselves. If so, He has a queer idea of mercy.

79. REPORT BY AN OFFICER OF THE AMERICAN STATION IN KHARTOUM.

1. On 11 July I proceeded west to the Wadi Abu Hamira to ren-dezvous with Firecracker. He did not appear, but I found his writ-ten report [reproduced in 73] buried in the roots of the acacia tree designated as a deaddrop. I left a message instructing him to report at this spot at 0200 on any day through 15 July. At 0200 on 12 July I found him awaiting me. Firecracker was in a highly nervous state and immediately asked me for one thousand pounds. He explained that he believed he might have to flee the country on short notice and he wanted to be well supplied with cash. I explained that his pay was being deposited regularly in Barclay's Bank at Kampala in accordance with our agreement. I gave him fifty pounds (sterling) in five-pound notes and secured his thumb print on the receipt (attached).

2. Firecracker was asked to identify "Richard." He was unable to supply details. He assumes "Richard" is a Soviet officer who will provide advice and support to the ALF during the remainder of "Golgotha" and thereafter. Soviet control in Dar es Salaam has provided no details as to the means of transportation to be used by "Richard." Firecracker is convinced that "Richard" will arrive by parachute, but that is, of course, pure speculation. I instructed

Firecracker to obtain a photograph and full description of "Richard" immediately on his arrival.

3. Firecracker stated that he fears for the safety of "Richard." The execution of Ahmed, on what other members of the ALF believe were Soviet orders, has produced great anger in some of the men. So far this has been directed toward the Soviets, and not primarily against Firecracker, who was Ahmed's executioner. Firecracker concedes that he has not been able to assume full control of the ALF headquarters since Ahmed's death. The latter was, it would appear, a more popular and powerful figure than Firecracker led us to believe. Firecracker now thinks it possible that some members of the ALF will kill "Richard" on his arrival in revenge for the death of Ahmed. Firecracker states that he has argued against this course of action, pointing out that it would mean the loss of the ALF's only source of money and arms. He believes that he will be able to restore his authority if given time, and stated his intention to radio Dar es Salaam recommending that "Richard's" arrival be postponed. I advised against this action, stating that any such radio message would have the effect of arousing the suspicions of Firecracker's putative Soviet superiors.

4. Because all ALF assault teams have been recalled on Soviet instructions, virtually the entire strength of the organization is now encamped at its headquarters. Although all six members of the team that attacked Christopher's camp are missing, only four bodies were found at the scene by ALF scouts. Firecracker claims to have had no prior knowledge of this operation. He does not know its purpose, or what orders were given to the assault team by Ahmed. Firecracker passed our information concerning Miernik to Ahmed on 7 July; the attack took place on 9 July. Firecracker states that he has not been able to discover whether Ahmed passed this information to Dar es Salaam by radio.*

---

*Intercepted radio traffic contained no reference to Miemik or the route of the Cadillac. It is assumed that Ahmed mounted the attack on his own initiative, possibly with the idea of kidnapping Prince Kalash, possibly as a means of demonstrating to Miernik the ALF's capacity to carry out independent operations. All indications are that Ahmed was a somewhat dashing figure, intelligent and courageous, but difficult to control.

5. ALF lookouts this date reported the landing of a police helicopter at the palace of the Amir of Khatar. It is assumed by them that this has some connection with the attack on the Christopher party. Firecracker seems unaware that Qasim himself was present in the Amir's palace.

COMMENT: If Firecracker has not yet lost his nerve, he is on the point of doing so. He is obviously in the toils of the double-agent syndrome. I believe that if his personal danger increases appreciably (or if he simply believes that it is increasing) he will attempt to escape to Uganda, probably with no prior notice to us. The presence of virtually the entire strength of the ALF in one place, and the apparent breakdown of discipline attendant on the execution of Ahmed, provides an obvious opportunity for the Sudanese. They may wish to move in at once, and there are persuasive reasons why they should do so while we are still able to assist through our control of Firecracker.

80. INTERCEPTED TRAFFIC FROM THE SOVIET TRANSMITTER (14 JULY).

1. Two companies of parachute troops equipped with automatic weapons and mortars will depart Khartoum by air during night 15 July. Destination El Fasher for quote routine maneuvers unquote.

2. Disperse all ALF personnel immediately. Abandon your headquarters.

3. Cancel rendezvous with Richard. Richard will contact Qemal 15 July at time and place of Richard's choosing.

4. Suspend all operations until consultation with Richard. Hide all arms and ammunition. Destroy all documents.

(Note: This message was not acknowledged by the ALF transmitter. The Soviet transmitter rebroadcast the message at hourly inter-

vals on 14–15 July. It was not unusual for the ALF transmitter to fail to acknowledge messages. Only Ahmed and Firecracker were trained to operate the radios. On date of message Ahmed was already dead. Therefore only Firecracker would have been able to receive the Morse signal, decode it, and understand the Russian in which it was written. At 0732 and again at 1932 on 16 July, the Soviet transmitter repeated this message *in clear,* in the Arabic language. This final attempt to contact ALF headquarters evidently failed. There was no acknowledgment.)

81. FROM THE FILES OF CHIEF INSPECTOR ALY QASIM.

Acting on my orders, Constable Mirghani rejoined the main force of the Anointed Liberation Front and delivered a letter from me to Qemal. Mirghani had been lightly wounded in the action at Kashgil and he was unable to travel until the night of 13th July. He told Qemal, again on my instructions, that he had been captured by the police, questioned by me, and given his freedom on condition that he deliver the letter. Qemal may or may not have accepted this story, but he took no action against Mirghani. Instead, he sent Mirghani back to me with a verbal message that he would meet Prince Kalash on the morning of 15th July at a place west of Mellit, about fifty miles west-north-west of El Fasher. He guaranteed that he would come alone and unarmed.

I informed Prince Kalash of these arrangements. He was provided with an escort from the Amir's household: two men armed with Sten guns and revolvers. On 14th July I requested the commander of the army troops to station a squad of picked men on the high ground surrounding the meeting place as additional protection for Prince Kalash. In the event of any untoward event, these men were to intervene at once. They took up their positions the night before. They were armed with machine guns, a mortar, and grenades in addition to their rifles. They were equipped with a radio transmitter. Other troops were positioned to intercept any persons attempting to escape the meeting place.

Prince Kalash took the man Miernik with him to the rendezvous. I had no foreknowledge of this incredible action. After the fact, I learned that the Amir believed he was doing me a service in delivering Miernik into the hands of the ALF. On 14th July, the day before Prince Kalash's meeting with his half brother Qemal, I had confided to the Amir my suspicion that Miernik might be a Soviet agent sent to take command of the ALF. The Amir decided to test my theory. "One assumed that Qemal was waiting for this foreigner," the Amir told me. "If Miernik joined him, then his guilt was established."

It was useless to point out to the Amir that Miernik's disappearance proved nothing. We can never be certain that the man was not abducted by Qemal and his thugs. By putting Miernik out of our reach, the Amir put him beyond proof of my suspicions. He also put in hazard all the carefully laid plans that depended on a successful meeting between Prince Kalash and his half brother. I feared that Qemal, seeing Miernik in Prince Kalash's company, would smell betrayal.

However, Qemal kept the rendezvous. He apparently had concealed himself some time earlier in the small trees that grow nearby. The troops did not discover him until he walked out of the trees and presented himself to Prince Kalash. Qemal's unsuspicious behaviour had something to do with the fact that Prince Kalash had left Miernik approximately one mile to the south, at the site of some stone ruins. Because the troops had no orders to watch Miernik—his presence had not been anticipated and therefore was not dealt with in their instructions—they kept no watch on him. (I digress to remark that this blind stupidity is typical military behaviour.)

Qemal agreed to assemble the personnel of the ALF shortly after dawn on 17th July at their headquarters. He gave Prince Kalash the precise location of this place. The main ALF camp was located between the east and middle forks of the Wadi Magrur, fifty miles west of Malha. Prince Kalash provided me with no details of his remarks to Qemal, except to say that he had greeted him as a brother. The lieutenant in charge of the troops reports that Prince Kalash, on meeting Qemal, embraced him.

After their conversation was concluded, Qemal disappeared on foot into the bush. Prince Kalash turned his Land Rover around and returned to the ruins where he had left Miernik. Miernik was not there. Prince Kalash was observed calling Miernik's name, and he and his bodyguards conducted a search of the area that lasted for the better part of an hour.

The troops did not interfere. They had earlier observed a second Land Rover, which had been concealed in the bush, proceeding in a southeasterly direction through open country. It contained four men but the distance was too great to permit identification.

Prince Kalash afterwards reported that he and his men found Land Rover tracks beginning at a point about two hundred yards from the stone ruins. The tracks led in a southeasterly direction.

Only after intensive questioning did Prince Kalash tell me that he had taken Miernik into the desert, and there abandoned him, on the Amir's orders. It was a bitter task for the prince. He felt that he had deceived, and perhaps killed, his companion. "Qemal got a look of madness in his eyes when I told him I'd brought Miernik along," Kalash said. "He went off snarling about the Russians. I tried to beat him back to the ruins. I wanted to get Miernik away from there. But he was gone. Prince Kalash was by now convinced that a mistake had been made. He wanted to pursue Qemal and Miernik in my helicopter, but I could not permit that. The Amir forbade Prince Kalash to involve himself in any kind of a rescue attempt. 'Kalash says this Pole is a harmless fool," said the Amir. "Aly states that he is a Communist spy, Qemal thinks he is a Russian. Let Qemal decide what to do with him."

82. FROM THE DEBRIEFING OF ZOFIA MIERNIK.

No one had any idea that Tadeusz and Kalash were going into the mountains together. They simply went. Ilona saw them from the window as they were getting into the Land Rover. As she told it later, she ran out to talk to them. Tadeusz told her they were going to look at some ruins—a morning excursion. Ilona thought so little of the incident that she didn't even mention it to me. I can understand why. It didn't seem important, much less dangerous. Living in that palace, which is really a fortress, surrounded at all times by the Amir's power, one readily forgets danger. What happened on the trip only a few days before seemed far away in time. It was inconceivable that anything could happen to any of us so long as we were guests of the Amir.

Kalash had been back for some time before I was given the news. I expect he had to talk the situation over with his father before telling Nigel and Paul. I was the last to know, and it was Paul who told me. He could easily have deceived me—made the situation seem less serious than it was. I would have been ready to believe that Tadeusz had just wandered away and lost his bearings. That would have been serious enough, but after all there seemed to be hundreds of people about the palace, so a search party would have been easy to organize. Almost anyone else would have thought it merciful to lie to me. But Paul told me the truth, and told it at once. We met in a small courtyard; it was a hanging garden, really, with vines and shrubs growing up the walls and over the top. There was a fountain—a fountain in that desert! It had some sort of an American device that circulated the same few liters of water forever. The American ambassador had given several of these pumps to the Amir, who quite adored them. It was a cool place. I went there every day, to read and exercise. We never saw the boys, you realize. It was a strict Muslim household where the sexes came together only for breeding purposes.

So I was a little surprised to see Paul, but very glad. I felt close to him. He is a sympathetic type, you know, and strictly speaking he saved my life at least twice in the space of a couple of weeks. As you seem to be interested in such things I may as well tell you that I was madly signaling to him that he was welcome to climb in the window whenever he wanted. I realize that I am not coming to the point very quickly. You must forgive me. I have a tendency to cry when I tell this story. I want to give you the facts as coldly as possible.

Very well. Paul comes into the garden. It must have been very early afternoon. The sun was overhead and strong. The floor of the courtyard was dappled with shadow. Shafts of sunlight, perpendicular columns of white sunlight. Paul walked through these, out of the shadow, into the light. It was a very theatrical effect. He sits down beside me. With no preliminaries—not even speaking my name in a tone of voice that might have warned me—Paul told me. Tadeusz was missing in the desert. Kalash thought he might have been abducted. No trace had yet been found of him. There had been talk about organizing a search party. The Amir had forbidden it. If Tadeusz had been kidnapped, we would hear from the bandits when they demanded a ransom. To approach the kidnappers now, with the threat of force, would create the risk that Tadeusz might be killed.

I just stared at him. What was he telling me? Paul's face was serious but not worried. He was watching my reaction very closely. I thought, Ah ha! He expects me to get hysterical. I said, "What do you think of his chances?" Paul said, "I don't know. Kalash says there's no possibility that your brother is merely lost. He's sure someone grabbed him. If he was taken by friends of the people we shot a few days ago, obviously his chances are almost nonexistent. But maybe not. I would think that men wanting revenge would simply have killed him where they found him. The other possibility is kidnap and ransom. Kalash tells me the local kidnappers are pretty honorable—if you pay, they give back the victim unharmed. It's a matter of business ethics. So we can wait and pay if the second possibility is the one we believe in.

I asked him how much the ransom was likely to be. Looking back, it seems insane, this conversation between Paul and me. For all we knew my brother lay dead out there somewhere—perhaps having been tortured—and we sat in a garden by a splashing fountain and discussed price. The fountain smelled of chlorine, by the way. The chemical smell of it made me angry: these damned Arabs with their American fountains, their Cadillacs, their pet lions, their harem filled with children. You know what it was. Subconsciously I was blaming Kalash for everything that happened. He was so supremely indifferent to other people, to life itself. Now he had done this to Tadeusz. To Paul I said, "How much do you think they'll want?"

"The Amir says that they usually demand only a modest sum. What he considers a modest sum I don't really know. Kalash guesses it would be a thousand pounds."

I had a good deal more than that in the rucksack. Sasha had given it to me, as you know. Bundles and bundles of dollars, worth millions of zloty. At the time I'd thought he was crazy—what did I need with all that money? Now I was glad I had it. I blessed Sasha, who . . . One of Sasha's sayings was "You cannot think of everything, but if you have enough money it's not necessary to think of everything." Even Sasha could not have thought of this— Tadeusz in the hands of bandits. Good God, who *could* in this day and age?

Q. Did you confide in Christopher about the money?

A. No, and I don't really know why not. I just nodded and said we'd pay. I said something like, "I have a little money." Paul didn't question me. He never questioned anybody, you know. Everyone confessed to him all the time, but he never invited it. My brother told him *everything*, and I assure you that was not like Tadeusz. There was something about Paul. One simply trusted him.

Q. Did you trust what he was telling you about what may have happened to your brother?

A. I trusted him. I had the feeling he was withholding his own opinion. At least I think that's what I felt. Be honest. Who knows after the fact what you knew and didn't know? Anyway, Paul told me that he didn't think we should just sit down and wait. He agreed that an expedition to rescue Tadeusz was a dangerous idea. I knew he would have to go out alone, if he went. Kalash would never help him.

Q. Why not?

A. Kalash did not like my brother. He thought he was a fool. By Kalash's standards he *was* a fool. Tadeusz lacked nonchalance-totally lacked it. That embarrassed Kalash, made him contemptuous. Nigel was nonchalant. Paul was nonchalant. Ilona was nonchalant. Even I, a little bit. That was the quality Kalash prized above all others. After the shooting that night, Kalash and Paul and Nigel were no different than they had been before. No emotion, no anger. They kept up appearances. Making no mention of the fact that Ilona and I were naked, never even referring to that fact is an example of what I mean. Drinking tea and chatting beside the dead bodies, all that was part of their style. Tadeusz ran behind the tents and threw up. For days afterward he was withdrawn, silent. His hands trembled. The other three rode through the desert eating oranges and making witticisms.

Q. How did Chistopher happen to take you with him?

A. I insisted on going. It's true he didn't oppose me, but I thought this was just another example of his sensitivity. He realized I would be happier taking part. He was my brother's only real friend in that crowd. I've told you he didn't interfere with others, didn't judge. When I said I wanted to go, he thought for a few moments. Then he said yes. So we went.

Q. What was Christopher's motivation, in your opinion?

A. His what? His motivation? Why did he do what he did? He wanted to find Tadeusz. He wanted to help. Simple friendship. Perhaps a certain regard for me as well as for Tadeusz. Paul and I *liked* one another.

Q. You didn't think he had any ulterior motive he wasn't telling you about?

A. Oh, for Christ's sake. Of course not. What could it possibly be? He was likely to get himself killed. It wasn't as if he hadn't had some experience with these madmen already, you know. He knew what those people who had Tadeusz were capable of.

Q. All right, Miss Miernik. Let's go on. We'd like you to describe what happened after you and Paul started out together. Just begin at the beginning.

A. The beginning I've already told you. In the garden we agreed that we'd go out together. We hadn't much hope that we'd actually find Tadeusz. We didn't know the country. If we had known more about it I think we wouldn't have tried at all. It's a hopeless place to search for anyone. Mountain after mountain, little valleys, forests of dwarf trees, caves. It's a labyrinth up there. I had the feeling that we were not on our own planet any longer.

However, we didn't foresee any of that. I went back to my room, with my girl trotting along with me—annoying, that, always having a servant with you—and changed into trousers and boots. I put some things into the rucksack on top of the money. I still thought the money would be useful, that we could buy Tadeusz back. Then I went back to the garden and waited for Paul. Pretty soon he came along and took me to the Land Rover. He had packed some of the camping gear and filled up the jerry cans with water and gasoline. Also, he had that portable radio set they had taken from the bandits, the walkie-talkie. And the Sten gun, lying on the front seat. Kalash was there with the big black fellow who let us in the night we arrived. He was a special chum of Kalash's—went everywhere with him. Kalash said nothing to me, absolutely nothing. At least for the time being he left off giving me looks of sexual invitation. That's beside the point. Kalash and Paul were looking at a map. Kalash drew a line on it, to show where he had last seen Tadeusz. They were as cool as could be; one would have thought they were discussing the best route between Geneva and Lausanne. The famous nonchalance again. Kalash folded up the map, handed it to Paul, and said, "Cheerio."

Cheerio. We drove away. It took us a couple of hours to reach the place where Tadeusz had vanished. There was no proper road. We bumped along, dodging rocks, reversing, finding the way as best we could. It was by this time late afternoon. We picked up the tracks of the other Land Rover and drove in them. Paul was remarkably skillful. Before we reached the crest of a hill he would stop the car, get out, walk to the top, lie down, and search the way ahead with binoculars. He had me keeping a lookout behind us and all around us as we drove. He knew just what he was doing.

We kept on until the last light. Paul returned from one of his scouting trips to the top of a hill and said he had seen water ahead. We drove on until we came to this place with a sort of spring and trees. It was not my idea of an oasis, but I guess that's what it was. He pulled the Land Rover into the trees and unloaded the tent and so forth. Then he covered the car with branches to camouflage it. We ate cold food out of tins. Paul didn't want to show a light, so we sat there in the dark. He was just an outline to me. There was no moon, only the stars. They seemed to be the same stars one sees in Poland, and this surprised me. Before there had been so much moonlight one couldn't see the stars properly. I expected strange stars, the Southern Cross. We hardly spoke. The whole trip was silent.

Paul got out the radio and tuned it in. Pretty soon, very faintly, I heard Kalash's voice. I don't know why this should have surprised me, but I was startled. My heart pounded. What I hoped, of course, was that Kalash would say that Tadeusz had come back. It was nothing like that. Paul just gave him our location. He and Kalash had marked the map—

Point A, Point B, and so on. "Twenty miles northeast of Point B," Paul said. "No luck." He repeated this formula. I heard Kalash say, "No luck here, either." Paul turned off the radio and hung it up on a branch.

Q. So nothing happened that first day and night?

A. Ah, here is the part you have been waiting for. Something happened.

Q. Something happened?

A. Yes. I seduced Paul Christopher. He had set up the tent and put my sleeping bag in it. His own sleeping bag he spread on the ground, in the open. He said to me, "Are you tired? We'd better try to sleep." I said to him, "I'm not tired." Then I crawled over to him in the dark and kissed him. He was not surprised; nothing surprised Paul. He kissed me back and we went on. Your files should show that he makes love gently and for a very long time. He has an honest body, just as he has an honest mind.

Q. I see. Well, this really isn't necessary, Miss Miernik. As you've said, it's a private matter.

A. There are no private matters in this world, my friend. Paul and I could not have found a place where we were less likely to be found making love than in that oasis. All the same, you were following us, weren't you? You did not actually walk into our camp and shine a torch on our bodies. You just want to look into our minds. The picture is still there, and that's better than the reality for you. Ordinary life, for you, is pornography. No, no, I'm not blaming you or any of the others who are like you from Russia to America. The South Pole as well, I suppose. It's what you do; it's a fact of existence. Please note that I am showing no anger. I am smiling. Some things cannot be taken down in writing.

83. REPORT BY CHRISTOPHER.

15 July. If anyone but Kalash had come to me with the information that he had lost Miernik in the mountains on an archaeological expedition I would have reached for my revolver. In Kalash's case, it was perfectly believable. "Miernik has been rooting in my father's library ever since he arrived," Kalash told me, "looking for a link between our family and the old sultans of west Sudan. He will not be convinced that we came from Arabia. One indulges these fantasies in scholars. I thought he'd like to see the ruins; there are some rather dim pictures on the old walls. As I was going right by on my way to see someone I offered to drop him off. I could not have been more astonished when he vanished."

I immediately assumed that Miernik had taken advantage of Kalash's expedition in order to make contact with the ALF. When Kalash told me that his meeting was with his half brother Qemal, I no longer had any doubt that Miernik had slipped away to take command of the guerrillas. In a way, it was amusing that Miernik had in the end outwitted me through such a simple device. While I slept the morning away, he got in a Land Rover and rode innocently away, making no attempt at concealment because he had equipped himself with one final perfect cover story. The ancient kings of Darfur. It was a pretty operation.

No doubt I could have accepted his disappearance as the proof we've wanted that he is the Soviets' principal agent to the ALF. But a mixture of duty and pride (mostly pride) made me think that I had to follow him to make absolutely certain. I was curious to know what change would come over him once he was freed of his cover personality and acting as head terrorist.

I did not imagine that Miernik would have been so careless as to leave any clues behind him, but I searched his room anyway. His clothes were all neatly hung and folded; there was nothing in the pockets. I felt the linings of his suitcases and looked for hidden compartments; it seemed possible that Miernik would use such devices. Finally, in a locked valise, I found three oblong metal boxes filled with file cards. These were covered with Miernik's large handwriting, in green ink and in Polish. There was nothing else. The small briefcase that Miernik always carries with him was missing. I took the card files to my own room and told my boy to let no one touch them in my absence.

Kalash agreed to let me have a Land Rover. He wanted to send along a couple of his father's men as protection, but I refused. Later I had cause to regret this: I could have used a couple of strong natives for some of the work that lay ahead. I thought the best protection I could have was Zofia Miernik. If there was anything genuine about her brother, it was his blundering love for Zofia. I didn't plan to use her as a human shield as I shot my way out of the camp of the ALF, but I did believe that Miernik would control his men if she was present. Also, I didn't want *her* disappearing while I was wandering around looking for Miernik. She agreed to come without hesitation. Her agitation over Miernik's disappearance seemed genuine.

After I left Zofia I went outside to load the Land Rover. Kalash was already on hand, and with him was Aly Qasim. They gave me a marked map and a walkie-talkie, and we agreed on a radio routine that would permit them to keep track of my movements as long as I didn't get out of radio range. Qasim was very direct. "I assume," he said, "that we have a mutual friend in Harrison Burbank.* He is a splendid chap. I will mention to Harrison what you are doing when I speak to him today. He will have a natural interest in the activities of an American citizen. I will tell you now what I shall have to tell Harrison later on—that I cannot offer you any protection once you are out of my sight. This is a very large country, very wild." Qasim unfolded the map and drew a circle around a spot on the middle fork of the Wadi Magrur. "I advise you to avoid this place,"

---

*The chief of the American station in Khartoum.

he said. "Good luck." He shook hands, smiled brightly, and walked into the palace.

Zofia and I found the ruins where Miernik had last been seen, and a little distance away the tracks of the other Land Rover. These led southeast for two or three miles, then turned straight north. As the ground rose, it became less sandy, and following the tracks became increasingly difficult. Mostly I guessed at the route: in that terrain, which is a jumble of flinty hills and gravel fields, there in nowhere to go except through the passes. Occasionally, on a patch of soft ground, I'd find a tire track, and once a smear of oil where the Land Rover had apparently been parked while Qemal and Miernik and their friends ate lunch: there were pieces of food strewn over the ground, and behind a rock a pile of human excrement.

The country was absolutely empty and silent, with not even a bird showing itself against the sky. The sun was very strong. I had taken the canvas roof off the cab of the Land Rover: I wanted to see behind me. Zofia rode beside me, not talking, not complaining. I put her to work as a lookout, wondering all the time if she would tell me if any of the ALF came sneaking over a hilltop. I more or less thought she would; she couldn't be certain that any armed men she happened to see belonged to her brother. *I* couldn't be certain that she knew anything about her brother's mission.

We covered perhaps seventy miles, mostly in first gear, before dark. We camped in an oasis and went separately to the spring to take bucket showers. I made contact with Kalash at nine o'clock, the agreed transmission time, before we went to bed.

Zofia had difficulty sleeping. I awoke about midnight when I heard her rummaging around in the Land Rover. She was look-ing for her cigarettes, she said. She sat down near me to smoke, and in the flare of the match I saw that her face was wet with tears. She has a silent way of crying—no sniffling or whimper-ing; the tears just squeeze out of the corners of her eyes and run down her cheeks. Zofia is a very appealing girl. She asked in a perfectly steady voice if I minded her talking to me. I told her to go ahead.

"Have you any curiosity about my brother at all?" she asked. "I'd like to know what you really think about him, Paul."

"What do you think about friends?" I said, shrugging into my wonderful-person role. "You take them as they are. Tadeusz is certainly a little more colorful than most people. I like him. It's natural to like a man who interests you."

"Not many people have ever liked Tadeusz. You and Sasha. My father never liked him. He was an ugly man, like Tadeusz. Perhaps he didn't want to be reminded of his own looks every time he saw his son. That's Tadeusz's explanation. He was badly damaged by our father's indifference. It was not cruelty. Father wasn't even unkind. He simply ignored his son. That's always been Tadeusz's fate, to be ignored."

"Well, he seems to have broken that mold with a vengeance. Half the people in these mountains are thinking of nothing but Tadeusz at this moment."

"Why do you say that?" Zofia said sharply.

"The obvious reason, Zofia. If he has been kidnapped, then his captors must be very much aware of him. I know I am. Kalash, Nigel, the Amir—your brother is in everyone's thoughts."

She drew on her cigarette in the darkness. "You sound exasperated," she said. "I guess I can't blame you. This really is a stupid situation, and it's all Tadeusz's fault. I'd like to blame Kalash, but that's unfair. My brother isn't a child. Why should Kalash have held his hand? He wouldn't have done it for you or Nigel. There would have been no need. With Tadeusz, there has always been that need. Things happen to him. He falls over everything."

I couldn't see Zofia's face, but the tone of her voice fitted the words she was speaking. Her speech was flat, bitter, hopeless. If she did not believe Miernik to be the man he pretended to be, she was a gifted actress. There were only marginal reasons to doubt her. (None of my relatives knows what I really do for a living. Why should Miernik's?)

"I will tell you a truth about Tadeusz," Zofia said. "This quality he has of being a victim is not a fault. It's his natural condition. It goes back to his birth. Each person is born intact, I believe, and is the same all through his life in spite of education, in spite of training, in spite of experience. No one ever changes. Tadeusz was born sad and clumsy. I'll tell you something else. I have tried all my life to love him, and I've failed utterly. Pity I can feel for him; ever since I can remember I've been anxious not to hurt him. I have always done everything I could to make him certain that I, at least, love him. I can't be sure he believes it, I don't know how he can. But I hope he believes. Some people can be absolutely hopeless, unable to do the simplest thing, and still be lovable. Tadeusz is merely irritating. The more he tries to please, the more annoying he becomes. Had he come to Bratislava to fetch me instead of you, I don't know what I would have done. I am so aware of his kindness, his loving nature. But I practically strangle with exasperation every time he does something for me. Of all the people my brother has ever known, only Sasha and you have been able to be patient with him. It's a terrible thing. A person like Tadeusz traps anyone who feels sorry for him; he imprisons you in your own pity for him."

Zofia fell silent. She was smoking one cigarette after another. Her voice, which is as light as a girl's voice can be, had fallen into a monotone. She was ashamed of herself, but she couldn't stop talking.

"When I was a child," she said, "Tadeusz liked to play with me. I don't mean games. He liked to dress me up, fondle me, it was like being a doll in a dollhouse. He would say something to me. Then he'd say, 'Now you say . . .' He'd give me my lines. It was Tadeusz speaking to Tadeusz out of my mouth, inventing my kindness. After Mother died he became my personal maid. I was very young, so I needed someone to help me get dressed and so forth. Each morning he'd wake me up with a wet kiss. Even as a young boy he had that very large head covered with black hair that stands on end, and big thick glasses covering his eyes. He'd get me up, wash me, dress me. He'd comb my hair for me. Everything he did with those hands of his hurt me. He pulled the hair right out of my head with the comb. He didn't mean to, of course, the poor boy was trembling with the desire to be gentle. But he hurt me all the time. I used to squeeze my eyes shut and bite my lips to keep from screaming. I knew he would be devastated if I showed any pain. Father let him do it—I suppose he had my same feeling that to prevent him would be sadistic. Sasha talks about my spending all my time with him in the attic. Well, I loved Sasha—but I was up there playing the guitar mostly because it was a way to get away from Tadeusz. Tadeusz would follow me into the attic. Sasha taught him foreign languages with a kind of game. They would write each other secret messages out of foreign books. You pick the first word on a line, and note down the page number and the number of the line. Tadeusz would have to read and translate hundreds of words until he found the right one for his message. Sasha has a gift for making difficult things fun to do. Tadeusz loved this game of the book code. He always wanted me to play, but I could only do it with Polish books. I can't tell you how glad I was when I reached an age where Tadeusz could no longer touch me. I don't mean there was anything sexual in what he did. It was never that."

Zofia gave a sudden deep laugh. "You know what I think?" she said. "I think my brother is a saint who was born too late. In the Middle Ages he could have gone into a monastery, where he would have been valued. By the time he was born, all the monasteries were closed. So he carries an invisible monastery around with him wherever he goes. In spite of everything he can do, the world keeps poking its fingers through the bars at him. Mouths whisper through the windows. Tadeusz cannot keep the world away from him, and now it *really* has got hold of him. I'll bet he's lying in some place a lot like this one, bound hand and foot, hungry and sore and thirsty and frightened out of his wits. And do you know what he's thinking? He's thinking, 'What will happen to Zofia without me? Will she finish university? Has she had a good supper?' It's maddening, Paul. He'll die, perhaps. And if he does, he won't die screaming with fright, but muttering with worry."

I remembered Miernik, kneeling in the moonlight at Kashgil with the Sten gun at his shoulder, and the tape recording of his session on the floor with Ilona, and the way he boxed me into going to Czechoslovakia, and a good deal besides. Zofia's explanation of the book code didn't much move me. To me Miernik didn't seem quite the passive bungler Zofia made him out to be. Or any more in need of love than the monk she imagined he should have been. Miernik had found his monastery, all right. It was one of the last ones left, I thought sardonically, and the abbot was Lavrenti Pavlovich Beria and his spiritual successors. This was my last sardonic thought about Miernik.

Zofia still couldn't sleep. I really could not listen to any more analysis of her brother. The girl and I lay in the oasis, talking about the stars. To keep her from telling me more about Miernik, I named all the constellations I could remember: Gemini, Orion, Perseus, Cassiopeia, Pegasus, Cygnus, Serpens. We calculated the distance to Alpha Centauri in miles and kilometers. Had Miernik been there he could have traced the connection between the prechristian myths after which the stars are named and the religious anxieties of the nuclear age. But he was down the road somewhere.

16 July. We started north again at sunrise. I was lightheaded and a little raw from lack of sleep. Both Zofia and I had painful sunburns. As we traveled north, the country became rougher and what little vegetation there had been ran out; we were only a hundred miles or so from the edge of the Libyan desert, and the air was hot to the touch, like the bottom of a cooking pot. The Land Rover, running in low gear and four-wheel drive most of the time, overheated. I kept on adding water from the jerry cans I'd filled at the oasis, straining out the green slime and the sand through a T-shirt.

I navigated as best I could with a compass and the relief map Kalash had given me. The map was an old British job and not always accurate; I thought often that I was lost when hills appeared before me that were not marked on the map, but finally I concluded that many features of the country simply had not been noted. I expected to find the ALF on the other side of every hill. The Land Rover, its motor roaring and its load rattling, seemed louder by the moment. Any terrorist within two miles could have heard us coming.

We had been moving north for about four hours when I faced the fact that we had lost Miernik's trail. I had seen no tire tracks, and no other sign of his Land Rover, for a couple of hours. There seemed to be no other route than the one we had taken (I'd turned off into five or six blind canyons before settling on the route we now followed through a maze of dun-colored hills). At ten-thirty I stopped the car, got out the walkie-talkie, and climbed to the top of the highest ground in the neighborhood. All I got on the radio when I tried to contact Kalash was static, so I concluded that we were out of range for daytime transmission. There must have been enough solar radiation in that scorched sky to block a fifty-thousand-watt station.

I was trembling from the strain of climbing a five-hundred-foot hill with a walkie-talkie in one hand and a Sten gun in the other. Therefore I had difficulty holding the binoculars steady, and on my first sweep of the country ahead I missed the object on the next hilltop. I caught it on the second sweep. It was about a mile away, a vertical thing different in color from the earth. The atmosphere was full of heat waves, and I thought at first I might be seeing a mirage. At the base of the object there was a steady flash of light, as if the sun were hitting a mirror. I adjusted the glasses and studied the scene, squinting in an effort to make it out.

Finally I slid down the hill and got into the Land Rover. I told Zofia nothing, but drove straight on toward the hill I'd been studying with the binoculars. We reached the bottom of the second hill in about five minutes. The summit was not visible from where we were. I told Zofia I was going to climb up to have another look ahead. I gave her a pistol and told her to shoot at anyone she saw. She looked at me round-eyed and bit her lip; I was sorry to frighten her, but it was better than taking her up the hill. By this time I had an idea what I was going to find at the top. There were Land Rover tracks all over the ground where we had parked.

I hung the Sten gun and the binoculars around my neck and started up the hill. I went as slowly as possible, partly because I wanted to have some breath and reasonably steady hands when I got to the top. Halfway up the slope I stopped and searched the ground below me with the glasses. There was no sign of life, only Zofia crouching in the shade of the Land Rover with her yellow hair catching a nimbus of sunlight.

Miernik was hanging by his heels on an X-shaped cross, one anlde tied with wire to each of its upper arms. His corpse was naked, and a streak of dried blood, as brown as dung, ran from his crotch down through the matted black hair on his chest. He was pretty badly cut up—all the fingers of his right hand had been lopped off and there were knife wounds on his feet and legs. His genitalia were stuffed into his mouth. None of these injuries was sufficient to kill him, and I found no gunshot wounds. Evidently Miernik had been left on the cross to bleed to death. I removed the trash from his mouth and buried it in the sand.

Around the base of the cross (I wondered where they'd got the lumber) was a jumble of stuff: Miernik's glasses, which explained the flash I'd seen through the binoculars; an Exakta camera with the film pulled out of it; Miernik's scuffed old briefcase. A few feet away I found his diary, page after page covered in green ink. There was a rosary, a psalter, a comb, and Miernik's copy of the pocket edition of *Democracy in America*. Also his passport. All his possessions had been abused: the glasses smashed, the camera bent as if someone had stamped on it, the rosary missing its cross, pages torn out of the books. I put everything back in the briefcase and took it with me down the hill.

There was no need to say anything to Zofia. She watched me as

I came down the hill with her hand shielding her eyes from the sun. The briefcase told her everything. She stared at it as I walked across the flat ground between us, and when I was close to her, she reached out her hand. I gave her the briefcase. She ran a fingertip over its pebbled surface, fingered the worn brass catches, and then lifted it to her face and kissed it. She got into the Land Rover and sat in the front seat, her eyes straight ahead.

I got a pair of pliers out of the toolbox and took the tent and a coil of rope back up the hill. I cut the wires around Miernik's ankles, and his body, still wired to the cross at the wrists, tipped over and slammed into the ground like a side of beef. I freed the wrists and dragged the corpse onto the outspread tent. Miernik was frozen into his spreadeagled position. It was impossible to move the rigid arms and legs. I didn't want to do his body any more violence, so I didn't try to break his limbs, but wrapped him as best I could in the canvas, tying the bundle with rope. His feet and arms protruded; I covered his ruined right hand with my handkerchief and tied it around the wrist. Some merciful person had cut the veins. I wasted a lot of energy pulling the cross out of the dirt and breaking it up.

Then I sat down beside Miernik and got out the binoculars once more. A couple of miles to the north I caught sun flashes. Focusing in, I saw what I supposed to be the camp of the ALF. There were a couple of Land Rovers with the sun on their wind-shields, a few camels, a dozen striped Bedouin tents, and twenty or thirty men moving around. There was no sign of anything but routine activity. I hoped they didn't have any scouts out.

Miernik in life had been a heavy man. Dead he was like a boul-der; it was impossible to lift the body. I took hold of the ropes and dragged him down the hill. The canvas slid easily over the sand on the steep slope, and by the time I got to the bottom I was digging in my heels and holding back the corpse. Miernik had an eager-ness in death that he had never shown when alive.

Zofia met me at the bottom of the slope. She knelt in the sand and touched the green canvas bundle. "I'd like to see his face," she said. There was no point in refusing her. I felt around until I found Miernik's head, and pulled the canvas aside. His eyes were rolled back so that only the whites showed, and his mouth was gaping, with black blood on the teeth. "Leave him a minute," Zofia said. She went to the Land Rover and came back with a jerry can of water; she leaned away from its weight, carrying it on her thigh. She poured water on a cloth and washed Miernik's face. We covered him and dragged him to the Land Rover. Zofia helped me lift him into the back. I lashed him down so he wouldn't bounce around, and wrapped the roof canvas around his bloody feet. Zofia scrambled in with Miernik and sorted out the sleeping bags and the food; she packed these under her feet in the front seat.

As nearly as I could make out, we were about forty miles west of the road that runs through the Tabago hills from Malha in the north to El Fasher. The map showed a long dry wadi alongside the road. I drove eastward and in an hour or so we found the stream bed. Its floor was fairly smooth, with great cracks running through the gritty dried mud. The Land Rover could make twenty-five or thirty miles an hour over this ground. I hoped we could make the El Fasher road by dark. I planned to continue driving until we got back to the palace. Miernik had already been dead for some time, and perhaps it was his ghost that whispered worriedly in my ear about the danger of corpses in a hot climate.

84. REPORT BY COLLINS.

A servant fetched me from my room before lunch on 15th July and led me to a parlour in the Amir's wing of the palace. There I found Prince Kalash and Ilona Bentley, together with a rather light-skinned Sudanese who was introduced to me as Chief Inspector Aly Qasim, of the Special Branch at Khartoum. I recognized Qasim as the man to whom Prince Kalash had spoken after our audience with the Amin a few days before. Prince Kalash told me that Miernik had wandered into the desert, or perhaps had been kidnapped by "bandits" while inspecting some ruins in the Tabago Hills that morning. It was feared that Miernik's life was in danger. Christopher and Zofia Miernik had gone out in a Land Rover, by themselves, to search for the missing man. "I am responsible for this contretemps," Prince Kalash said. "Of course I should be in the search party, but my cousin here has convinced my father that I should remain in the palace." He appeared to be genuinely embarrassed, an entirely new mood for Prince Kalash. The attitude of Ilona Bentley was equally out of character. She sat on a stool with a handkerchief in her fist, her eyes reddened and her hair somewhat dishevelled. Miss Bentley was obviously (rather too obviously, I thought afterwards) fighting for self-control.

2. Chief Inspector Qasim stated that he wished to interview us. I asked if he was acting in an official capacity. "A disappearance is a police matter, and I am a policeman," Qasim said. His manner was cold but correct." He asked me when last I had seen Miernik, and I told him the night before. Had Miernik mentioned his intention of accompanying Prince Kalash this morning? No. Qasim wrote down the answers to these pointless questions in a notebook. He asked Miss Bentley the same set of questions—with more revealing results for me, at least. Ilona Bentley had seen Miernik just before his departure; she had observed him and Prince Kalash from her window as they got ready to climb into a Land Rover parked in the central courtyard. She had run out of the palace, hoping that they might take her with them. "It's tedious, hanging about one's room all day. If there was to be a lark of any kind, I wanted to go along. Prince Kalash refused to consider it. I thought it beastly of him. There was a bit of an argument, as Prince Kalash will recall." Qasim said: "A friendly argument, I expect?" Prince Kalash answered: "It was a spat. Ilona is a wilful girl. You can ignore that incident, Aly." Qasim was by this time staring fixedly at Miss Bentley's bare thighs. "One never knows what small bit of evidence will crack the case," he said in a voice filled with sexual

innuendo. "I will write it down." He did so. Prince Kalash glowered at Qasim's bad form. "Then write down that she forgave us before we left," Prince Kalash said. "She wished us a happy day. In fact she went back to her room and fetched a camera for Miernik. She hung it around his neck and—I hope this will not drive you wild with envy, Aly—she kissed him good-bye. Miernik agreed to take pictures of the ruins for her. Miss Bentley is an enthusiastic photographer." To Miss Bentley I said: "I hope it wasn t your new Leica, Ilona." "No," she said, "it was an old camera I carry as a spare."

3. During the remainder of the day there was a great deal of activity at the palacemen coming and going, Prince Kalash occupied every moment with his father and Qasim. It was obvious that something more important than Miernik's disappearance was worrying them. Qasim had arrived in a police helicopter, and he frequently dashed out of doors, leaped into the aircraft, and clattered away for an hour or two. When I protested to Kalash about the danger to Christopher and Zofia Miernik, he shrugged. "Paul is quite able to take care of himself," he said. "I think they're in no great danger. And they won't be alone out there for very much longer." He refused to elaborate on this last statement. When, the following morning, Christopher had not returned, I asked to see the Amir. It was my intention to demand that a party be sent after the American. Apart from the competitive aspect of the situation, I was anxious about him. Unlike Miernik, Christopher had no bona fides that would impress a band of Communist guerrillas. The Amir regretted that he could not see me. Whilst I was waiting in an anteroom of the Amir's suite, Qasim entered—accompanied by a lieutenant-colonel of the parachute regiment in battle dress. Qasim smiled agreeably and said: "Good day, Captain Collins. We hope to have some news of your friend soon." Qasim was pleased with himself for having let me know, with that reference to my army rank, that he had a file on me. At about ten o'clock that night, Prince Kalash came to my bedroom. "Nigel," he said, "I have some

rather distressing news. Paul had a radio with him, and he was supposed to contact me morning and evening so that we might keep track of him. There was no word from him this morning, nor again this evening. Perhaps he is out of range, or trying to transmit from low ground. But I think not. I think he may be having some difficulty." The true dimensions of this incredible muddle became apparent to me. I spoke angrily: "Well, then, we'd better go out and find him. Really, Kalash, the situation is intolerable. First Miernik is carried off by a lot of cutthroats, and then you permit Christopher to go out alone-with a *girl*, Kalash—and lose him too. It's too stupid. I'm beginning to believe you're willing to get us all killed in this damned desert." Prince Kalash then said a very curious thing: "Not *all* of you, Nigel," in a tired voice. "Be ready to leave at dawn. The boy will wake you up." He strode out of the room.

4. At dawn on 17th July I went outside to find Prince Kalash and Chief Inspector Qasim standing by the helicopter. Qasim opened the door and gestured for me to get in. I sat in the back with a silent Prince Kalash. The pilot, very smartly turned out in starched khaki, buckled our safety belts for us. He asked Kalash's permission to touch him, but not mine. The helicopter lifted off very rapidly and headed north. "We have searched all this ground," Qasim shouted, "but there is no sign of any of your friends. If they were there, we would be able to see them from the air. However, we will look again. Keep an eye out and tap the pilot on the shoulder if you see anything." The terrain was a perfect blank—eroded bare hills and wadis, an occasional patch of stunted trees. I saw nothing. At the end of an hour, the pilot put the machine into a steep climb, and then hovered at about four thousand feet. Qasim squirmed round in his seat and pointed out the left-hand window. Below us, as if drawn on a map, lay a large blue lake shaped like a bird's claw. A battle was being fought in the space between two of the toes. Scores of parachutes blew over the floor of the desert. Soldiers skirmished towards an encampment in which a half-dozen large striped tents were afire; as we

watched, a row of vehicles under camouflage netting went up in flames like a string of firecrackers. Inside the camp, men in native robes were running about through a heavy mortar barrage, firing off rifles. These men had no cover of any kind and they were being knocked over rapidly by the exploding mortar bombs and by small arms fire from the attacking troops. The soldiers advanced on three sides, firing automatic weapons and heaving a prodigious number of grenades; they seemed to be taking almost no casualties. Some of the men in the camp threw down their weapons and attempted to surrender. They were shot out of hand. In less than fifteen minutes, the fight was over. Qasim watched its progress with guffaws of delight; Prince Kalash looked on with indifference. Qasim spoke in Arabic into a microphone. Someone on the ground must have told him it was safe to land, for he gestured at the ground with an arrogant thrust of his thumb, and we went down.

5. The helicopter landed a few hundred yards from the camp. The lieutenant-colonel I had met the day before was standing by a map table with a gaggle of staff officers. He touched his cap to Qasim, bowed to Prince Kalash, and gave me a fishy look. Bursts of automatic fire split the air, the unmistakable sound of British weapons. I heard no return fire, so I assumed that the troops were dealing with their prisoners. It was impossible to see what was going on, as a small hill lay between us and the site of the battle. I asked no questions. It was hardly necessary. The Sudanese obviously had located the main camp of the Anointed Liberation Front, and were destroying it. Qasim spoke to the lieutenant-colonel for several moments, leaving Prince Kalash and me to fidget in the heat. At the palace he might defer to the prince; here he was in command. As the firing died, Qasim approached us. "I'm afraid there is no trace of your friends in the camp," he said. "That can be taken as a good sign. Perhaps Miernik is merely lost after all. Of course, it's also possible all three have been murdered elsewhere. We have taken a number of prisoners, and naturally I will interview them. As soon as I have any sort of information,

you shall have it as well." I remarked that it was unlikely any prisoners of the bandits could have lived through this attempt to rescue them. Qasim shrugged and said to me: "I have brought you here on Prince Kalash's personal assurances, Captain Collins. We have known for some time of the existence of this gang of bandits. They were the same ones who attacked you at Kashgil. Criminals of the worst sort, ruthless men—a rather atavistic phenomenon, I'm afraid. They were given every opportunity to surrender and submit to a fair trial. But Colonel Shangiti tells me they refused all appeals to reason. I'm afraid all but a handful of them were killed while resisting arrest. All well and good—a suitable end to a bad lot. If your friends have perished, they are the last victims of this scum. But we are trying to build a nation in Sudan. Publicity over brigands like these only encourages others of their kind. Also, it is, I will be frank, an embarrassment internationally that we should still have such elements in our country. Therefore I ask you to keep what you have seen to yourself, so far as the press and the idly curious are concerned." Qasim smiled brilliantly. "I am sure you will be discreet, Captain Collins. If you must discuss this—and I know it is a temptation, perhaps even a duty to do so—be so kind as to discuss it only with men who are as discreet as yourself." Qasim and Prince Kalash growled at one another in Arabic for a moment or two. Two soldiers accompanied by a shouting officer came into our area on the double, carrying a stretcher with a dead body on it. Qasim, Prince Kalash, and Colonel Shangiti inspected the corpse. Prince Kalash returned to me. "I came specially to talk to that chap, he was a brother of mine, but they've killed him," he said. "The army wants you and me to clear out now." We got back into the helicopter. The pilot apparently was as curious as I about the fate of the "bandits." He hovered for a moment over the camp. Nothing remained of it except a few scorched places where the tents had been and a pillar of smoke from the burning motor park. The dead had been arranged in a long rank at the edge of the camp. I counted more than fifty corpses. There were no wounded; only the dead. Four men in native robes were being marched under guard towards Qasim. I expect they were later subjected to what Qasim calls "interviews."

6. As we flew over the wadi, Prince Kalash told me there had been a cloudburst the night before. More than two inches of rain fell on the hills in the space of an hour. The guerrilla camp had been flooded. *"Allah akhbar,"* Kalash shouted with a grin, "God is great. These fellows were wringing out their stockings when the army dropped in." The wadi had been transformed into a lake—shaped, as I've said, like a bird's foot. From the tip of the eastern-most claw a long smear of mud ran along the bed of what was normally a dry stream. It was apparent that a crude earth dam of some sort had been taken out by the sudden weight of the water. For a few moments, the dry stream must have been a torrent; now it was empty again, its slippery surface already beginning to bake and crack in the sun. Christopher had not been captured by the guerrillas. Kalash was now convinced that he was alive and well. "Perhaps Paul tried to strike across the hills to the Maffia road," Kalash said. "Keep an eye peeled." We flew low over the glistening mud, nosing round hills. For a long time there was no sign of life. Then, in a steep defile between two brown cliffs, we saw Christopher's Land Rover. It lay on its side in the mud with its bonnet open and the canvas roof ripped away. It was quite empty. Downstream was a trail of gear, scattered by last night's flood—jerry cans, pots and pans, tins of food. We saw no human beings.

7. The pilot landed the helicopter and the three of us got down into the mud and poked aimlessly at the wreckage. The Land Rover was not damaged, apart from a soaked engine. It was obvious what had happened. The flash flood, roaring down the steep bed of the dry wadi, had caught the Land Rover from behind and turned it over, spilling Paul and Zofia into the water. "Probably it wasn't raining here," Prince Kalash said. "They would not even have heard the water coming along behind them over the noise of the engine. The sand deadens the sound—these floods come very

quickly. The water can be six feet deep in a narrow place like this. Eventually it just subsides into the sand." A few hundred yards downstream I found Zofia's red rucksack, caked with drying sand. I took it with me back to the helicopter.

8. I sat in the rear of the chattering machine, staring at the back of Kalash's head. I thought it impossible that Christopher and Zofia Miernik could have survived the accident. Death by drowning in the desert seemed a fitting end to this farcical adventure. It has been a waste of friends from beginning to end. Prince Kalash, without turning his head, reached back and seized my arm with his huge hand. The helicopter made an abrupt turn, the horizon revolving beyond its perspex cabin. When it resumed course I looked downwards and saw Paul Christopher and Zofia Miernik standing on a bald hill. They were holding hands, calmly watching the helicopter as it settled to the ground, raising dervishes of sand around them. I learnt that Miernik was dead. Christopher had found him with Ilona's Exakta beside him. That discovery answered the question as to the purpose of the homing device. Prince Kalash and I were left alone on the desert when the helicopter left to take Christopher and Zofia back to the palace. We found Miernik's body not far from the place where the helicopter had landed. Prince Kalash gazed stolidly at the abused and bloated body of his friend. I said: "Odd that they should have killed only Miernik, isn't it?" Prince Kalash shrugged. "Miernik was the one they found," he said. "With how much help?" I asked. The prince went still like the future amir he is. "My dear Nigel," he said at last. "Miernik was bound to be killed by his friends. Be glad *you* didn't have to do it." He took my arm and walked me away from the corpse.

85. FROM THE DEBRIEFING OF ZOFIA MIERNIK.

After we found my brother's body, Paul made the only mistake I've known him to be guilty of. He took the wrong fork of the wadi. A few miles east of where we found Tadeusz, the dry stream branched off—one section led straight into Malha, where the road to El Fasher begins, and the other ran south, parallel to the road. Paul wanted to go to Malha but somehow we got off on the second wadi. Normally, Paul would have checked the route with the compass. I suppose he was not himself after finding Tadeusz. He omitted some of the precautions he usually took. By the time he realized his mistake, we were too far along to turn back. Besides, he was not anxious to drive in the direction of the bandits. He told me later he had seen their camp from the hilltop where my brother died. We decided to drive down the wadi, which joined the road forty or fifty miles to the south. It was the intelligent thing to do. I was in no condition to be intelligent. Had Paul suggested walking I would have agreed.

Q. Why didn't you camp that night, instead of pushing on?

A. Because of Tadeusz. Neither of us was sleepy, you understand. The body was beginning to decompose. We didn't discuss it. It was perfectly plain that we had to get back to the palace as quickly as possible. Actually, we would have been all right but the Land Rover kept overheating. We had to stop every few moments to let it cool off. Finally Paul did something to the radiator—removed the thermostat, I think—and after that it ran better. Nevertheless, we were still in the bed of the wadi when night fell. Darkness comes like the closing of a nursery door out there. We continued, but much more slowly, because the headlights were not much help. It's not like a road, it's like driving on the snow—you cannot see the difference between the road and its edges. Paul had to concentrate very hard to keep us in the stream bed. Otherwise I think he would have heard the water coming down the wadi behind us, or sensed that something was wrong. That's how much faith I have in Paul Christopher—he would have needed a sixth sense to have saved us. A wall of water in the desert? Who could imagine such a thing? I didn't even know it was the rainy season.

When the water did come, it was a total surprise. I was just *seized* by it and flung away. One instant I was sitting in the Land Rover and the next I was at the bottom of a river. I didn't believe my senses. I thought I had gone insane. I expected to see Paul beside me at any moment, to be back in the Land Rover. I was astonished. Quite rationally I said to myself, "I didn't know that Tadeusz's murder and riding with his body behind me had such an effect—I didn't know I was going to lose my mind this way." Then I began to swim. It was pure instinct for survival. My mind told me to relax and breathe: the water was a hallucination. The water in my nose and mouth was real enough, however. I got to the surface and swallowed some air and was immediately pulled under again. I struggled less, tried to go with the water. Every few seconds the flood would spit me out for an instant and I could breathe. I kept trying to swim toward the edge of the water. After what seemed an eternity I felt the bottom. I kept swimming. Finally I got out. I ran, falling down and getting up, falling down and getting up, until I was far away from the flood. I fell on my face and retched. My mouth was full of sand and I had swallowed some of the water. The flood was just liquid sand, you know—like porridge. I can still taste it.

There was nothing to be done. I wasn't hurt. I was exhausted. I curled up and went to sleep. When I woke up, the sun was overhead and Paul was beside me. He was a wretched sight—his hair full of mud, his clothes ruined, his face scratched and filthy. I practically exploded with love. He had been thrown out of the flood at almost the same spot as I—it was a place where the wadi widened, and I suppose the water just suddenly got shallow and released us. We must have been tumbling along side by side under the surface the night before, never knowing it.

Paul still had his compass and a pocketknife. Everything else had been lost. We walked along the banks of the wadi and found some of our canned fruit half-buried in the sand. We ate a can of peaches and Paul bundled up the rest in his shirt so we could carry them. He said there was no point in wasting our energy looking for the Land Rover as it would not run. There was no sign of Tadeusz. "We'll come back for him," Paul told me. "We won't leave him here." I wondered why he insisted on this. Of course I realize now he was afraid I would get hysterical. Perhaps I *was* hysterical. If I was, it had nothing to do with my brother—he was beyond help. As for his body, I didn't care what happened to it. The person was gone from it. My hysteria had to do with Paul. I was mad with joy that he was alive like me.

Paul got out his compass and decided we should walk eastward over the hills. The road we wanted was fifteen or twenty kilometers in that direction. We began to climb. When we got to the top of the first hill we heard the helicopter. Paul dumped the cans out of his shirt and waved it. The helicopter flew right by, sounding like a gun firing. Then it turned and landed a few feet away.

Kalash shot out of the door and scrambled toward us with his arms hanging down and the rotor blades flashing a few inches above his head. He gave me hardly a glance, but threw his arms around Paul and lifted him off the ground. He stood there with Paul dangling in his embrace for quite a long time. Nigel meanwhile had come up to me. He was carrying a light coat and for some reason he draped it over my shoulders. It was 120 degrees in the sun. "'Your brother?" he asked. It was the first time anyone but Paul had mentioned Tadeusz since we found him. I meant to give Nigel a calm reply. When I opened my mouth, nothing came out but a series of shrieks. Nigel's face, always before so cold, twisted in pain and he put his arms around me. He held me upright, muttering into my hair and patting my back, until I got control of myself. They put me into the helicopter. Paul joined me. The pilot flew us to the palace. Kalash and Nigel waited where they had found us—the machine could carry only four people.

I learned later that Kalash and Nigel found Tadeusz. They brought his body back, tied to the landing gear. I never saw it. By the time I knew he had been found, they had sealed him up in a coffin. I never saw any part of his dead body except the face. Perhaps it's just as well.

Q. But you did learn what had happened to him?

A. That man Qasim, the policeman, told me something about it. Apparently a couple of bandits seized him while he was poking around in the ruins. Qasim couldn't understand why they had killed him instead of holding him for ransom. He kept asking me if Tadeusz was carrying a large sum of money. I didn't know. I didn't think so. *I* had all the money, in my rucksack. Nigel found it, as you know, and gave it back. The rucksack contained Tadeusz's briefcase when I lost it, but the briefcase was gone when I got it back. All the money was there—over ten thousand dollars. But the briefcase was gone. Paul said I may not have put it into the rucksack after all, but I remember quite clearly. It doesn't matter. Nothing of value was lost except my brother's diary. I don't think I would have read it in any event. What could his diary tell me that I need to know?

Q. How did you interpret Ilona Bentley's reaction to your brother's death?

A. She was distressed. Ilona came to my room almost as soon as I returned to the palace. She kissed me, which I didn't particularly like. She said nothing for a long time. Actually she just stood there trembling from head to foot. She had to sit down in order to get hold of herself. Ilona told me she had loved Tadeusz. "I realize you won't believe me," she said, "but I did rather love your brother. You and I are different sorts of women, Zofia. I am able to love a great many people all at the same time. Tadeusz was loved by me." I expect she was telling the truth. What she said was a comfort to me in a queer way. She had been generous with Tadeusz, sleeping with him, whatever her intentions and whatever the results. All that was over. I found myself sympathizing with Ilona for the first time.

Later on, after we had taken Tadeusz to Khartoum, Ilona came along to the funeral. They all did. They were all absolute atheists, except for Kalash, and he was hardly a good Catholic. But they sat through the mass with me, all very correct. I don't mean that to sound contemptuous—probably their thoughts of my brother did him as much good as the priest's ritual and my prayers. We had to have him cremated, of course. This was done after the requiem mass. Theoretically the Catholic dead are not cremated. But I didn't want to bury him in that damned desert. I wanted to take him back to Europe with me. Nigel and Ilona arranged all that. I'm sure it was very difficult, but they took care of everything.

Ilona turned up at the plane, when we left with Tadeusz's ashes, with a bouquet of flowers. I don't know where she got them in that climate—they were roses. She asked if I minded her having the box containing the urn opened, so she could put the flowers inside. I agreed, and she knelt on the tarmac in the beating sun by the open crate, arranging the roses around the ashes. She was weeping. It was kind of her, I thought. There was no question at all that she was tremendously sorry about Tadeusz. No doubt she always had been.

86. FROM THE FILES OF CHIEF INSPECTOR ALY QASIM.

Of the sixty-three terrorists who were engaged by troops of the Parachute Regiment in the main camp of the so-called Anointed Liberation Front on the Wadi Magrur at 0640 hours on 17th July, only four survived. Of these, two were seriously wounded, and despite conscientious treatment by army medical staff, both died before I was able to complete my interviews with them. Of the two remaining prisoners, one was a low-ranking illiterate who was unable to supply any useful information. The other, Fadl Baballah, had been second-incommand of the ALF under a certain Qemal, who unfortunately was killed in the morning's action.

Baballah stated that he had joined the ALF in the belief that it intended to serve Islam. He was recruited by the late Ahmed, who was a boyhood friend. Ahmed told him that the USSR was a country governed by devout Muslims who wished to restore the purity of the faith. When Ahmed was executed on orders from the Russians, Baballah was disillusioned. He no longer believed that the Russians were friends of Islam, and he desired revenge for the death of his friend. He decided to kill Qemal, and on 12th or 13th July threatened him with a pistol.

What follows is a stenographic transcript of Baballah's description of this incident and certain of the results that flowed from it:

"The Russian radio told Qemal to kill Ahmed. He did so without hesitation and without giving Ahmed a trial. Always before when a comrade made a mistake, he was judged by a tribunal of the freedom fighters. They would decide his guilt and prescribe his punishment. If it was death, the sentence was carried out in a proper way by comrades of the condemned man. His error was explained to him before he died. But Qemal lured Ahmed into the desert and killed him by trickery. This was a terrible act. Soon all in the ALF knew about it. There was great anger. Comrades came to me and said, 'Fadl, you must get rid of Qemal and take command of the movement. Qemal killed Ahmed out of ambition. The Russians cannot order the death of a comrade in that way. It is wrong.'

"Qemal was a clever man and very brave. However, I never trusted him. I never believed that his heart was with the cause, as Ahmed's heart always was. I thought it best to kill Qemal exactly as he had killed Ahmed—go with him as a friend and shoot him.

But when I tried to persuade Qemal to come with me one night, he refused. 'Fadl, I know what you are thinking,' he said. 'I am thinking the same thing, that these Russians are no good. They betrayed us. You are angry because Ahmed is dead. How do you think I feel? It was I who killed my friend because the Russians told me to. I feel so badly I wish you would kill me, and if that is what you want to do I will turn my back now and let you shoot me.' I said, 'Very well, turn around, because I certainly intend to shoot you in the head.'

"Qemal showed no fear. He said, 'I agree. But first, listen to what I have to say, so that after you have killed me you can save the cause. You will be a great leader, Fadl. I have always thought that you, who are a pure man untouched by foreign ideas, should have been the commander of the ALF instead of Ahmed or myself. I wish to die knowing that Ahmed will be revenged and that the cause will triumph.'

"Qemal said that we must first of all get rid of the Russians. Ahmed had been saying this secretly for some time, and many of us agreed with him. He saw the truth about the Russians, and that was why he was killed. They cared nothing about Islam, nothing about Sudan, nothing about the ALF. All these three things, which meant everything in the world to me and the other comrades, were only a joke to the Russians. They are imperialists just like the rest of the Europeans. Now Qemal too realized the truth. 'We must fight on,' he said, 'but it's better to fight on alone than to take orders from the Russians.' I put away my pistol; I hadn't the heart to kill him. Besides, he was an educated man and we needed him.

"After that we had many planning sessions, Qemal and I. We agreed that we should have an important Sudanese as the titular head of the movement. This man would have no power, he would be a symbol for the masses. Qemal said he thought that his brother, Prince Kalash el Khatar, might join us if he understood our purpose. This had originally been Ahmed's idea. He had sent a team of comrades to capture Prince Kalash, but all of them except one was killed in the attempt by Europeans who were guarding the prince. The Europeans had machine pistols and our men had only the old American rifles and submachine guns the Russians had given us. Those rifles are no good against modern weapons. You saw what happened this morning. Your soldiers had machine guns and mortars; we had no chance with the old guns the Russians gave us. They never gave us enough ammunition. That was one of the ways they controlled us. If there was to be an operation, a plane would come over and drop a few boxes of bullets. Otherwise we had only twenty-four rounds per rifle. The Russians condemned us to death by not giving us bullets, the same as they condemned Ahmed.

"Qemal arranged to meet Prince Kalash two days ago. Another man called Siddik and I went along with him. Qemal had promised to meet alone with his brother, so we hid nearby. Now I remembered that on this same morning a Russian called Richard, which was a code name, was supposed to join us. I realized that we were very near the place where Richard was supposed to wait for us. Ahmed, before he died, had told me about the rendezvous arrangements. Qemal never said anything about it, but I supposed he just intended to leave the Russian alone in the desert—not meet him. There were certain arrangements. I had met Russians before, with Ahmed. We used to find them with a small radio. You turn on the radio and it makes a sound like an automobile horn. The louder the sound becomes, the closer you are to the Russian. The Russian carried another small radio that sent out a signal. This was necessary because a stranger cannot find his way in the desert. We always kept the location of our camp secret even from the Russians, and we moved all the time. Then, too, the Russians always came by parachute and sometimes the wind would carry them away from the place they said they were going to land. So the radio device was very useful.

"As Siddik and I waited for Qemal it occurred to me that the Russian might be nearby. I had the radio device in my Land Rover, which used to be Ahmed's vehicle, so I got it out and turned it on.

The signal came out of it quite strongly. We walked in one direction and another until it got louder. Then we simply followed the signal until we found the Russian. He was standing in the ruins of an old house, looking at them and muttering to himself. He was rather fat, as Russians usually are. I sent Siddik around behind him, and then I stepped into the ruins. The Russian did not see me at first, he was interested in something written on one of the walls. When he did see me, he leaped in fright. Then he smiled and made salaam.

"There was a password. I gave it because I wanted to be sure he'd come along willingly, not suspecting anything. I said, 'Heaven is far away,' which was the password the Russians had sent. The Russian peered at me through his glasses, still smiling foolishly, and said, 'God is great.' That was not the prescribed countersign, but these Russians are never straightforward; they don't always come right out with things like passwords. I said 'Where is God?' The Russian said, 'Allah is everywhere and near at hand.' That was the countersign, or near enough. I shook hands with the Russian, told him how glad we were to see him, how grateful we were to him, and so on. He kept on being suspicious. At first he was not going to come with me, but when Siddik stepped through the broken wall behind him with his rifle, the Russian stopped arguing and walked to the Land Rover with us.

"Qemal was astonished when he came back and found that we had taken the Russian. I took him aside and told him how I had found him. Qemal was extremely pleased. 'Good,' he said, 'now you can have your revenge for Ahmed, and we can leave a signal the Russians cannot misunderstand to show that we are finished with them.' Qemal said the Russians would certainly come looking for their man if he did not radio to them that all was well. He said we should kill the Russian and cut off his balls and hang him up the way we had done the others. Then we would radio the Russians and tell them to look on a certain hill for their Richard, who was unable to carry on and wished to return home.

"So that's what we did. The Russian tried to dissuade us. At first he kept telling us in Arabic that he wasn't a Russian. He got out his passport which showed he was something else. Qemal read the passport and said it came from a country that was a colony of Russia. He talked Russian to the man. The man answered in Russian. We took him a long way, almost to the camp, before we killed him. He argued with us right to the end. 'You are making a mistake, a terrible mistake,' he said. 'I am not this Richard. I know no Richard. I am a friend of Prince Kalash el Khatar. He is nearby. He will tell you.' Qemal laughed at him. 'Prince Kalash is my brother,' he said. 'I just spoke to him. He said nothing about any Russian friend. Prince Kalash has no Russian friends.'

"The Russian, in the end, was very strange. He saw that we were going to kill him. He was a powerful man; he could have fought. But he did not. He submitted like a sheep. Siddik went to the camp and got the boards while Qemal and I talked to the Russian. When Siddik came back, we tied him on the crossed boards. Qemal took no part in any of this; Siddik and I did all the work. It was Siddik who used the knife.

"The Russian hung there upside down, talking some foreign language in a voice that got louder and louder as Siddik cut him. It sounded like prayers. Only once did he make any fuss. He fainted when Siddik cut off his fingers. I slapped his face until he woke up. Then Siddik told him what he was going to do. When the knife went between his legs, the Russian roared, a huge sound. Not a scream. He roared like a stabbed lion. Then, naturally, he went unconscious again. I wanted to shoot him but Qemal said no-let him bleed. But before we left him I cut his wrists."

"I don't think Qemal ever radioed the Russians where to find their man. He was going to do it this morning after we broke camp. But there was the rain in the night and then you attacked us. So it was all for nothing."

One cannot read the mind of a dead man, so it is impossible to know for certain what Qemal hoped to accomplish by the murder of Miernik. The Pole's true identity did not matter to Qemal; perhaps he genuinely believed that Miernik and the Russian agent "Richard" were one and the same. Leaving aside the confusion over identity, Qemal's motive seems clear enough: Baballah and the other terrorists wanted to kill *someone* in revenge for Ahmed's execution. Better, from Qemal's point of view, that they kill Miernik than Qemal. By encouraging, even ordering, Miernik's death, Qemal demonstrated to his underlings that he was as angry at the Russians as they, and that he was free of the Russians' control.

87. REPORT BY CHRISTOPHER'S CASE OFFICER.

1. Christopher delivered his excellent though typically literary report on the ALF/Miernik episode in Khartoum at 0230 on 21 July. This written account adds flesh to the bare bones communicated in my cable of 18 July, which was based on a hurried verbal debriefing of Christopher conducted by this officer in El Fasher. At both meetings the agent appeared to be in excellent physical condition. However, he has been through a somewhat trying experience, and his morale is understandably impaired.

2. This officer notes, not in criticism but as a matter of observation, that Christopher is more than usually prone to believe that his understanding of this operation is more accurate than that of the case officer, the station, or the country desk at Headquarters. The death of Miernik made a vivid impression on him, and he gives it undue weight in his estimate of the overall value of the operation. The fact that he has become emotionally involved with Zofia Miernik undoubtedly colors his judgment to a certain extent.

3. Christopher has reverted to his earlier view that Miernik was not, in fact, a Soviet agent. So convinced is he of the correctness of his view that he is able to rationalize all the evidence to the contrary that has come to us from a wide range of sources, including the information made available to us by the Sudanese Special

Branch and by British liaison, whose own agent on the scene contributed valuable corroborative reporting, particularly on the role
of Ilona Bentley.

4. At Christopher's request, his argument in support of his view
in reference to Miernik was tape-recorded, and it is here presented
verbatim (as edited by Christopher).

CHRISTOPHER'S STATEMENT

This operation is now terminated in the field. The ALF
has been neutralized, the Soviets have been thwarted—and
Miernik is dead. In addition to all the evidence Headquarters
will have from far-flung sources I think it is important that
the analysts have my view of the situation. Of all the dozens
of people who worked on this project, I alone was on the
scene, knew the people, witnessed the events. That is an ego-
tistical statement on its face, but I want my judgment on the
record even if it is to be discounted.

It's in the nature of our work that we never know how matters are going to turn out. We begin and end in the dark.
There is an overlay of efficiency in everything we do. I'm
convinced that there is no more intelligent or unemotional
group of men on earth than ourselves. That, if I may say so,
is our principal weakness. Because our people are so bright,
because our resources are so huge, we consistently tinker with
reality.

The Miernik operation is a classic example of this tendency.
We began with a vague suspicion: that Miernik was being
defected by the Poles. Tentative conclusion: Miernik is an
agent. Obvious question: What is his assignment?

What we had at the beginning was a set of assumptions. It
was proper to test those assumptions. After all, that is our
job. But the testing process—calling up our own resources
and those of friendly services all over the world—creates an
almost irresistible psychological force. We are experts in sus-

picion. We search diligently for evidence that will confirm our suspicions. To transform a supposition into a fact is the sweetest reward a desk man can know. We do it all the time, and usually we are right. But sometimes we are wrong, and I believe that there is no possible way for us to know this.

You will recall, not without impatience, that I believed in the early stages of this operation that there was a strong possibility that Miernik was innocent. I am trained to regard all behavior as cover. At no time did I spontaneously believe anything Miernik said to me or indicated to me through his overt personal conduct. But I had an instinctive feeling that all the indications that he was an opposition agent were, just possibly, false. That attitude was also part of my training, and I am sure that Headquarters shared my reservations.

The difference is this: I knew Miernik personally. For you, the reservations were intellectual—routine professional skepticism. For me they were intestinal. There is no way to argue an intestinal case in cables and dispatches, or even in clandestine conversations with a case officer whose proper function is to discount the emotional reactions of his agent. We are, quite properly, interested primarily in information that is stripped of the background noise created by the personality of the source.

In the end, my training brought me around to the conclusion that Miernik was, in fact, an agent. There was no other rational explanation for many of the things he did: the book code, the contact with Sasha Kirnov, the heavy-handed dramatization of his plight, the expertise with weapons, the mixture of self-revelation in unimportant matters and obsessive secrecy in others. I never entirely got rid of the instinctive feeling that he was genuine, and therefore innocent. But in a conflict between instinct and what appears to be objective evidence, the latter must always win.

In order to go on with what I was doing to Miernik, I had to believe that he was an enemy. Otherwise my activity, for all its surface of cleverness and technique, was stupid. My conclusion that Miernik's behavior confirmed our suspicions was not—as I believed it to be—a return to objectivity. It was a flight from it. My change of heart turned me (and, to the extent my reporting influences its judgment, turned Headquarters) away from a search for the truth. Everything after that was an attempt to achieve operational results.

All the evidence said to us: "Yes, Miernik is a Soviet agent." All the evidence, that is, which we saw fit to consider. Existing simultaneously with the information that confirmed our suspicions was a second body of evidence, like a planet identical to Earth on the other side of the sun, which just as conclusively demonstrated that our suspicions were incorrect. We hadn't the technique to see it. This is no one's fault; it is in the nature of our equipment.

What we overlooked was this: *there was no purpose in what Miernik did.* His behavior from beginning to end was inconsistent with the simplest rules of tradecraft. Leave aside for a moment all the thoughts we put into his mind and into the minds of the Soviet service we assumed was handling him.

Concentrate on this: why, if the Soviets wanted to provide an extremely sensitive operation like the ALF with a white Communist as principal agent, would they choose to send him into the Sudan in a Cadillac with an American agent, a British agent, and a Sudanese aristocrat who had every reason to be hostile to anything that threatened the established order? Why expose him—virtually confirm his identity—to such an array of enemies? Why not just drop him into the desert on a moonlit night?

For that matter, why insert a KGB man into a highrisk situation like the one in which the ALF operated? His capture guaranteed the very thing the Soviets presumably would have wanted to avoid at all costs: confirmation that they were equipping and controlling the guerrillas. Even if they were too dense to realize that the ALF could not succeed and would eventually be swept up by the Sudanese, they must have seen that the presence of a Polish principal agent was unnecessary (they had perfectly adequate control through Ahmed and Qemal and their radio link) and unbelievably insecure.

I am going to say a very harsh thing that is directed as much (or more) against myself as against all you people who sit inside, making the plans that I carry out. *I think we ran Miernik as we did primarily for the fun of it.* We have come to look on our work, in the field at least, largely as a sport. Miernik provided an opportunity to match wits with the opposition. We knew from the start that we would win: we had physical control of their alleged agent, we had access to the Sudanese police and military, we had penetrated the ALF. All the opposition had was Miernik and a bunch of deluded tramps who couldn't think for themselves or maintain decent security. It was a chance not just to beat the Russians for the umptyumpth straight time, it was an opportunity to humiliate the bastards. We would not have been human if we hadn't seized this opportunity.

It cost Miernik (not to mention Firecracker and sixty other Arabs) his life.

When I found Miernik hanging on that cross with his scrotum in his mouth I saw in my mind's eye all the complex machinery that had produced this simple result. It was our questions about Miernik (questions formulated by the best and most honest minds of a great nation) that drove Miernik to what he undoubtedly would have called his Golgotha. An illiterate tribesman with a knife provided Miernik with a final opportunity for the cheap dramatics that embarrassed me into suspecting him in the first place. We didn't actually send him out to be killed. His death arose from a misunderstanding. Miernik's murder is not, technically, on our heads. In fact, the man we sent into the desert wasn't Miernik at all—that person was a creature of our imagination built out of spare parts left over from our previous experiences with wily Poles and sinister Russians. The real Miernik was that carcass on the cross, clumsy and ridiculous even in death, with the wounds he tried to show me at last made visible.

5. Despite his obvious reservations, Christopher has continued to operate with his normal loyalty and efficiency. He has obtained Miernik's diary (transmitted herewith for translation and analysis), and he has intervened with Zofia Miernik with a view toward making her available for a full debriefing by the Geneva station. In order to provide Miss Miernik with an incentive for cooperation, Christopher has been instructed to tell her that our interviews are a normal procedure preliminary to granting her status as an immigrant to the United States under the Polish quota. Christopher had suggested that Miss Miernik be granted immediate citizenship under a special congressional bill, but he is now persuaded that the interests of the government, and those of Miss Miernik, will be better served through the quieter process of ordinary immigration.

88. PERSONAL LETTER TO CHRISTOPHER FROM THE CHIEF OF HIS OPERATIONAL DIVISION.

12 August

Dear Paul:

There are a good many things I want to say to you that are better said in a personal letter than in an official communication. I hope that you will read this note patiently and with an open mind—and with some awareness of the value I place on our friendship and the high regard in which you are held by the company as a whole.

First of all, I think (and so does everyone else) that you did an absolutely first-class job in connection with Miernik and the ALF. Knowing your feelings about this assignment, I hesitated a long time before writing up a proposal that you be decorated for your work. I suspect that you do not want recognition of this sort, in this particular case, but all here agree that you richly deserve it, and perhaps in later years you will look more kindly on your medal. (Not that you'll ever actually look on it—after it's awarded it will be locked up forever in the Director's safe along with all the others earned by men like you.)

All of us here have considered very carefully the reservations you expressed to Bill concerning the mistake you think we made about Miernik. It was an eloquent and persuasive statement. I do not for a moment discard the possibility that your judgment is correct. If it is true that we shoved Miernik toward a useless death out of a misunderstanding of his role, then we have a great deal to be sorry for. However, I believe that the evidence is sufficiently weighty on the other side of the question to merit *your* keeping open the possibility that Miernik was exactly what we suspected him to be.

I will not review all the bits and pieces you already know about, although I think you should give some consideration to such things as his being in exactly the right place at exactly the right time (with a radio homing device in his camera) to be picked up by the ALF.

(We do have information from a sensitive source in Warsaw that a colonel in the Polish intelligence service—the man in charge of their part of the ALF operation—was demoted *at the request of the Russians three days after the ALF was destroyed and Miernik got himself killed.* Moreover, on the day of Miernik's contact with Firecracker [Qemal], the Soviet transmitter in Dar es Salaam made no fewer than six attempts to raise their agent "Richard" in coded broadcasts to the ALF. They got no answer. If Miernik was not Richard," then where was the real "Richard"? The Sudanese scoured the desert for this elusive character, but never found him. Isn't it possible that *you* found him, hanging on that cross?)

I would like to tell you about Miernik's diary, which is available to us thanks to your good work, and which we have had translated. It is a remarkable document. It reveals a man torn between two parts of his nature. One part is the one you came to believe in so strongly—the sensitive, intelligent, ugly, and misunderstood Miernik. The other part, less specifically drawn, but nevertheless very easy to see between the lines, is the one we believe to be the "real" Miernik.

After reading the diary, there is no question in my mind that he was an agent, and an exceptionally clever one. This conclusion is not based on any specific confession of Miernik's, but rather on the style and tone of what he wrote. The diary is a chart of his inner thoughts. The dominant thought was a fear of discovery, a suspicion of the motives of everyone he came in contact with, a determination to do his duty however distasteful he found it. If you wish, you can read the whole thing the next time you're home; I think that doing so would make you feel better—but I think, too, that you should put a little time between yourself and the events that have so disturbed you before you sit down with the diary. The file cards carried by Miernik are a detailed rundown on every aspect of the country and its leading personalities. It is impossible to explain why he would compile such data in the absence of an operational purpose.

Whether Miernik was or was not the agent sent out by our friends in Moscow to case-officer the ALF is, in reality, beside the point. We could not foresee that events would develop as they did, but in the end the Sudanese dealt with the ALF in a way that made Miernik's presence irrelevant. There was some revulsion here over the methods used by the Sudanese army and police: all that killing really was unnecessary and counterproductive. The fact that Firecracker was killed out of carelessness was particularly hard to take. We felt that we owed him something better than that. The Sudanese not unnaturally decided to keep the whole affair quiet, so the idea we had for a really embarrassing exposure of Moscow's hand in Africa went by the boards. Personally, I think this is just as well: the heroic death of the ALF martyrs was more likely to be an inspiration than a discouragement to other potential terrorists.

You may read the foregoing paragraph as confirmation of your belief that your own assignment was without value. Far from it: we wanted to cover all bets, and you covered Miernik in a style that few could equal. I believe we had the right man, did the right thing, and produced the right results. That's all that matters. Forget Miernik and go on to something else. You have a brilliant professional future before you. Let's get on with it.

I can understand why you want to avoid any further reporting on the people who were with you in Sudan. As Bill has already told you, we think you should drift out of these relationships as naturally as possible and as soon as possible for security reasons. We have some residual curiosity about Ilona Bentley. There's no question that she fingered Miernik, although the results were not what she expected—and maybe not what the Russians expected, either. We taped a pretty hysterical encounter between her and her Soviet case officer, a fellow named Kutosov who operates out of Paris. She accused the Soviets of having murdered Miernik. Kutosov denied it, of course, and blamed it on the stupidity of natives. And on us. They've guessed that Firecracker belonged to us, and they naturally conclude that we put him up to the killing of Miernik. Bentley may even believe this, for all we know. As nearly as we can make out, the Soviets recruited her around 1957, promising special treatment and perhaps even release for a Hungarian she knew (knew in the biblical sense) in return for her cooperation. After she got involved, she grew to like the work for its own sake. Kutosov is still running her on a variety of low-grade operations, according to our cousins in London. We don't imagine that she'll hold up for very much longer, considering her emotional pattern and the fact that she's thoroughly blown to half the services in the world.

If I were you, I'd abstain from any more quick tours of Czechoslovakia. The Czech officer commanding the area of the frontier where you crossed over with Zofia defected a couple of weeks ago. His superiors began to wonder where he was getting all his money. Among the things he told the debriefers was this: Sasha

Kirnov was shot dead by the KGB man, Shigalov, in the woods behind you as you made your way across the frontier. There are any number of ingenious theories as to why this was done. The most probable one is that the Soviets thought Kirnov had been doubled. He was in contact with a third-country agent in Vienna named Heinz Tanner who had been co-opted by the British. And one of our people in South America had been seeing a lot of Kirnov socially, trying to set him up for defection or recruitment. Our fellow had no luck. Neither, in the end, did Sasha.

We hope to see you before much longer. Betty still wonders when you'll find the right girl and has a whole platoon of prospective brides lined up in anticipation of your next visit to Washington. If I were you, I'd leave all that for old age. If I have anything to do with it, you're going to be too busy for a family for a long time to come.

Best regards,
JACK

89. FROM THE DEBRIEFING OF ZOFIA MIERNIK.

The months have gone by, and now we never speak of what happened in Sudan. It's curious how little difference Tadeusz's absence makes. When Father died, there was a hole in the world. Tadeusz left no trace of himself. Perhaps I'm older and more used to things. One does get used to things, I've found.

I don't even have a photograph of my brother. I suppose the only pictures of him in existence are in the files of the Polish police; even Tadeusz couldn't escape their cameras. He used to say that the police alone can certify that one is alive, with their passports and identity cards. I can certify that he is dead. I have a witness in Paul Christopher, and I still have Tadeusz's ashes in their urn. I keep them at the back of the closet. There seemed to be no point in burying them in some Swiss cemetery that I would never visit. This way I am obliged to think of him every time I open the door to take down a dress. Tadeusz doesn't haunt me. God knows where his ghost has gone—back to the Polish woods where our mother was killed, perhaps.

The others tried for a while to keep up their friendship, but it didn't work. In the old days they were held together by humor and good times. They all realized, after we came back from Sudan, that they'd have to look elsewhere for those things; they couldn't give them to each other any longer.

Of all those who were involved, I think Ilona suffered most. She lost Nigel completely. What happened between them I don't know. It was almost as if Nigel blamed Ilona for all that had happened. He was brutal toward her—if she came into a café to meet us, Nigel would simply get up from the table and leave. For weeks Ilona was absolutely haggard. She'd come to see me in the middle of the night, and then just sit in a chair with her eyes closed, saying nothing. She told me she had begun to dream of Belsen for the first time since her childhood. I see her sometimes in the city. She always has someone with her—she can't be alone, and she's lucky to have such looks so she doesn't have to be without a man.

Nigel rings me up sometimes and takes me to dinner. He has been awfully kind. Once in a while I see Kalash, always with a different little female. He wears these girls like scarves—they flutter around his neck till his mood changes, and then he puts on another.

For a time I saw Paul constantly. When we got back to Geneva, it seemed natural to stay at his flat. I didn't want to be alone, and I didn't know anyone here. Even if I'd been a native *genevoise* I would have found a way to live with Paul. I love him. When we found my brother's body in the desert, I took about fifteen minutes off to mourn Tadeusz. Then all I thought about or felt had to do with Paul. I could have sung, to be beside him under that awful sun, alive in that awful dead place with Tadeusz's corpse behind us in the Land Rover.

While we were living together I tried to create an atmosphere of happiness. It lasted for forty-three days. Paul did his best, really he did. I bought cookbooks, and tended his clothes, and kept the flat neat because he hates clutter, and made him drinks at the end of the day. I really wasn't very good at any of that, but he has a gentle way about him and I thought for a while that all those things didn't matter so long as we had the other thing. As time went on, Paul became more and more quiet. I took his loss of gaiety for a sign of love.

Then, on a Saturday afternoon in September, I coaxed him into bed. It was a lovely day; we'd had lunch on the terrace and drunk a lot of wine in the sun. It was wonderful for me to be with Paul. I used to cry afterward, foolish with happiness. On this particular afternoon I noticed his body more than I usually did. For the first time I was aware of something I suppose had only registered on my subconscious all the other times. When pleasure runs through the body of a lover, you can feel it. I felt nothing like that in Paul.

I opened my eyes and saw his face above me. It was the first time we had done it in the daylight. In his eyes I saw the truth. I guess he had drunk too much wine or was too tired to save me from it. Paul did not like to make love to me. I waited until he went to sleep, and then I left. Paul never tried to find me.

So what I have is Sasha's money and Tadeusz's ashes, and the absolute conviction that I am going to live to be an old, old woman.

END